The brilliantly conceived sequel to
The President's Plane Is Missing:

Air Force One Is Haunted

President Jeremy Haines:	His second term is beset by staggering problems and impossible decisions ...but will the pressure drive him to push the buttons for World War III?
Doctor Jessica Sarazin:	The Commander-in-Chief has come to her with a secret that is potentially lethal to National Security. Is he losing his mind—and is she losing her heart?
General Duane Collison:	Since the President lacks "the right stuff," Collison wants to do his duty—and wipe out the Russian threat forever....
Franklin Delano Roosevelt:	Is he a figment of Haine's imagination—or America's last ghost of a chance?

AIR FORCE ONE IS HAUNTED

ROBERT SERLING

ST. MARTIN'S PAPERBACKS

AIR FORCE ONE IS HAUNTED

ISBN: 0-312-90029-5

Printed in the United States of America

St. Martin's Paperbacks edition/October 1985

10 9 8 7 6 5 4 3 2

For their professional skill and treasured friendships, this book is dedicated to the doctors in my life:

Luther Hall
Bob Johnson
Kathy Henry
Wayne Bixenman
Leonard Joffe
Phil Philbin

“Do I believe in ghosts?
No, but I’m afraid of them.”
Marquise du Deffand

“No man will ever bring out of
the Presidency the reputation
which carries him into it.”
Thomas Jefferson

AIR FORCE ONE IS HAUNTED

NATIONAL

REPORT

Dream into Nightmare

A troubled President goes from glory to Gethsemane in only two years

The midway point of his second term finds President Jeremy Haines probably wishing he had never run for reelection.

As Haines returned last week from an inspection tour of West Coast electronics plants working on a U.S. anti-missile system, his spanking-new Boeing 747 traversed a country torn by the worst recession since the 1930s (unemployment is nearing the 13 million mark) and threatened by the intractable hostility of the Soviet Union.

The President himself draws a gloomy parallel between the problems facing his Administration and those of his political idol, Franklin Delano Roosevelt. At a Los Angeles party fund-raising dinner the night before he left for Washington, Haines pointedly recalled "the courage and wisdom that FDR demonstrated in facing the twin specters of economic disaster and sword-rattling, ruthless dictatorships."

It was not the first time this Republican President has invoked FDR's name and memory. Haines firmly believes his Democratic predecessor of more than a half-century ago was America's greatest President—"a man with human weaknesses massively overshadowed by God-given purpose and unquenchable spirit," he told graduates at Harvard's commencement exercises last summer.

No President since FDR had ever won another four years in office with greater popular support nor a brighter future for both nation and world than Jeremy Haines. Six years ago, Haines squeaked into the White House; two years ago he was reelected in a landslide triumph that saw him winning forty-seven states and grabbing all but twenty-three Electoral College votes.

The President rode to the crest of popularity and trust on the strength of his detente agreement with the Soviet Union, a pact signed against a backdrop of tragic intrigue. As every American now knows, Haines dispatched Air Force One on a phony vacation trip to Palm Springs as a coverup for his secret meeting with Soviet premier Alexei Bujesky at Camp David. En route to Palm Springs, the Presidential aircraft ran into a violent thunderstorm and crashed, killing all aboard—including the President's cousin, who had doubled for Haines at the night take-off from Andrews Air Force Base.

When searchers failed to discover Haines's body in the wreckage, the carefully orchestrated plot threatened to come apart as fast as Air Force One, the now-discredited Amalgamated Condor. Haines, sworn to secrecy by his Russian peer, could not reveal his whereabouts until the nonaggression pact—aimed squarely at belligerent Peking—was signed and Bujesky was on his way back to the USSR.

Not until columnist Jack Anderson broke the story two weeks after the pact's signing did the nation learn how close the United States had come to igniting a nuclear war with China, while Haines was still missing. Anderson's shocking report (his source was an unidentified cabinet officer widely rumored to have been then-Transportation Secretary Harvey Brubaker) disclosed the details of an alleged dramatic cabinet meeting presided over by Vice President Frederick J. Madigan, who, according to Anderson, had actually won narrow cabinet approval to launch a preemptive nuclear strike against Peking. Only Haines's last-minute appearance prevented Madigan's horrifying decision from becoming reality.

There has never been a flat Administration denial that such a meeting took place—only a lame, rather halfhearted rebuttal claiming that the columnist "somewhat exaggerated the event in question." Madigan himself called the Anderson story "99 percent fiction," a denial disbelieved by 99 percent of official Washington. Such skepticism was largely instrumental in convincing Haines that the inept Vice President would be a distinct handicap in his reelection bid, and Madigan was dumped from the ticket in favor of Arizona Congressman Geoff Mitchell.

By now, Haines must be wondering why he didn't follow Fred Madigan into political obscurity. The former Vice President is happily serving as president of the Midwestern Toy Corporation, where the only war buttons he can push are on the firm's popular "Space Wars" video game. The contrast between Haines and his onetime bête noir is startling. "I'm having a ball," Madigan says. "Running a toy company makes me feel like a kid again." But the man he served so ineptly is a noticeably aging, harassed and lonely man (a widower when he entered the White House, Haines has never remarried), one whose deteriorating appearance underscores the stresses of the world's toughest job. His once-straight shoulders are stooped, his steel-gray hair is the color of fresh snow, and the natural grin that endeared him to millions of visually impressed voters is now as obviously forced as a chorus girl's smile.

No wonder. Premier Bujesky died within six months of the signing of the nonaggression pact, and his hard-line, American-hating successor, Andrei Magoyan, promptly rendered it meaningless by inking a similar agreement with Red China. With his Chinese border flanks protected, Magoyan launched a campaign of vituperation against Haines unmatched even in the coldest days of the Cold War. And while he flung insults and wild accusations against the United States, the frog-faced Russian premier sent his red legions into every Iron Curtain country displaying the slightest wavering of allegiance to Communism and USSR domination.

One by one, as the Free World watched in helpless horror, the Soviets clamped their steel military grip on Poland, Yugoslavia, Bulgaria, and Czechoslovakia—each nation, once an island of defiant independence, crushed into total subservience as had been Afghanistan before them. Beset by domestic troubles, Haines has had to sit by in frustrated futility. Badly shaken by the collapse of his spectacular detente coup, the embattled chief executive is under fire from within his own Administration as various disenchanted officials clamor for a stronger posture against the Soviets.

The loudest voice of all comes from the chairman of the National Security Council, former Air Force chief of staff General Duane Collison. That towering, brilliantly articulate hawk figuratively slapped the President's face last week.

"We have failed miserably to learn from past mistakes," he told the National Manufacturers' Association. "Premier Magoyan is no less a menace than was Adolf Hitler, and we know only too well that Hitler nearly triumphed because weak, vacillating leaders did not recognize the threat."

In almost any other country but the United States, such caustic, scarcely veiled contempt would have resulted in Collison's dismissal. Significantly, the President's response fell short of even a mild rebuke. "The general has a right to his opinion," Haines allowed, "and in many ways I can't blame him for his frustration."

Washington observers, surprised at Collison's open insubordination, were stunned at the President's Milquetoast reaction. "Haines carried turning the other cheek too far," the *Washington Post* grieved. There is growing belief in world capitals, including America's, that Jeremy Haines has lost his ability and even his will to lead. If this is true, Franklin Delano Roosevelt must be turning over in his grave.

ONE

ONE

While waiting for the patient to arrive, Dr. Sarazin read the letter for the third time.

UNITED STATES NAVAL MEDICAL CENTER
Bethesda, MD 20856

Personal and Confidential

Dr. Jessica Sarazin
5300 Garland Road
Potomac, MD 20854

Dear Dr. Sarazin:

Herewith the complete medical records of the patient I have asked you to see; I have taken the liberty of sending them via courier because of their confidential nature and to provide you ample time for study prior to the initial session.

As I explained in our recent telephone conversation, I have called on you for help in view not only of your splendid professional reputation but your known interest in the field of parapsychology.

If this were a simple matter involving hallucinations under stress (and, frankly, that would be my considered diagnosis), I would have preferred to confine this case to my own office. But the identity of the patient dictates the necessity of seeking for him the very best in psychiatric analysis and aid.

I would, of course, appreciate your keeping me advised of any development you deem worthy of my attention and/or consultation.

Sincerely,

Catlin Baxter, Captain
Chief of Psychiatry

Jessica Sarazin put down the letter and picked up the thick medical history file; she did not open it again but merely hefted it, almost absentmindedly, as if the very weight imparted the contents. Not that there was anything clinically significant amid the voluminous medical reports, fairly typical of a reasonably healthy male of sixty-one—with one exception. Dr. Sarazin had noted a tendency toward elevated blood pressure, kept under control with 0.1 milligrams of Catapres twice daily until three months ago. At that time the dosage was increased to 0.2 mg. The most recent blood-pressure check, only four days earlier, showed 158 systolic over 85 diastolic. Not bad for a man of his age and life-style, yet Jessica had zeroed in on a coincidence. The doubled dosage was prescribed just about the time the patient had reported what Captain Baxter had discreetly described as "psychiatric deviation."

Baxter was probably right in his informal diagnosis, Jessica decided. Hallucinating under severe stress. Except that Dr. Sarazin's curiosity had been aroused by something else Baxter had written in his carefully phrased account of his last interview with the patient.

> . . . although one thing does not jibe with this very tentative analysis. He is a man who has handled maximum stress with exceptional ability in the past and his own reaction to his psychiatric difficulty is one of unusual calm and detachment. He exhibits none of the expected fear or hysteria usually associated with experiences of this kind and this in itself leads me to suspect a deeper trauma of serious proportions . . .

Well, Jessica thought, that was the job of a good psychiatrist. To dig deep and to probe widely for hidden, unsuspected causal effects. Events, incidents, words, relationships planted so far down in the subconscious that their existence has to be mined. Except for the medical file, she would be starting virtually from scratch with this patient. Baxter deliberately hadn't told her the specific nature of the hallucinations—"I want *him* to tell you as if he's getting it off his chest for the first time," he had explained, "and in that way you'll both be on an even keel, so to speak."

Then he had blurted, most unprofessionally, "It's the goddamnedest thing I ever heard!"

Dr. Sarazin glanced at the wall clock. Only five minutes until the appointed time. She rose and peeked outside her office to make sure that Sue, her secretary, had gone home. Baxter's instructions—they were more like flat orders—were most specific. There were to be no patients in the waiting room nor anyone else for at least an hour before the patient arrived and a half-hour after he left. Obligingly, Dr. Sarazin had postponed three other appointments and given Sue the afternoon off. Yet such arrangements were hardly presumptuous. She knew the patient's identity.

The President of the United States.

With her receptionist gone, in accordance with Baxter's orders, she had left the door to her private office open so she could keep an eye on the reception room. A small sign at the door of the waiting room instructed patients, PLEASE RING BELL, but maybe Presidents didn't have to observe such requests. The bell rang however, followed by the entry of two husky young men in blue business suits so similar that they looked like twins. Haines trailed them in, and Dr. Sarazin rose from her desk. She was about to walk into the waiting room but the President entered her office before she could reach the door, murmuring something to the two men, who nodded and took seats in the waiting room.

Haines himself closed the door of Jessica's office. "A moment of great import," he chuckled. "Except for such occasions as going to the bathroom and to bed, this is one of the few times I can tell the Secret Service its presence is unwelcome."

She liked that. She had heard he had a sense of humor, and it boded well for the relationship. It showed a vein of introspection that could be valuable in therapy. A man able to find humor in one of the most confining aspects of his life had a kind of pliable objectivity.

"Mr. President," Dr. Sarazin said, holding out her hand, "this is an honor."

Even as she voiced the conventional obeisance, she had begun to study him clinically in a visual sense.

Although Jessica had seen Jeremy Haines countless times on television and in news photographs, she was not quite prepared for the first sight of him in person. He was handsomer than she expected. Well over six feet tall. A lean, strong, outdoorsy face, with thin lips framing a wide mouth and a jaw that could have been the jutting prow of a sleek cruiser, more graceful than massive so that it managed to soften the ruggedness of his features. His eyes, deepset and gray and disturbingly expressive, reflected the man's moods as if they were the lens of a movie projector transmitting images.

But he also looked older than she had anticipated. She could remember pictures of him during his first administration, when his hair was just a fraction away from a crewcut, so closely clipped at the temples that it was difficult to tell where the graying began. The hair was much longer now and pure white, not unattractive yet creating the illusion that the roots had somehow managed to work their way down so they had sprouted into lines on his tired face.

Fatigue was her initial impression of him. He wore it like a heavy cloak that slumped his shoulders forward. But her second impression came from his eyes—first piercing as they studied her face, then frankly inquisitive, with a faint undertone of amused mockery. He's skeptical, she decided instantly, but he's willing to listen—or, better yet, to talk.

Haines took her hand with a gentle squeeze. "I suspect it's going to be more of a pain in the neck than an honor," he said wryly.

She motioned him into a leather armchair in front of her desk and he smiled slightly.

"I was afraid you were going to put me on a traditional couch," he observed. "I see you have one."

"That's for my naps," Jessica assured him lightly.

He smiled again and Jessica sat down at her desk facing him. She started a tape recorder. Haines frowned unhappily but did not protest and his next words told the banter was over. This, she decided instantly from his expression, was a worried man.

"Dr. Sarazin, how much do you know?"

"Captain Baxter has briefed me in general terms and I've been going over your medical history." She patted the file in front of her.

"Did he tell you what I've been seeing? Or thought I saw?"

"You've been seeing ghosts."

He nodded, his forehead screwing itself into tiny

crevices. "The obvious conclusion, then, is that I'm cracking up. Bonkers, as the younger generation would put it. One hell of a situation for the President of the United States."

"Mr. President, what is your honest opinion of my profession?"

"It would be a subjective opinion," he hedged. "You're the first shri— psychiatrist I've ever seen. Other than Cat Baxter, of course."

"You started to say *shrink*, which indicates that your opinion is somewhat negative."

"I'm sorry. I should . . ."

She interrupted. "No apology necessary. A good psychiatrist, if he or she is honest, will recognize the limitations of the profession. Psychiatry, Mr. President, is easily the most imperfect branch of medicine. Too often we have to deal with intangible theories and pure guesswork. A surgeon can spot cancer. An ophthalmologist knows when he has a patient with glaucoma. A general practictioner can diagnose a case of measles. But psychiatry deals with the human mind, the most complex and least understood of all living organisms. So let's establish something right from the start. I'm not sure I can help you. I'm not even sure there's anything wrong with you. But I'm going to try to help. And for that, I will need total honesty and unquestioning cooperation on your part. Is that clear?"

"Perfectly," he said, but she had the sudden notion that it took an effort to keep his voice from cracking.

She gave him a warm smile, and Jeremy Haines found himself relaxing in spite of himself. Her voice was so calm it was almost hypnotic, low and modulated yet with such perfect diction that she seemed to be speaking louder than she was. The voice went with the woman, he decided. Jessica Sarazin was tall—about five feet nine he guessed—with patrician features and black hair, streaked with gray. She wore her hair rather long; parted on the left, it fell carelessly around the shoulders of her white, V-neck blouse; Haines noticed she had a habit of brushing the strands away from her right eye. He also observed an almost total lack of makeup except for a pale shade of lipstick, and the simple turquoise pendant that hung from her neck almost to the cleavage of the blouse; there was no jewelry on her hands, and her nails, while neat, were devoid of polish. The blouse itself was reasonably well filled out; she was rather small-breasted for a tall woman, Haines thought, but still strikingly attractive. Probably in her early forties, he figured—maybe older, considering her medical reputation. Cat Baxter, a man of discerning cynicism and dour appraisals, had grudgingly labeled her "pretty damn good."

". . . have you ever believed in ghosts?" she was saying.

"To about the same extent I believe in flying saucers. In other words, I doubt their existence but I'm willing to believe anything's possible. I keep remembering that line from *Hamlet,* 'There are more things on heaven and earth than are dreamed of in your philosophy.' If you asked me if I believe in ghosts *now,* I'd have to answer yes. The alternative is to admit I'm crazy, or going crazy, isn't it?"

She shook her head, her dark brown eyes sober with an understanding that he could feel. "Let's start with psychiatry's so-called explanation," she said. "Which holds that ghosts are merely manifestations of various emotional stimuli. Unconscious wishing that takes the form of very powerful fantasizing. Terrible grief. Guilt feelings buried far deeper than a person realizes. So the theory is that the subconscious mind is capable of creating two-dimensional images in whatever form the mind desires. A wife mourning a dead husband, for example, has the ability to conjure up his ghost. Not really, of course, but in her own mind a visual apparition that can be terrifyingly real. Do you follow me?"

Haines nodded but frowned. "You used the expression *so-called explanation*. Sounds like you don't quite buy the official line."

She leaned forward, cupping her hands and looking at him steadily. "No, I don't. It's too pat, too glib, and it leaves a whole bunch of unanswered questions. In other words, at best it's only a partial explanation that doesn't fit every case. Your UFO analogy was excellent. You can provide logical, satisfactory solutions for 90 percent of such sightings, but that still leaves 10 percent that can't be resolved so easily. No, Mr. President, seeing ghosts does not mean you're going bonkers. As a psychiatrist, I may find that what you've seen fits the conventional doctrine. You're obviously under enormous stress, and stress can play havoc with the subconscious. But I'm also a parapsychologist, if you know the term."

"Something to do with ESP, isn't it?"

"ESP is only one aspect of parapsychology. A more generalized definition would be the study of all psychic phenomena, and that would range from poltergeists to mental telepathy. Up to the 1970s, most scientists considered parapsychologists as first cousins to cranks, charlatans, and outright con artists. Respectability came in the form of acceptance of parapsychology by the American Association for the Advancement of Science. And rightly so, for parapsychology *is* a science—rather inexact, like psychiatry itself, but still requiring all the tools and objectivity of any scientific research. For whatever reason, pyschic phenomena do exist and deserve to be studied—and explained, if possible."

A look akin to bitterness slid across Jeremy Haines's face. "I doubt whether you can find any explanation for what's happened to me short of concluding that I'm on the verge or even in the middle of a nervous breakdown."

"That, too, is possible."

Her bluntness surprised him and he could not smother a slight smile that was more wry than humorous. "In other words," he observed a little sadly, "I *am* going nuts."

"I didn't say that. Like most laymen, you overgeneralize when it comes to medical terminology. A nervous breakdown is not synonymous with insanity. Seeing ghosts may well be a symptom of nerves frayed to the point of severing the mind from reality but . . ."

"Which seems to be a polite way of calling me insane. Severing the mind from reality? My God, Dr. Sarazin, isn't that a classic definition of insanity?"

She instantly regretted her phraseology. He was, quite naturally, vulnerable and sensitive to any nuance yet he was too intelligent to be coddled and soft-soaped. "There is," she said cautiously, "the crucial element of degree. The severance can be temporary, relatively mild, highly concentrated in one or two particular areas, and potentially reparable. That doesn't add up to insanity. In your case—and admittedly, at this stage I'm guessing—I suspect you've compensated well for all the stress of your job except for one weak spot. What that is, I have no idea, but it's my job to identify it. The apparition or apparitions you've seen probably represent the one point at which your nervous defenses have weakened."

"You should use the singular," he said with an enigmatic smile.

"I beg your pardon?"

"Apparition, not apparitions. I keep seeing only one particular ghost."

He was a widower, she knew. "Your late wife?"

"No, nothing like that. So you can forget your deep grief buried in the subconscious theory. I only wish it were that simple. Tell me something, Doctor. Do *you* believe in ghosts?"

"I can't give you a simple yes or no."

"That's a politician's reply, not a psychiatrist's. Nor a parapsychologist's."

Jessica laughed. "I suppose the psychiatrist in me would say no, there are no such things as ghosts. The parapsychologist in me would give you a fairly strong *maybe*. Perhaps even a *probably*."

The President smiled, but again, there was no mirth in his expression and those gray eyes were filled with unconcealed tension. "At this point," he said with a touch of grimness, "I think I'd prefer hearing from the parapsychologist in you. Incidentally, would you object to my lighting up a pipe? I find it relaxes me."

"Not at all. I like the smell of a pipe."

Jessica watched as Haines went through the pipe smoker's ritual: dipping a well-worn briar into a leather tobacco pouch, tapping the contents into the pipe bowl, and then lighting it with a match torn from a blue and gold matchbook. Her sharp vision caught the inscription on the cover; the words AIR FORCE ONE embossed just under the Presidential seal. Haines sucked the flame into the top of the bowl, extinguished the match with two flicks of his wrist, and puffed away, staring at her through smoke tinged with a pleasant aroma.

She sniffed as delicately and unobtrusively as possible. "Nice. Smells like vanilla."

"Mixture 79 is the brand. I've smoked it for years. And thanks. Telling a man his tobacco smells good is like complimenting a woman on her perfume."

She had the feeling he had used the pipe-lighting interlude as a respite, like the one-minute rest between the rounds of a fight. The gray eyes were fixed on her face, asking silent questions. Jessica Sarazin cleared her throat.

"You asked how parapsychologists feel about the existence of ghosts or spirits. The answer depends on one's definition of ghost. If you mean a ghost is the spirit of a dead person, someone who has managed to remanifest in the dimension of the living, then I'd have to raise a yellow flag of caution. Acceptance of that definition amounts to belief in life after death, and this is something neither I nor a great many parapsychologists are prepared to concede. There are other theories and explanations just as valid."

"Such as?"

"A British parapsychologist I admire holds that a ghost is a form of very powerful personal energy that somehow persists even after a person dies. There's considerable support for this theory. Studies have shown that the human body can transmit a kind of electrical energy even when all other organic life has ceased. The energy persists apparently indefinitely and in rare cases is so strong that it forms the image of its original source, or so the hypothesis goes.

"Many of the other theories are variations of the electrical energy supposition. One researcher claimed that we generate a form of personal energy that in its strongest quantity can continue after death. Another believed that all space and matter contains an unknown substance capable of preserving the impressions or images emitted by the living. He called the substance 'psychic ether,' and not a few parapsychologists think there may be some scientific validity to it.

"There's a common denominator in all this. Imagine that psychic ether, assuming it exists, is like an invisible photographic film. Obviously, not everyone who dies generates enough energy to leave a permanent imprint on this film—if everyone did, we'd have more ghosts than people. But the parapsychological theory is that the energy is recorded on the psychic film under exceptionally traumatic circumstances. The victim of a murder or an execution, for example. A person dying violently and unexpectedly, such as in a plane crash. A mother who at the very moment of death worries not about death itself but its effect on those who survive her—a beloved husband, son or daughter."

Jeremy Haines's pipe had gone out, and as he relit it, Jessica noticed that the hand holding the match shook slightly. But his voice remained calm, almost detached. "Fascinating," he commented, "but if it's true it would seem that a great many people would be seeing a great many ghosts. Violent, traumatic deaths are not uncommon."

"The answer—and again I'm speaking mostly of theory—is that the images recorded on this psychic film are suspended in time, invisible until they encounter the mind of a person who's sensitive to psychic stimuli. Such stimuli could have several sources. Stress, grief, fright, guilt—they all can trigger the mechanism that allows them to see that piece of film."

The President was frowning. "Do you believe this—this psychic film stuff?"

Dr. Sarazin framed her answer carefully. "Let's just say I believe it's an interesting explanation for events and instances that are not scientifically explicable in themselves."

Jeremy Haines sighed. "I'm afraid that doesn't help me one damned bit. First of all, I don't think I'm the type to be sensitive to your psychic stimuli—if I were, I should have seen my wife's ghost by now." He hesitated, and when he resumed, his voice was an octave lower and almost husky. "I loved her very much and not a day goes by that I don't think of her and miss her. So this film script of yours makes no bloody sense."

Jessica had the urge to reach across her desk and

take his hand. She said gently, "It's not necessarily my script and I didn't claim it was valid. But your not seeing your wife as some kind of ghost doesn't make it invalid, either. Those who accept the psychic film or energy explanation would merely point out that she apparently didn't give off enough energy to record an image. Was her death accidental or natural?"

The gray eyes flashed anger. "She died of cancer. Lingering and painful. Christ, she didn't have any of your goddamned energy to spare for herself, let alone some harebrained theory!"

She could have kicked herself for asking the question. She had allowed him to go from interest to bitter skepticism, from a desire to be helped to a brittle defensiveness, yet this was one of the hazards of her job. The probing and the searching could touch a raw nerve and a patient's resentment came with the territory.

She said, with a coolness she did not really feel, "But you *have* seen something, Mr. President, and we have to find a reason for it. I can appreciate your reluctance to swallow these 'harebrained' theories as gospel—I've already conceded they are far from gospel. Yet perfectly sane, well-balanced people have experienced similar phenomena. We can deny, scoff at, or reject the theories as nonsense, but we can't dismiss the phenomena themselves."

She could see the tenseness on his face dissolve into an expression she could not quite fathom. The interest was back but accompanied by a coating of wariness that warned her to tread carefully. His eyes had narrowed into half-slits, imparting an intensity not entirely free of anger.

"Doctor," he said quietly, "when you repeated my use of 'harebrained,' I take it you were parroting me, not agreeing with me."

"Mr. President, there have been too many verified instances of psychic phenomena for me to label any explanation, however theoretical, as harebrained."

"I'd appreciate hearing some examples."

"It would take the rest of the day to cite just the better cases from England alone. The British take their ghosts seriously, and with good reason. Psychic investigators of unimpeachable reputation have testified that there really are haunted castles, inns, and homes. Some apparitions have even been photographed, with no evidence of fakery or doctoring. I've seen copies of them, and they're impressive. One was a snapshot taken of a car in a funeral procession. The driver presumably was alone but in the back seat was the image of a woman—the woman who was being buried that same day."

Haines was staring at her, eyes now wide open. "No chance that somebody faked it?"

"A great deal of effort went into trying to prove it was a hoax, but without success. As far as anyone could tell, a member of the family took the picture on impulse and was totally shocked when it was developed."

"Ghosts by Kodak," the president muttered. "Maybe I should keep a camera with me, if only to prove my sanity."

"Maybe you should," Jessica agreed, and Haines looked at her, surprised.

"Are you kidding?"

"No, I'm not, although there's no certainty the camera would record anything. Ghost photographs can be rather perverse. Some investigators have taken pictures of apparitions visible to their eyes and come up with absolutely nothing on the film. Yet some people have photographed what were apparently normal scenes and objects—but when the film was developed, the results were weird. Faces of perfect strangers, of long-dead relatives. This may be part of the psychic film theory."

"These all occurred in England?"

"Incidents have occurred here, too. Legitimate American ghost stories are far less frequent and the evidence not as conclusive—after all, we're a much younger nation than Britain. As a matter of fact, the White House itself is supposed to be haunted by the ghost of Abraham Lincoln, although he hasn't been seen for many years."

The President grimaced. "If old Abe showed up in my bedroom tonight, I wouldn't be a damned bit surprised."

She studied his solemn, concerned features. "Perhaps it's time to talk about your own particular ghost," Jessica suggested. "Exactly where have you experienced this psychic phenomenon?"

Haines snorted. "You mean exactly where have I seen the damned ghost?"

She could not help but laugh. "I'm sorry. Too often we psychiatrists slip into jargon. Okay, where has your damned ghost appeared—in the White House?"

"No. On Air Force One. Always on Air Force One."

Her eyebrows went up. "That's a pretty big airplane, isn't it? And it can carry a lot of people. No one else has seen it?"

Haines hesitated, and the furrows reappeared on his brow. "My God," he murmured, "when I told this story to Cat Baxter, he thought I was crazy. He tried hard not to show it but that look on his face—I'll never forget it. It was like watching the countenance of a judge about to pass sentence."

"I'd like to hear the story," Jessica said calmly.

"The . . . the thing I keep seeing appears only when I'm alone on that airplane. Have you ever flown in a 747?"

She nodded.

"Well, then you know it has an upper compartment behind the cockpit, reachable via a spiral staircase. On Air Force One, the upper level is set aside mostly for my own use. There's a lounge area with armchairs, a couple of sofas and a desk. Also a small stateroom and a private lavatory. I've established the rule that nobody goes up there without my permission. A Secret Service agent stations himself by the staircase in the lower cabin and makes sure nobody goes up without my approval—which I don't give very often."

He paused to fill and to light his pipe again—once more, Jessica thought, he was giving himself a chance to formulate words before he spoke—and resumed.

"I don't know know whether this is clinically significant to a psychiatrist, but I prefer being alone. More so these days than before, although I've always been something of a loner since my wife died. I mention this because of what I'm about to tell you. The ghost has appeared every time I've been alone in that upper lounge. And I've flown on Air Force One precisely six times in the past four months."

"Four months ago is when you first saw it?" she asked.

"Correct. And I might add I saw it just as clearly and vividly as I'm seeing you now. There was no shrouded figure, no wavering, shimmering wisp of ectoplasm, no indistinct shadow. It was so real it was flesh and blood. I might as well have been talking to someone as alive as you."

Dr. Jessica Sarazin felt, simultaneously, a chill and a sense of anticipation. "You saw someone you once knew?"

"Not exactly. This particular ghost died in 1945, and I was fourteen years old at the time. But I knew a lot about him, Doctor. You see, I discovered an interesting coincidence. Does the date January thirtieth mean anything to you?"

She shook her head.

"It will. It was on January thirtieth, four months ago, when I was returning from California on Air Force One, that I first saw him. A man who was born January thirtieth, 1882, over a century ago. Doctor, please turn off your tape recorder."

"I can't, Mr. President. If I am to study your case thoroughly and objectively, I must have an absolutely accurate, verbatim record of what you tell me."

"Do you realize the consequences if a tape of this session was to be heard by anyone else?"

"I have indeed. I assure you, the tape will never be heard by anyone other than myself. It will be placed in a locked steel box that, in turn, will be kept in a safe for which I alone possess the combination. Does that ease your mind?"

"No, it doesn't. But I suppose there's nothing I can do about it. Baxter trusts you and I'm afraid I must, too."

"And I won't violate that trust. Now tell me about this man who was born more than a century ago."

"I'm a little surprised you haven't already guessed. The ghost I saw, Dr. Sarazin, and have subsequently met five other times and always in the upper lounge of that 747, was Franklin Delano Roosevelt."

— TWO

Most of all, he remembered, he had been terribly restless on that night of June 30—more so than on any flight he had taken as President.

He felt a gnawing, frustrating feeling of helplessness that trickled into depression. He yearned for companionship and simultaneously rejected it as a sign of the weakness that seemed to have invaded his faculties. The awesome loneliness of the Presidency had been grafted onto his own penchant for solitude, and it was a deadly, debilitating combination; he knew it was wrong and yet he could do nothing about it.

It frightened him that he wanted desperately to talk to someone on his own intellectual or even political level—a peer, a confidant, an administration colleague—and that he did not dare. He was afraid to. He had become too pliable, the steel of resolve and judgment so weakened by constant exposure to the searing heat of crisis that he bent willingly to the views, opinions, and advice of others. Where once he had welcomed the give-and-take of discussion and debate as mere input into his own decision-making process, now he was swaying to whatever verbal wind was blowing in his direction.

"President Haines seems pitifully vulnerable to the influence of the last person he talked to," *The New York Times* had commented in a recent editorial. Jeremy Haines had read it without anger because privately he acknowledged its truth. Even this concession bothered him. During his first administration, virtually any editorial containing even mild criticism used to infuriate him; now he was accepting criticism as gospel.

He hated himself for this flabbiness. He should have fired that insubordinate bastard Duane Collison long ago, just as Harry Truman had sacked Douglas MacArthur, and there was a time when he would have swung the ax with hardly a second thought. But no longer. He had found himself listening more and more to Collison with a kind of respect that once would have sickened him. He could sense the general's contempt and hostility toward him, so thinly masked by the layer of obsequiousness a military man allows Presidential authority. Yet Jeremy Haines had found himself wondering if Collison's pugnaciousness wasn't a wiser course than his own fumbling ineffectiveness when it came to curbing the Russians.

Collison was on Air Force One tonight, at the President's own invitation; Haines had deemed it both courteous and expedient to let the chairman of the National Security Council see for himself how the laser anti-missile system was progressing. They had said little to each other during the trip, except for exchanging prescribed pleasantries within earshot of others, but Collison had asked for a private meeting sometime during the return flight. The general was waiting, Haines knew, to be asked up to the upper lounge sanctuary before the 747 landed at Andrews Air Force Base.

But Jeremy didn't want to see him. Not in this frame of mind. Not when he felt increasing envy for Collison's aggressive confidence, so sharply contrasting with his own growing weariness and vulnerability to persuasion. No, Haines decided, it would be better for him to be alone. In the old days, he might have wandered up to the flight deck to chat with the crew. He particularly loved to visit the cockpit when Colonel Marcus Henderson was commanding Air Force One, first on the old Boeing 707 and then on the ill-fated Condor after it replaced the original Boeing. But Henderson had been among the victims when the Condor crashed en route to Palm Springs; Haines had not only grieved his death but felt guilt that he had indirectly caused it. Perhaps, subconsciously, he had deliberately avoided getting close to Henderson's replacement on Air Force One, Colonel Joseph Cardella.

He liked Cardella, a stocky, cigar-smoking fireplug of a pilot with a brusque, no-nonsense air that invited both respect and instant compliance from his crews. Like Henderson before him, he flew airplanes by the book; the safety and well-being of the President and anyone else on Air Force One were his highest priority. It was typical of Cardella that even as he secretly wished Haines would have the same easy rapport with him that the President had shared with Henderson, he understood why it had never developed. On more than one occasion, he had been on the verge on inviting the President up to the cockpit but had held back. Haines was not the same man who used to sit for hours on the cramped flight deck, smoking his pipe and listening to the crew's irreverent banter, and Joe Cardella knew it.

On this night of January 30, a discreet chime sounded—the signal that the President had pressed the cockpit button on his lounge telephone—and Cardella flicked his own communications switch marked Upper Lounge.

"Flight deck, Cardella," he answered.

"Colonel, this is the President. I was wondering where we are."

Cardella, who had just checked their position seconds ago, replied, "About forty miles south of Albuquerque, Mr. President. Right on schedule, sir—we're estimating Andrews in three and a half hours. Might even be a little less than that if this tailwind holds up."

There was a moment's silence at the other end of the line and Cardella felt uncomfortable, as if he was supposed to provide more information and didn't know exactly what was wanted. "Everything okay back there, sir?" he finally asked.

"Everything's fine. I . . . was just curious. Thank you, Joe."

The intercom clicked off. Now that was something, Cardella thought—the first time the President had ever called him by his first name. He hadn't been aware Haines really knew his first name. Sounded a little bored, Cardella mused, and maybe lonely. The pilot had a sudden urge to call him back and invite him to the flight deck and actually had a finger on the switch when he decided Haines probably would rather be left alone. Anyway, Cardella was one of those airmen who instinctively resented the presence of outsiders in his working environment.

Yet even as he made that decision, he sighed. He had a curious disturbing sense that he was wrong. And at the very moment his forefinger touched the lounge communications switch, only to withdraw, Jeremy Haines was blinking his eyes in disbelief at what he was seeing . . .

The President was sitting in one of the well-padded, swivel armchairs by a lounge window. Unwilling to summon any of the three Air Force stewards assigned to the Presidential plane, he had mixed himself a Scotch and soda from the lounge bar and was sipping it meditatively, his gaze directly ahead toward the bulkhead and small door that led to the communications section and, beyond that, the cockpit. Seldom did he venture through that door; it was an area containing a bewildering complex of electronic consoles, including the computerized war codes and the means of transmitting their deadly signals to the Strategic Air Command, to naval units, and to missile centers all over the world.

It also was an area grimly reminding Jeremy Haines that Air Force One was more than his personal airplane. It was a flying command post from which, with the touch of a few coded, computerized buttons, he could launch an armada of nuclear weapons toward any spot on the globe. At his fingertips were the means to destroy civilization, yet he could never forget that somewhere in the giant enigma that was Russia were similar consoles capable of igniting the same holocaust. Maybe, he was thinking, that was one reason for not wandering up to the cockpit. He would have to go through the door into the communications area, always manned by a cold-eyed Air Force officer with a briefcase containing the war codes strapped and padlocked to one leg. He had used the room a few times to send routine messages, but the sight of the padlocked briefcase invariably unnerved him. A smaller version of the installation had been built in the White House basement; it even bore the same name, War Room. He hated both locations. They spoke silently of the potential horror, the ultimate nightmare, that every President must face.

Cardella had guessed right. Jeremy Haines had wanted to visit the flight deck and to absorb, as he had with Marcus Henderson, the cheerful yet brisk efficiency of a well-drilled crew—a sanctuary of sanity in the midst of insanity. But he could not get himself to walk through that door, like the bulkhead itself bulletproofed with a special alloy lighter and stronger than steel.

Haines was staring idly at the door, resenting its restraining influence that somehow imparted a feeling of evil, when his gaze fell on the armchair directly ahead of him, its back to him. There was something unfamiliar resting against its side, so unfamiliar that for a moment he did not even recognize what it was and thought a steward must have left a broken part of a serving cart in the lounge. Almost simultaneously, he felt a clammy chill in the warm cabin.

His brain identified what his eyes rejected as impossible. It was a steel crutch, twin-legged, with a rubberized horizontal grip at the top. Then his brain rejected what his eyes saw. A hand closed on the grip and the chair swiveled 180 degrees around on its base so that its occupant faced him.

Jeremy Haines gasped.

"Good evening, Jeremy."

The voice was no less familiar than the occupant's face, the tone rich, cultured, mellifluous. Those features—Haines instinctively blinked, not just in wonderment but to focus a confirmation of what he was seeing—the leonine head with its bulldozer jaw and patrician profile; the deepset eyes, embedded in parchment skin so discolored that it looked like tobacco stains; the massive shoulders and chest. Even the clothing was familiar—a cape draped over those shoulders, the same cape, Haines thought unbelievingly, that he was wearing in Warm Springs, Georgia, at 1:15 P.M., on April 12, 1945, when an artist was sketching his portrait, a painting never to be finished. "I have a terrific headache," that magic voice had said. Only it wasn't a mere headache. It was the pain of a massive cerebral hemorrhage that stilled the voice forever.

"Good evening, Jeremy . . ."

Until now.

Haines swallowed hard and found his own voice. "This is one hell of a dream," he said hoarsely.

"Are you quite sure it's a dream?" The inflection was faintly mocking.

"I prefer dream to hallucination." He was staring at the apparition's blue suit under the cape. He remembered reading once that Franklin Roosevelt was wearing a suit that color when he was stricken. My God, this thing seemed alive. All that was missing was the famous cigarette holder, jutting from the strong lips like the aft flagstaff of a ship. And as if the apparition could read his mind, it chuckled. "I'd ask you for a cig but unfortunately you smoke a pipe and anyway that little vice of mine is no longer possible."

. . . for a cig." Roosevelt had never fully articulated *cigarette*—it was always *cig*. Haines shuddered involuntarily and the voice said sympathetically, "I know this is rather hard to take, my friend, but believe me, you're not dreaming."

"I have to be," Haines breathed. "You're too damned real to be anything but a dream."

The massive head tilted back and laughed. "I hate to disappoint you, Jeremy, but to paraphrase slightly from my favorite author in my favorite story, I'm not sitting in your stomach like an undigested bit of beef, a blot of mustard, a crumb of cheese, a fragment of underdone potato. That's what Ebenezer Scrooge said to Jacob Marley's ghost. By God, I still remember those lines. I used to read Dickens' *Christmas Carol* to my children and grandchildren every Christmas Eve." The voice had turned wistful at the memory and then hardened almost to the point of harshness. "I'm afraid, old boy, you'd better accept what your mind and intellect tell you is utterly impossible. You're talking to a ghost."

"I don't believe in ghosts."

"Can't say that I blame you. I didn't either." That hearty laugh again. "Of course, I do now. I seem to be one."

Haines decided wryly that if this crazy nightmare was going to persist, he might as well go along with the illusion. It might even be enjoyable. "Okay," he obligingly agreed, "if you're a ghost, what the hell are you doing here—on a modern jet at forty-five thousand feet traveling six hundred miles an hour?"

Roosevelt looked around the big lounge, apparently for the first time. "Quite an airplane," the ghost commented. "If I had one of these, I might have enjoyed flying more than I did. Actually, I hated going anywhere by air. Give me a ship or a train anytime. My God, I'll never forget that trip from Albany to Chicago in 1932. Flew there to accept the nomination in one those damnable Ford trimotors. Just a stunt, y'know. A way to prove that a polio cripple could be President—flying was supposed to be only for the ablebodied men who were brave."

He guffawed. "Brave? My God, Jeremy, I was airsick the whole flight and absolutely petrified. I didn't fly again until the war, when I had to. Can't even remember what planes I used. One was a big flying boat. The other was some four-engine airplane Douglas built. Otis Bryan of TWA was my pilot. Grand fellow, Otis. Once we were going into Malta and . . ."

Haines interrupted him, gently but firmly. "Even if

this is a dream, I have to ask you what you're doing here. What do you want?"

"To help you," Franklin Roosevelt replied. "That is, if you'll accept help. I gather you need some fresh ideas. Fresh input."

He might as well go along with the dream, Haines decided again. At least the conversation was getting interesting. "Mind you, I still don't believe I'm talking to the ghost of FDR. A predecessor, I might add, whom I respect tremendously—which is probably the only reason I'm continuing this asinine game."

"You're going to find it's not a game."

"I'll find it out when I wake up."

"My friend," the ghost said softly, "you're not asleep. As you're going to discover any moment now."

Haines was still looking at the apparition in front of him when, out of the corner of his eye, he saw the War Room door open, and there emerged the barrel-shaped figure of Colonel Cardella. In the split second it took for the President to spot the pilot and then to look back at the ghost, Roosevelt had disappeared. He tried to compose himself as the commander of Air Force One approached, his craggy, bulldog features creased with concern.

"Thought I'd drop back and see how you were doing," Cardella said pleasantly. "You sounded, uh, a little depressed."

Haines tried hard to keep his voice calm. "I'm fine," he said, but controlling himself verbally fell far short of hiding his appearance.

"You're as pale as a ghost," Cardella said, with an

innocence that made the President smile grimly to himself. "Sir, are you all right?"

"Depressed was the right word," Haines allowed. "I appreciate your asking, though. Matter of fact, your company's welcome. It probably sounds sacrilegious, sitting in the midst of sheer luxury, but I guess I was going stir crazy."

The pilot nodded, more in agreement than sympathy. "That's really why I came back, Mr. President. Thought you might like to stretch your legs and pay us a little visit up front. Major Jackman says he'd rather smell your pipe than my cigar." He gestured toward the intercom phone on the cabin wall next to the President's chair. "I would have called you first, but I figured you might be napping and I didn't want to disturb you. That's why I came back in person."

He was rambling a bit, a little ill at ease, Haines realized. "I think I'd like that visit very much, Joe." The President looked at his Rolex, rose, and followed the colonel toward the cockpit. The communications officer on duty in the War Room apparently had climbed to his feet the minute he saw the lounge door open and was already saluting as Haines entered.

"At ease," the President laughed. "No need for formalities on this plane, son." The officer, wearing captain's bars, was a whipcord-slim youngster with a dark complexion, straight black hair, and high cheekbones that hinted at some Indian heritage. Haines had met him at the start of the trip from Washington; Cardella always introduced his crew to the Number One passenger. "Captain Ferguson, isn't it?" the President inquired.

"Yes, sir."

"Well, it isn't necessary to rise and salute every time I walk through here. I appreciate the gesture but I'd prefer informality while we're flying."

"Thank you, sir." Ferguson refrained from confessing that the salute was more for Cardella's benefit than for the President's. The colonel was a stickler for military protocol.

"Good-looking young officer," Haines observed to the command pilot as they proceeded toward the cockpit.

"Very competent, Mr. President. He's about one-quarter Apache, you know. The crew calls him Geronimo."

A thought suddenly crossed Haines's mind. What should he call that damned ghost—Mr. President? Now *that* was a stupid thing to worry about. He was still dreaming all this. Even as he stepped into the flight deck, with its array of complicated instruments and the peculiar yet not unpleasant leathery odor of all airliner cockpits, he was sure it was a dream. It had to be.

He watched Cardella maneuver himself laboriously into the left seat, nodding to his copilot, Jackman, who removed the oxygen mask he was required to don anytime the command pilot left the cockpit. It was one of those fascinating, small but vital niceties of flight deck discipline that Haines had learned from Marcus Henderson. Curious that a dream should be so detailed and authentic; dreams were supposed to be full of illogical situations, yet there was nothing illogical about what he was experiencing now. The easy, friendly greeting from Major Jackman, whose rotund body matched his pixie face, and a respectful handshake from the flight engineer, Lieutenant Curtis, a towering beanpole of a man with freckles and a bristling moustache. Nothing illogical about the way Cardella suggested that the President don a headset and listen to the air-to-ground communications between Air Force One and Air Traffic Control. That's what Henderson had suggested every time they flew, and what Haines invariably did.

He had the headset on now.

"Air Force One, this is Albuquerque Center. Please ident."

"Roger, Air Force One identing."

"Thank you, Air Force One. You're nice and clear on our scope. Please confirm ground speed and altitude."

"Air Force One is at forty-five thousand and we're showing five hundred eighty knots ground speed. Estimating over Amarillo in six minutes."

Some dream, Jeremy Haines thought once more. Even the dialogue's authentic. He listened to the metallic-sounding chatter for a few more minutes, then lit his pipe. The familiar odor of the tobacco tossed another challenge at his confidence. This was a dream in which everything was routine and frighteningly normal. It wasn't supposed to be happening this way . . .

". . . like the smell of that pipe, Mr. President," Jackman was saying. "Now take our colonel's cigars. They smell like burning engine oil."

"You don't laugh at my jokes," Cardella growled, "so you might as well learn to put up with those cigars."

Haines resorted to doing something that he hadn't

done since childhood nightmares—he tried to force open eyes that already were open. He *had* to wake up, he kept telling himself. The very logic of what he was experiencing made the whole thing illogical. He closed his eyes, opened them again, and saw Cardella turning the knob of the autopilot with the careful dexterity of a surgeon probing an incision. Jackman's hand delicately manipulated the throttle settings. The smooth precision of their movements contrasted incongrously with the light talk, as if their minds were linked to the red glow of the instruments and not to their tongues. Too, too real. Jeremy Haines shuddered again.

When he finally decided to leave the cockpit, it was more from frustration than boredom. He had expected the visit to confirm he was dreaming; it had done the opposite. Gravely, he thanked Cardella, nodded pleasantly to Jackman, and shook hands with the flight engineer. "I'd like to do this more often," he said as he paused at the doorway.

"You're always welcome, Mr. President," Cardella said in a pleased tone.

After the door closed behind Haines, Cardella playfully slapped the copilot's shoulder. "Told you he just wanted to be asked," he chortled.

"Yeah," Jackman agreed. "Seemed to be enjoying himself, too. He had that headset on for fifteen minutes. God, Joe, he's aged."

Cardella nodded soberly. "When I went to invite him up here, he looked sick. Absolutely no color in his face. Which reminds me, Curtis, what's the duct temp gauge show for the upper lounge?"

The flight engineer peered at an instrument on his dial-studded panel. "Eighty, sir."

The colonel frowned. "Eighty, huh? The zone temp control should give that area about a nice seventy-two. Funny."

Jackman glanced at him furiously. "Was the President complaining of being cold?"

"No, matter of fact, I was. When I went back to see him, I felt the damnedest draft. Like somebody had opened a window."

"At forty-five thousand feet?"

"I said it felt like it. Just for a few seconds."

Jackman shrugged. "Want Curtis to go back there and look around?"

Cardella considered this but shook his head. "I don't think it's necessary. While I was escorting Mr. Haines to the cockpit, I walked right by the lounge emergency exit. It seemed tighter than a new drum. No sound of an air leak or any misalignment—that draft, or whatever it was, didn't come from there and that door's the only possible source outside of the heating ducts themselves. Seems crazy, doesn't it?"

"Well," Jackman philosophized, "this bird's got four and a half million parts, and that's four and a half million possibilities for some screwy troubles."

Cardella just grunted. "Never felt a draft like that before," he commented more to himself than to the others. "Gave me the creeps—like I was walking by a graveyard at night."

When the President left the cockpit and returned to his lounge seat, he made a point of checking his watch. He had been in the cockpit for thirty-one minutes. Dreams do not last for thirty-one carefully logged minutes, not unless the passage of time is part of the subconscious illusion that constitutes a dream. Considering this possibility, he mentally began to retrace every aspect of the flight from the time he boarded in Los Angeles. At no time could he remember closing his eyes, even for the luxury of momentary relaxation.

He had sat in the lower cabin for the takeoff—the Secret Service insisted on this because it would be easier to evacuate him if something went wrong on takeoff or while landing; the upper-lounge emergency exit was equipped with an evacuation slide, but the lounge was some thirty feet from the ground. He hadn't fallen asleep during takeoff—he remembered he was sitting next to Wayne Dillman, his press secretary, and talking with him until they reached cruising altitude. Then he had told Wayne he was going to the upper lounge and had added, "No visitors." As soon as he went to his private quarters, a steward had served him a snack that he only half finished before summoning the steward to remove the tray. He vividly recalled mixing that Scotch and soda the minute the steward left via the spiral staircase, and he was still sipping that same drink when the ghost appeared.

When, Jeremy Haines asked himself desperately, had he fallen asleep?

The truth hit his brain simultaneously with the return of that clammy aura that seemed to fill the lounge like a bone-chilling fog. Heart pounding, he stared at the empty seat that faced his. He thought he saw a small mist forming just above the seat, a tiny, swirling blur replaced instantly by the fully dimensional, non-transparent figure of the ghost.

Haines sighed. "Your entrances and exits are rather sudden," he said with false calmness.

"I don't mean to startle you," Roosevelt said, "but rapidity seems to be my mode of travel. Still think you're dreaming?"

"I don't know what to think. All I'm sure of is that I could never tell anyone about this. They'd have me committed. I wish that pilot had shown up a few seconds sooner. I might have had a witness."

"If he had shown up a few seconds sooner, I would have disappeared a few seconds sooner," FDR said. "The fact is, Jeremy, I'm afraid the only person who'll ever see me is you. And only on this plane."

"Why?"

"The reason is inconsequential. Only the fact that I'm here is important. My presence is one of those mysteries to be explained after each person dies. When each of us finds out whether death is simply everlasting sleep or whether it involves some kind of afterlife."

"You seem to be proof of the latter," Haines observed dryly, and Roosevelt threw back his head and laughed.

"Don't jump to conclusions," he advised. "If you want to believe I came straight from something called heaven, I can't stop you. Of course, some of my old Republican friends would prefer to believe I came straight from the other place."

"A decided possibility," Haines murmured. "After all, I'm a Republican. I may have admired you greatly, but I also thought you were a devious, manipulating son of a bitch."

"Only too true," FDR agreed delightedly. "For me, the ends justified the means. Which is the closest to idealism any politician can get. You're not so bad at the art yourself, by the way. Far more adept than some of your predecessors—Carter and Reagan, for example. Each well meaning and sincere but far too rigid. Poles apart politically and philosophically, yet strangely alike in some of their faults."

"You seem to have a great deal of knowledge about what has been happening to this country."

The noble, almost sculptured head nodded. "I'm aware of many things. *How* is beside the point—one of those mysteries I'm not at liberty to solve for you. You must remember, Jeremy, that politics constituted almost my entire life. I've followed with almost indecent interest the careers of your more recent predecessors."

The conversation, Haines decided, had taken on the quality of an absurd fantasy—discussing politics with a Franklin Delano Roosevelt who had been dead for almost a half-century. Yet the unreality, not to mention the growing suspicion that he was hallucinating, were not enough to quell curiosity. The discussion was following so natural a course that Haines had the crazy impulse to offer FDR a drink. What was his favorite? Haines searched his memory.

"Do ghosts drink?" he asked innocently. "If memory serves me, you were not averse to dry martinis."

Roosevelt smiled, a bit wistfully, Haines thought. "No thank you. In what you might term my present state of being, neither tobacco nor alcohol are possible. You might say I seem to have lost the urge. Now, what were we talking about?"

"Your successors, my predecessors. I'd be interested in hearing your opinions of them."

"Gladly. Starting with Truman—of course, gutsy little fellow—what he did to that pompous ass MacArthur warmed the cockles of my heart. No great intellect, of course, but a politician with a consummate instinct for survival. His campaign against Dewey was masterful. Y'know, I never wanted to run for a fourth term. I knew I was sick. But the thought of leaving the country in the hands of that two-bit district attorney absolutely petrified me. What was it Harold Ickes called him? Oh yes, he said Dewey reminded him of the groom on a wedding cake." FDR laughed lustily. "Perfect description, don't you think?" He rushed on before Haines could open his mouth.

"I never told anyone this, but I give you my word if I hadn't thought Dewey could lick any Democrat except me, I wouldn't have run in 1944. There was only one Republican I would have trusted to bring the war to a successful conclusion and to establish the United Nations. I'll give you one guess."

"I am unable to come up with the name of any Republican you respected," Haines said weakly.

"You're wrong. There was one. Wendell Wilkie. He damned near beat me in 1940, but by God, Jeremy, I liked him. Didn't agree with his domestic politics, but he had vision. He had the ability to learn and he knew the isolationists in his party were dangerously, stupidly wrong. When it came to foreign relations, he was always on my side of the fence and I admired him for that. Y'know, after I won in 1944 I toyed with the idea of making him my Secretary of State, but I was talked out of it. He was an internationalist and would have been the perfect bipartisan choice. But Harry Hopkins got his dander up and convinced me to name Ed Stettinius, whose only real qualification was that he *looked* like a Secretary of State. Harry told me, 'You're going to be your own Secretary of State, so what's the difference?' I should have followed my own judgment—I could have gotten along famously with Wendell. I had already proved I could work with enlightened Republicans—Harry. Stimson was one of the best cabinet choices I ever made, and Frank Knox didn't do a bad job in the Navy Department." He paused. Even ghosts have to catch their breath, Haines thought.

"From all I've read, you seemed to have relied on Hopkins a great deal," he ventured.

"Harry was completely loyal to me. Stubborn fellow but absolutely brilliant. But I'm digressing—an old failing of mine. You asked me about other Presidents. Well, I've already given you my opinion of Truman. Petty vindictiveness was his worst fault, but he wasn't alone in that. It was a quality I observed in Lyndon Johnson. Nixon, too, and also Carter. And Jack Kennedy had a mean streak—he hated pretty good. Remarkable young man, Kennedy. But we'll get to him later. Let's see—Johnson? Grand politician with a terrible temper. He dug his own grave with Vietnam, otherwise he might have gone down as a great President.

"I guess I could say the same about Richard Nixon. Y'know, Jeremy, I felt a great deal of sympathy for that man. Insecure, overly suspicious, defensive, and amoral. Yet in some ways I had to admire him. Considering his detestable political leanings and background, he showed great vision in foreign affairs. It took a lot of courage to mend fences with Red China. I consider that the greatest achievement of his administration, one no Democratic President could have pulled off without getting crucified.

"I almost forgot Eisenhower. And I'm going to surprise you. Ike was very much underrated as a President. No great intellect, a rather simple man, in fact, but tougher than people imagined—the right man at the right time. He knew when to conciliate and to compromise and when to stand up and be counted. I may be prejudiced, of course—I happened to like him very much personally and he did a grand job for us in the war.

"Now Jimmy Carter, I always felt sorry for him. He picked the wrong time to become President. He didn't have the personality or charisma to lead at a time when the nation was begging for leadership. That's one thing I can say about that fellow Reagan—he could lead, even though in my opinion he was usually wrong about the direction in which he was going. Like most of us who have held our office, Jeremy, his intentions were good. It's amazing there have been so few real scoundrels in the White House. Even Harding was well meaning. Now, I seem to have left out somebody."

"Kennedy," Haines reminded.

"Fascinating young man, absolutely fascinating. If he had lived, I'm convinced he would have ranked as one of our greatest Presidents. Provided that he could have kept his love life out of print while he was in office."

Haines could not resist it. "After you died, it came out that you hadn't been a paragon of fidelity yourself."

FDR smiled ruefully. "No, I wasn't. For reasons we won't go into. I'm not proud of what happened but I'm not ashamed, either. I respected Babs tremendously." It took Haines a minute to recall that Babs was the name FDR always used for his wife. "Bob Taft used to say that the country elected the wrong Roosevelt, and Babs was always a great help to me. She traveled around as sort of my own personal ambassador. The funniest line I ever heard Bob Hope pull was his definition of war strategy. He said it was figuring out when to take the offensive and how to keep Eleanor out of the crossfire. Y'know, I was the one who gave her the wartime code name of Rover—amusing touch, don't you think?"

Haines smiled. "Very, but dwelling on the past doesn't solve my problems. Andrei Magoyan is the present and the future with which I have to contend."

"Ever meet him?"

The question surprised the President. "I would think you already knew. You seem to know everything else."

"Not quite everything. There are a few gaps in my education about one Jeremy Haines. Come to think of it, though, I do remember—you never did meet him."

"Never. There have been a few overtures on his part for a meeting, and I suggested it once myself. Nothing ever came of these efforts. Frankly, I think he wanted a face-to-face meeting for the purpose of intimidating me. He insisted that Moscow be the site. My own advisers kept telling me it would be more of a collision than a meeting of minds."

"They're probably right," Roosevelt said. "Reminds me of what happened at Yalta. Joseph Stalin could be a charmer, he also was a liar and a hypocrite of unbounded proportions. In his own way, a tyrant as evil and deadly as Hitler. My God, Jeremy, Magoyan is just as bad. Virtually a reincarnation of Uncle Joe—damnation, what a falsely benign nickname."

"Speaking of names," Haines said, "you keep calling me by my first name. I'm at a loss to decide what I should call . . ."

"Call a ghost?" FDR finished up helpfully. "Pardon my little vanities, but I suggest you refer to me as Mr. President. During those twelve years I spent in office, I rather got used to the sound of it. Now, as one President to another, how can I help you?"

"A more apt question," Haines said with a touch of grimness, "is how a ghost can help me. I may not be dreaming but I'm pretty damned sure I'm hallucinating. Excuse my candor, *Mr. President,* but I prefer to regard you as an aberration, a temporary departure from sanity. As such, I can't accept advice from a source that may well be in my own exhausted mind."

"A natural reaction," Roosevelt said sympathetically. "Perhaps I'm moving a bit too fast. You need a little more time to get used to the idea."

"That I'm going off my rocker?"

"That my presence is real. And that I'm here to help you. We have a great deal in common, my friend. Your problems are remarkably similiar to those I faced. You even said so yourself, in that Harvard commencement speech. That's when I decided to . . . well, return. Grand touch, by the way. Harvard was my alma mater, y'know." He imparted this unnecessary piece of information with such obvious pride that Haines, in spite of his disturbed state, had to laugh.

"Your alma mater," he repeated. "I once heard that a Harvard man was the kind of guy who could follow you through a revolving door and come out first."

"Bully!" FDR exclaimed. "A marvelous definition. By God, Jeremy, if you can crack jokes, you may be coming around."

"To what? Believing in haunted airplanes?"

"To accepting my help. Not tonight. You're still upset and uncertain. Besides, in a few minutes that phone of yours is going to ring. It'll be General Collison, asking to come up. You might as well see him because I'm going to leave you for now with just one piece of advice. You don't have what I had—a Harry Hopkins, the only person I ever knew who didn't come into that Oval Office asking for something. A Harry Hopkins who served as a buffer between the President and everyone who demanded, urged, and sought. You used to have one in Phil Sabath, but he died in that crash, God rest his soul. So my first piece of advice, *Mr. President,* is to start being strong again. Be yourself, or what you once were. As long as you're in office, Jeremy, you're the President of the United States. Oh, you'll make mistakes. That goes with the territory. But mistakes are part of making decisions, and decisions are the first priority, the ultimate responsibility, of any President. God knows I wasn't perfect—when I tried to pack the Supreme Court, for example, or the day I let Hugo Black talk me into canceling the air-mail contracts. That duncehead Benny Foulois told me the Army could do the job. Jim Farley warned me it was too drastic a step, but Black kept . . ."

"Mr. President," Haines interrupted softly, "you're digressing again."

"So I am. Well, are you ready to see Collison?"

"Under duress, yes."

"Bully. Remember, just be the boss. I believe you're flying to Florida next week for a speech. I'll see you on the way down."

The ringing of the phone coincided exactly with the ghost's disappearance—one second, he was there, and the next, just an empty chair.

Haines picked up the receiver. "Yes?"

"Duane Collison, Mr. President. Do you have a few minutes?"

"Just a few, General. I'll tell the boys to pass you."

He pressed an intercom button and gave the order. Then he hung up and drained the last of the Scotch and soda. His fingers drummed restlessly on the arm of the seat. He was thinking it had been a long time since he felt no fear of confronting the chairman of the National Security Council. Now it was not fear he felt but a kind of nervous annoyance; he was uncomfortably aware that Collison wanted to discuss what they had just seen of Operation Umbrella, the massive multibillion-dollar anti-missile project that had been under development for more than a decade.

While the trip had been announced officially as a tour of the West Coast electronics plants working on the system, these inspections were cursory and somewhat of a blind for the main purpose—a top-secret briefing by project directors and scientists on recent major technological breakthroughs. The media had been banned from both the plant tours and the briefing, much to their natural displeasure, having to be satisfied with the crumb Haines tossed as he boarded Air Force One for the return flight.

"All I can tell you is that good progress is being made but we're a long way from home," he told reporters.

He had deliberately understated that progress. Operation Umbrella was on the verge of implementation, Collison had been visibly impressed by what had been divulged at the briefing. Brilliant man, the general, Haines conceded. He had been the President's personal liaison with Umbrella's planners but, typical of Duane Collison, he had exceeded that role. He had cajoled, extorted, and cut enough red tape to fill a 747's cargo bin—all in the name of the President, Haines had to admit.

"The President wants this done . . . the White House will not accept that explanation for delay . . . Mr. Haines won't be happy with this kind of procrastination . . ." Always pushing, shoving, driving, a man possessed with a mission yet curiously selfless.

Jeremy Haines heard the quick footsteps mounting the spiral staircase; the sound pushed a sliver of foolish resentment into his tired mind. Once *he* had climbed steps with the rapid pace of a man in a basement hearing the phone ring in his kitchen; now he moved up the 747's stairs wearily and laboriously. Collison, only a year younger than the President, was jogging.

Haines inspected him as the general entered the upper lounge. He was three inches taller than the President but much thinner—more a basketball player than a fullback. Collison's ice-blue eyes were his most distinguishing feature, so piercing that they managed to harden the pale, almost feminine contours of his matinee-idol face. Joe Cardella, who knew Collison when the latter was Air Force chief of staff, once insisted, "He looks like a 1925 Arrow Collar ad and has just about the same depth." But then Cardella, like so many of his flying colleagues, always held a jaundiced view of superiors who were more administrators than pilots. And even the colonel had to admit that Duane Collison's forte was administration, at which he was ruthlessly efficient—and public relations, at which he was smoothly adroit.

Inevitably, Collison was often compared to Douglas MacArthur. Collison was a spellbinding speaker with perfect oratorical timing and a convincing air of sincerity, a master of facts and irrefutable logic. His voice was his chief weapon—deep, strong, and subtly dramatic. It also offset the ascetic quality of his thin frame and pale face. It was a voice like a sound track dubbed into an unlikely body.

"Hello, Duane," the President said, motioning him to sit in the chair recently occupied by the apparition. "Care for a drink?"

"No thank you, Mr. President. I've already had my quota. These Air Force stewards mix a wicked martini."

The two men studied each other momentarily with the wariness of two fighters starting a cautious first round. It was Collison who finally said, "I hope you're as pleased as I am about Umbrella's progress."

"Very pleased. They've accomplished miracles in

the past two years. It's hard to believe that in 1983, when Ronald Reagan first proposed an anti-missile system, the consensus was that it amounted to a scientific improbability, requiring the expenditure of untold billions with little chance of success."

Collison smiled faintly. "Well, it *is* expensive. Ninety-eight billion dollars so far and that doesn't include the cost of putting it into orbital operation." His matter-of-fact tone suddenly took on an almost evangelistic fervor. "But considering what's at stake, you have to agree it has been money well spent."

Haines said laconically, "If the damned thing works."

"Oh, it'll work. After what we've seen and been told, I'm absolutely convinced we are on the verge of changing the balance of power between the United States and Russia."

"Which will last only until they come up with an Operation Umbrella of their own."

The general leaned forward, the tapering fingers of one hand cupping his chin. "Mr. President, you know as well as I do those bastards are a year behind us. Umbrella isn't just a shift in balance of power—it's a one-hundred-eighty-degree turn."

"But temporary," Haines repeated.

"Granted. That still gives us a year."

"In the context of modern times," the President said soberly, "a year is just a heartbeat."

Collison shook his handsome head. "Time enough to change history."

Haines frowned. "Change it in what way?"

The frown hadn't escaped Collison and he decided

to walk a careful, oblique course. "Change it for the better, I'd say."

The President said sharply, "Knock off the pussy-footing, Duane. What the hell are you suggesting?"

"I'm suggesting that Umbrella, assuming it works, gives us the chance to take a firmer stand against the Soviets. They not only respect strength, they fear it—if the strength is owned by the other guy. They're bullies, and like any bully they'll back down if somebody bigger and tougher than they are rolls up his sleeves and invites 'em outside."

Haines said dryly, "Your analogy is a bit over-simplified. You're implying we should threaten them with nuclear war, and that, my friend, is no minor let's-step-outside-the-bar brawl in some alley."

"We don't have to threaten them directly," Collison argued. "Once they know Umbrella's up and that they couldn't touch us with a thousand-missile attack, they'll see the light and very quickly. They'll be demanding peace conferences and disarmament."

"They're always demanding peace conferences and disarmament," the President reminded. "Peace on their terms and disarmament by everybody but them. The only real effect of Umbrella on the Soviet Union would be an accelerated effort to match us. We'd spend that year of so-called grace listening to the usual warmonger accusations with an occasional coo of a phony dove. No, Duane, I'm afraid all Umbrella gives us is a year in which we're assured they won't jump us, and after that—well, the same Mexican standoff that exists today. Nobody wants a nuclear holocaust, and we aren't strong enough to beat them with conventional weapons.

In that sense, we're paying a ninety-eight-billion-dollar insurance premium for a twelve-month policy."

Collison's eyes flashed with the intensity of sunlight on an ice floe. "You seem to regard Umbrella as a boondoggle. But you backed its continued development, Mr. President, from the day you took office. As did every President from Reagan on down. Are you now telling me it was an enormous waste of time and money?"

"I'm telling you nothing of the kind. I agree that Umbrella is absolutely essential for the national security. It's a permanent shield against nuclear attack, but one that inevitably will have a Soviet counterpart. And when that happens, we're back to Square One. Both systems, we hope, will prevent nuclear war and mutual destruction. I can only thank God we're getting our shield up first. If the Soviets had beaten us to it, they might have wiped this country off the map. Or at best, blackmailed us into submission."

The cold eyes narrowed. "Sir, that is precisely my point. We *are* getting our shield up first. Shouldn't we be considering doing exactly what they would have done if they had won the race?"

"Blackmail?"

"I don't care what you call it. I repeat, for one year we can call the shots. We're impervious to attack and they're relatively wide open."

"What in God's name are you proposing—that we attack *them?"*

Collison hesitated. "Attacking them from behind Umbrella's protection would have to be categorized as a last resort. I'm suggesting, sir, that we at least consider using Umbrella as a weapon of persuasion, a club held in the hand of a nation that makes it clear it will not be afraid to swing it."

Jeremy Haines stared at the general, ripples of disbelief flowing across his tense face. He said slowly, "As long as I am President of the United States, General Collison, I will not threaten anyone, including the Soviet Union, with nuclear war. I do not intend to go down in history as the man who pushed the button for the end of the world."

Duane Collison uncoiled his lanky body from the armchair and stood up, his patrician features a little flushed. "With all due respect, Mr. President, your attitude dooms Operation Umbrella to failure even if it works. We would have been better off with your Mexican standoff and spending the ninety-eight billion dollars on conventional weapons."

The President's weariness suddenly returned, unwelcome and discouraging, like the reappearance of a malaria fever he thought was under control. Or, he mused unhappily, spending ninety-eight billion on the poor and the sick and on scientific research that wasn't aimed at mass murder or at preventing mass murder. Aloud, he said diplomatically, "I appreciate your input, Duane. We'll be talking again—after all, Umbrella's still not proven. If just one or two missiles get through the screen on the test, we may have to go back to the drawing board."

Collison said rather stiffly, "I'm quite sure that isn't going to happen, Mr. President. And I'd like very much to discuss with you further the, ah, implications of a successful test."

But he was thinking, "A hell of a lot of good that discussion will do. He's still a procrastinating, spineless weakling . . ."

As he turned to leave the lounge, Haines said, "Tell McNulty no more visitors, will you?"

"Yes, sir."

The President's eyes followed Collison as he disappeared down the spiral staircase, then shifted to the chair in front of him. And there sat Franklin Roosevelt. Again, Haines had the curious feeling of being in a dream that somehow had acquired the logic of reality. He wasn't, he realized, even surprised.

"Interesting fellow," the ghost observed. "Reminds me a little of Doug MacArthur."

"Interesting and potentially dangerous. I take it you heard the conversation?"

"I did."

"Any conclusions?"

"Well," FDR said, "he doesn't have much respect for you."

"His opinion of me doesn't matter. I'm far more concerned with his opinions of Umbrella's impact. He seems to think it'll give us carte blanche to throw our weight around."

Roosevelt nodded. "He did seem a little, ah, belligerent. However, as you yourself pointed out, the system's still unproven. I suggest it would be grossly premature to make any decisions along the lines the general proposed. We have too many domestic problems demanding our immediate attention." He paused, clasping his big hands against the back of his head. "Fascinatin' idea, though, this Umbrella. Marvelous name, by the way. Worthy of being one I would have thought up myself."

Haines looked at him curiously. "I really didn't expect to see you again tonight. From what you said, I was supposed to have a little time to get used to . . . to a ghost."

"Couldn't resist a few more moments with you. Wanted your reaction to Collison. The man absolutely intrigues me. Tell me something, Jeremy, do you trust him?"

The President shook his head, a gesture more of indecision than a negative response. "I'm not sure what you mean by trust. He's an extremely capable person—without him, Umbrella probably would be two years behind in development. He's made it virtually a personal crusade. So I trust his ability and dedication. Whether I trust his loyalty to me and to my administration is another matter. He has been openly critical of my failure to contain Soviet aggression, although God knows there hasn't been any real choice. Containment at this stage means war."

The ghost bobbed his head sympathetically. "Dissent within an administration isn't unusual, Jeremy. That irascible old goat Harold Ickes fought with everybody. Even Jim Farley finally deserted me over the third term issue. You must remember that strong leaders invite controversy. They thrive on it—I know *I* did. General Collison's opposition is not really a breach of loyalty. It's an honest difference of opinion."

Haines snapped, "It's a goddamned important difference. He sees Umbrella as the means to get tough."

FDR said soothingly, "I'm sure we can determine the wisest course eventually, my friend. Let me leave you with this thought for now: The truly great men of history knew precisely where to draw the line between compromise and surrender. President Haines, I will see you in the very near future."

The ghost disappeared, leaving behind a disturbed Jeremy Haines, brooding over far more than his sanity. He was wondering exactly how dangerous Duane Collison was.

"I've left out certain matters involving security," the President said to Dr. Jessica Sarazin, "but I've given you the essential facts. That was how it all started."

— THREE —

The only sound in the room was the faint whir of the tape recorder.

Jessica shut it off and leaned back, studying the President's strained, solemn face. "And did the ghost reappear, as promised, on your flight to Miami the following week?"

"He did. And on four subsequent flights."

"Always the same way—one minute there and the next minute gone?"

"Like the characters I once saw on a couple of ancient television shows. I don't remember what they were called, but one was about a female genie and an astronaut. The other had a witch who was married to some advertising man."

"'I Dream of Jeannie' and 'Bewitched,'" Jessica said promptly as if she were competing on a quiz show. The President looked surprised and she added, "I happen to be a nut on TV trivia, and I remember both shows. I used to watch them in my younger days. The characters would appear or disappear in the time it took to blink your eye."

"And that's exactly how Franklin does it."

"You said he appears to be fully dimensional. There's no transparency at all?"

"None whatsoever. As I told you before, he might as well be flesh and blood." He hesitated, frowning. "That's unheard of, isn't it?"

"Unusual, but not unheard of. There was one documented case that occurred as recently as 1963. A prominent and very respectable British theologian named J. B. Phillips reported seeing the ghost of author C. S. Lewis, whom he had met only once but had corresponded with for quite a while.

"As Phillips told the story, Lewis suddenly appeared in his living room one night while Phillips was watching television. The ghost looked very natural and lifelike—surprisingly healthy as Phillips recalled the incident. Lewis spoke to him about problems Phillips was having at the time—I believe Phillips used the phrase 'revelant to my difficult circumstances.' The same thing happened again a week later, and once more they had a perfectly lucid conversation. No, Mr. President, yours was an unusual but not unique case of a so-called flesh-and-blood manifestation."

"Is that supposed to make me feel better?"

"It's supposed to assure you that the circumstances of your encounter have psychic precedents. She turned on the recorder again. "That clammy chill you mentioned—is it present every time he appears?"

Haines nodded. "Yes, although the intensity varies. It's like a damp fog, only colder. A fog you can feel but can't see. It lasts for only a few seconds."

"That, too, is not an unfamiliar phenonemon associated with ghosts. Tell me something—the first appearance was on January thirtieth and there were five others over the past four months. Yet you didn't see Captain Baxter until last Thursday. Why did you wait so long?"

"Because I was fairly certain I was going insane and I was afraid to have my diagnosis confirmed."

"What made you decide to see him, to confide in him, despite that fear?"

"It seems," Jeremy Haines said slowly, "I was beginning to listen to the ghost's advice."

"Well, that's expectable. From all I've read, Roosevelt was an extremely interesting, complex . . ."

"You don't understand, Doctor. I do more than listen to the advice. For the past three months, I've been following it."

FOUR

The senior Senator from Florida, the Honorable Benjamin Shub, had his nose out of joint.

He had boarded Air Force One for the flight to Miami supremely confident that he could bend the President's ear during the two and a half hours they were airborne and convince him that Medicare taxes must be raised another 20 percent. It wasn't necessary to tell Jeremy Haines that Medicare was on the verge of bankruptcy—the President already knew that. But he had to be reminded that Ben Shub, his friend and sometime supporter, was going to have one hell of a time getting reelected two years hence if the Haines administration didn't do something about it. After all, approximately one-third of Shub's constituency was collecting regularly from Medicare.

His conversation with Haines, conducted just before the 747 took off from Andrews Air Force Base, lasted three seconds.

"Good morning, Ben," the President said. "Glad to see you." Even as he shook the Senator's hand, he turned to talk to Press Secretary Wayne Dillman. "Wayne, sit with me on takeoff—couple of things I'd like to discuss."

"I have to see you," Shub pleaded, but the President already had taken Dillman's arm and was heading for the lower cabin conpartment reserved for the President and his aides. The Senator would have intruded, but he reasoned there still was plenty of time to make his pitch before they landed in Miami. Haines simply *had* to say something about the Medicare crisis in that speech tonight. He was invading the stronghold of the elderly and it was absolutely essential that he allay their fears. More than any President since Woodrow Wilson, Haines wrote an unusual proportion of his speeches himself and was always tinkering with them, almost up to the moment of delivery. So there still was plenty of time for Shub to contribute a few well-chosen sentences.

But there wasn't. The Senator's next glimpse of Haines was the President's tall frame walking briskly by Shub's seat toward the spiral staircase. Shub jumped to his feet and followed him, but the President was already halfway up the stairs and Shub found his path blocked by the huge, subtly menacing form of Secret Service Agent Mike McNulty.

"Sorry, sir, but the President doesn't want to be disturbed." McNulty's voice was soft and pleasant but managed to convey the impression that there was a .45 aimed at Shub's head.

"Well, would you mind going up there and telling him I have to talk to him?"

"Sir, when he tells me he prefers to be alone, that includes me."

"He's in another one of his goddamned Greta Garbo moods," the Senator sputtered. McNulty smiled faintly and shrugged his barn-door shoulders. Shub turned away, muttering to himself, McNulty still smiling behind his retreating back. Like every agent assigned to the White House detail, he worshipped Jeremy Haines.

In truth, however, McNulty didn't like Haines's growing insistence on inflight solitude anymore than people like Senator Shub or General Collison. He believed that at least one agent should be close to the President at all times. Not that anything was likely to happen aboard Air Force One—the entire crew, from Cardella down to the newest steward, had been subjected to a security check as stiff as those he and his fellow agents had undergone. But that didn't satisfy McNulty, who worried about the President. To him Haines appeared to be a man headed for a coronary, or maybe a nervous breakdown. His complexion seemed sallow despite his tan, and his obvious fatigue was combined with either lethargy or apathy—McNulty wasn't sure which. Whatever the case, this was not the active, dynamic Jeremy Haines of two years ago. The President did seem peppier and more cheerful on this flight, though; more like his old self than the agent had noticed for a long time.

McNulty sighed and hoped that this newfound energy wasn't analogous to the intense glow of a light bulb about to fail. Alone in the upper lounge, the President could conceivably have a heart attack and be unable to push the red emergency button on his intercom that would summon help. Just thinking about it gave Mike McNulty a chill, a feeling that happened to coincide with his awareness that a cold draft was coming from the upper cabin . . .

* * *

"I see you kept your promise," Jeremy Haines said to Franklin Roosevelt.

"Of course," FDR said cheerfully. "And I might say, old fellow, I'm absolutely delighted that I was expected. Shows a certain acceptance of me on your part."

"How do you know you were expected?"

"Oh, your general demeanor. I sense more of an element of belief, even expectation. The fact that you hightailed it up here as soon as you could—my word, you practically ran up those stairs. And I loved the way you brushed off that obnoxious person in that perfectly awful sports jacket. Who was he, anyway? A Republican, I'll wager."

"Senator Ben Shub, Republican, from Florida. Once again, I'm surprised when you ask me something like that. You seem so omniscient about things in general, I have to assume you're aware of the identities of members of Congress."

The ghost waved his arm airily. "Oh come now. I'm not *that* omniscient. Please get over the idea I'm some kind of super-ghost. Y'know, it's wrong to assign omniscience to anyone, and our worst failing as a people is our mistaken belief that our Presidents are somehow blessed with it. Omniscience is nothing but a myth, perpetuated either by the wishful thinking of those who want to believe their leaders are infallible, or those leaders whose egos are so huge they can't admit when they're wrong. Hitler was one of these, and Stalin, too. You might say theirs was ego carried to the extreme, and that's what differentiates a dictator from a civilized political leader.

"Now, take Churchill. Winston was one of the most egotistical men I ever knew, but he never thought that admitting a mistake was a sign of weakness." Roosevelt wagged a finger at the President. "Now *there* was a great man, Jeremy. I loved him. I'll never forget the time he was staying in the White House and we had been arguing for hours over some issue—I can't remember exactly what it was but the gist was that I didn't think he was telling me the whole truth. He broke off the argument to take a bath and I was still pretty sore. Well, I rolled my wheelchair into his bedroom to continue the discussion, and he had just climbed out of the tub. He stood there with that roly-poly pink body of his, absolutely naked, and yelled at me, 'I want you to know that the Prime Minister of Great Britain has nothing to hide from the President of the United States!' My God, Jeremy, I could hardly stop laughing. On another occasion . . ."

"Mr. President," Haines smiled, "didn't we have business to discuss?"

"Damnation, Jeremy, there I go again! Indulging in useless nostalgia when we have things to do. Let's talk about that speech of yours tonight. What kind of an audience will we have?"

The President was faintly amused at the use of the pronoun *we*. Roosevelt was thoroughly enjoying this personal involvement—to such an extent, Haines mused wryly, that he seemed to be reliving his old days of glory. He was acting for all the world like an old warhorse sniffing the smoke of distant gunfire.

"A party fund-raising dinner," he replied. "A partisan occasion on which I'm supposed to make some partisan remarks. Such as praising our friend Senator Shub, and delivering a few prosaic platitudes about keeping faith with the elderly. Deliberately vague assurances, I'm afraid, because there isn't a hell of a lot I can do about the elderly. Our Medicare program is just about down the tube. Raising taxes again is not only repugnant to me but useless. In one year or less, we'd be back in the same hole."

"I take it you have a prepared text of tonight's remarks?"

"More or less. I have a speech all typed out but I often ad-lib during the delivery."

"Ad-libbing can be very effective. Makes a speech sound much more natural. I remember once during one of my earlier Fireside Chats—marvelous name for such occasions, don't you think?—anyway, it was during one of those chats that I found myself desperately needing a drink of water. The White House wasn't air-conditioned in those days, and it was beastly hot. I stopped right in the middle of my speech and asked an aide for a glass of water. Then I apologized to my unseen audience, saying, 'It's a hot night in Washington, my friends.' Jeremy, the CBS announcer covering the White House—I think it was Bob Trout—he told me it was the most human touch he had ever heard in a Presidential speech. It put me right in the living room of every person listening to me. Of course, that wasn't my best line. The time I accused the Republicans of not being satisfied with attacking me, my wife, or my sons—now they had to include my little dog Fala." Back went the great head and out came the loud laugh.

"By God, that was the highlight of my entire oratorical career. Now, where are we?"

"We're not anyplace," Haines sighed. "I just mentioned that I like to ad-lib now and then."

"So you did. What you'll need tonight is a kind of preplannned ad-lib. Something that won't be in your prepared remarks that can be tossed in at just the right moment. Something dramatic, startling, newsworthy."

Haines said, in a tone that mixed resignation with sarcasm, "Such as declaring war on Russia?"

"Let's not be petulant," FDR said goodnaturedly. "Mind letting me see that speech?"

Haines fished the text out of a briefcase and handed it to the ghost, who riffled through the pages, scanning the contents rapidly, frowning or nodding alternately at what he was digesting. Still holding the pages, he finally looked up. "No ginger, my friend. No fire or spirit. It sounds as tired as you look, if you'll pardon my candor. You should change ghost writers, and I don't mean that as a play on words."

"I wrote most of it myself," Haines said tartly.

"Oh? Well, maybe it's time you accepted a little outside help. Presidents shouldn't have to write their own stuff. I never did. I'd tell the boys what I wanted to say, and when they came up with something, I'd edit it and contribute a few of my own choice phrases. Wasn't bad at the latter, either. Did you know I thought up some of my best lines? 'Nothing to fear but fear itself' was my idea. So was 'a little left of center' and 'a day that will live in infamy.' Oh yes, I almost forgot what I said about Mussolini when he invaded France. 'The hand that held the dagger has struck it into the back of its neighbor.' Very effective, although I must say the State Department wasn't very happy about my choice of language. But to get back to my point. We have to be more forceful and positive in this speech." He tapped the stapled pages but Haines was hardly listening; he was still mesmerized by the sound of the rich, unforgettable voice, mimicking perfectly the tone of the original.

"The hand that held the dagger . . ."

He had heard recordings of that June 1940 speech several times, as he had other Roosevelt speeches. It chilled yet enthralled him to hear that famous line again from the lips of this professed ghost. He could no longer tell himself it was all a dream, for now it was sound added to sight that convinced him. He couldn't be hallucinating, either. It was impossible to imagine that even a sick, fatigued mind could manufacture the inflections, the rhythmic lilt, the persuasive power of that voice. *Dagger* had come out *daggah, neighbor* was pronounced *neighbah*—the incredible anomaly of that cultured, aristocratic enunciation somehow possessing the ability to sway even those to whom a Harvard-tinged accent was an object of scorn. No President had ever matched the dramatic qualities of FDR's delivery—not even Reagan, with all his film training. Haines wasn't a bad speaker himself—he was very good, in fact—but he was an oratorical plodder compared to Roosevelt.

"Now let's talk about this Medicare problem," the ghost was saying. "Y'know, I was very proud of instigating the social security system, but I never intended that it become the major source of retirement income. Not to mention paying two-thirds of a retired persons's medical bills. It was supposed to be totally self-supporting and basically just a supplement to privately financed pensions. Nor did I ever envision anything like Medicare. Vitally necessary, of course, but draining the rest of the social security system to the point of collapse. So it seems to me, my friend, we've got to do something about financing this Medicare monster. Something dramatic, yet practical. Something innovative, yet sound. I've been thinking hard about this, Jeremy, and I've come up with a few exciting ideas. We'll just tidy up this speech of yours with a few additions—my God, I wish Bob Sherwood was here to help us. He was the best speechwriter I had. Fearfully bright fellow, Sherwood. He had the knack of fitting his words to my speaking style; we made quite a team. Now, this is what I have in mind . . ."

For the next ten minutes, Jeremy Haines listened transfixed to that half-hypnotic, virtuosic voice with its perfect diction and slick timing. A chameleon of cadence, a vast repertoire of dramatic timbre that first shocked, then intrigued, fascinated, and finally convinced—a logical progression of manipulated reaction by the master of manipulation.

At the end of the ten minutes, the President of the United States had delivered himself completely to the influence of an implausible, impossible being.

And at the foot of the spiral staircase, Secret Service Agent McNulty thought he heard the President conversing with someone, then reasoned it must be Cardella or another crew member. His own intercom light blinked.

"McNulty, this is Colonel Cardella. Is anyone up there with the President?"

"No, sir. Not unless he's talking to one of you guys."

"Well, nobody's left the cockpit since we took off. I went back to check something with Ferguson in the comm room and I heard voices in the upper lounge. Just wanted to know who was up there."

"Nobody," the agent said, mystified. "I haven't taken my eyes off the stairs of one second."

"That's funny," Cardella worried. "I know I heard voices."

"Maybe he was talking to somebody on the intercom," McNulty suggested.

"Guess that must be it. Just the same, I think I'll take a little walk back there and make sure. Mr. Haines told me before we left he didn't want to be bothered during the flight. Said he was going to work on his speech for tonight."

The intercom light winked off before McNulty could protest that no one could pass his station and go up those stairs without being intercepted. A little nettled, he stared accusingly at the occupants scattered throughout the cavernous cabin, illogically centering on Senator Shub, who was at that moment talking vociferously to Wayne Dillman. The agent continued to watch them, idly yet with a certain amount of alertness because Shub was obviously angry and McNulty didn't like any angry person within ten miles of the President. Shub's voice was so loud and argumentative, McNulty wished an agent had the authority to tell a Senator to shut up. The intercom went on again.

"McNulty."

"Cardella. You were right, he was on the intercom, talking to Dillman. He said he had just hung up when I came into the lounge. Sorry to bother you."

"No bother," McNulty said, and went back to observing the arm-waving gyrations of the senior Senator from Florida. Then it suddenly occurred to him that Jeremy Haines couldn't have been talking to his press secretary at any time during the last five to ten minutes. The discrepancy was fleetingly disturbing, but McNulty decided it must be inconsequential—even Presidents could lose track of time. Haines must have talked to Dillman before the press secretary got involved with the irate Shub. Or he was talking to someone else just before Cardella checked and didn't want to tell the pilot who it was. That had to be it.

Except that his Irish intuition kept telling him something was wrong.

Ben Shub emerged from an elevator in the lobby of the Miami's Sheraton River House and accosted Wayne Dillman.

"Well, I saw him," Shub barked angrily, "but it didn't do me one goddamned bit of good. Wouldn't tell me what he's going to say tonight and he wouldn't accept any of my suggestions. I tell you, Dillman, that boss of yours is too independent for his own good."

Only two weeks ago, the press secretary mused, Shub had castigated Haines for being too vulnerable to persuasion. Aloud, Dillman said soothingly, "I happen to know, Senator, he's going to make a few remarks praising your work for the elderly. It's in the prepared text."

"Prepared text, my ass! I asked to see that prepared text and he told me it would be a waste of time. Naturally, I asked him what he *was* going to say, and he had the audacity to tell me he wasn't quite sure because his ideas hadn't fully jelled. Can you imagine that? The dinner's only two hours away and he hasn't even written a speech yet."

"He likes to speak off-the-cuff," Dillman reminded him, although privately he was beginning to share the Senator's concern. Why the President seemed to have almost totally scrapped what he had written previously was a mystery. Normally, Haines was more than considerate about such matters, knowing that Dillman needed a relatively final text as soon as possible so it could be photocopied and distributed to the media. If the Senator was to be believed, the President hadn't even started his rewrite.

"He asked me to come up as soon as he finished with you," Dillman said to Shub. "I'll remind him to mention you in the speech."

Shub, mollified, looked at him shrewdly. "Something's up, Dillman. Something's brewing in that mind of his. Something so big he didn't even dare confide it to me, one of his greatest supporters. And I don't mind telling you, I resent it."

Wayne sighed. "I'm only his press secretary, Senator. I'm not privy to anything he's thinking until he's damned well ready to tell me."

"Well, I realize you have to get up to his suite. I'm in five-twelve, by the way. I'd appreciate your phoning me if . . . if there's anything you think I should know." The Senator's eyes narrowed. "Dillman, you're no naïve babe in the woods when it come to politics. I'm already on the ropes in this state. A weak, do-nothing President is gonna floor me for good. Yet why do I have this gut feeling the son of a bitch has a gun in his hand ready to go off? I'd sure as hell like to know what kind of ammo he's using."

They rode up on the same elevator, Shub getting off on the fifth floor and nodding perfunctorily as he stepped out. Dillman found himself pondering what Shub had said, the feeling that something was ready to explode. Wayne Dillman had the same feeling, without Shub's resentment at being left in the dark. The press secretary wasn't overjoyed, either, but he was nothing if not loyal to a President he alternately admired and pitied.

Dillman, waiting for a response to his knock, said to McNulty at the door, "I hope he's in as good a mood as he was earlier. When he got off the plane, he was almost bouncing."

"Hard to tell," the agent said. "When he called me in to tell me he'd see you and nobody else, he seemed downright cheerful but a bit preoccupied. Better knock again, Mr. Dillman. I don't think he heard you."

The second knock produced a "Come in," and the press secretary entered to find the President at the suite's writing desk, a hillock of yellow, lined foolscap paper in front of him.

"Thanks for coming up, Wayne," Haines said pleasantly. He gestured toward the foolscap. "I just finished revising the speech and I apologize for being so late—I haven't given you much time for typing and distributing I'm afraid. Who'd we bring along from the secretarial pool?"

"Jo Millner, Mr. President. She's fast and she's accurate. The hotel has the mimeograph equipment all ready."

Haines smiled. "I suppose some of you would have preferred one of the swankier places on Miami Beach but I've always stayed at the River House. Actually, it was my wife's favorite hotel in southern Florida—she introduced it to me."

"It's very satisfactory, sir, and I've heard no complaints."

The President chuckled. "Jo may have a complaint when she tries to decipher my handwriting. You're one of the few people who can read it. Better look it over, Wayne, in case Jo has any questions."

He handed the pile of yellow sheets to the press secretary, who digested the contents swiftly—Dillman was a self-taught or instinctive speedreader. The first few pages were prosaic—Dillman noticed the President had mentioned, in words of satisfying if not fulsome praise, the name of Benjamin Shub—but as he continued to read, Wayne's eyes widened and a low whistle escaped his lips.

"Jesus Christ," he murmured, "this is dynamite. It'll lead every newscast and hit every front page in the country. And it may give our friend Senator Shub a heart attack."

"He'll die happy," Haines observed dryly. "He's been demanding action and I'm giving it to him, provided Congress agrees. Wayne, get out your notebook. Call Walt Markel and tell him I want to see the Senate and House leaders in the White House at eight o'clock Monday morning. Our esteemed congressional liaison aide is going to have to help me sell this program. Second, get hold of Bill Webster. I want him to scrub and reshedule all afternoon appointments. I need at least two hours for that meeting with the insurance people."

"What insurance people, Mr. President?"

"You haven't come to that part of the speech yet. I've been on the phone since I got here, talking to top people at Prudential, Metropolitan, Equitable, Travelers, New York Life, Aetna, and everyone else I could think of. They've agreed to meet me in Washington Monday afternoon and discuss this plan—actually, to pledge their support publicly. I've already been promised that, along with their help in setting it up. One more thing, Wayne. Better tell Webster there'll be a cabinet meeting at ten Monday morning. And he's to inform Secretary Don Nickels at HEW. He's to invite Mary Jackson to the meeting—as head of the social security system, she can't be left out. Got all that?"

"Yes, sir." He put the spiral notebook back in his coat pocket and emitted another whistle. "Boy, this'll shake up the troops. Frankly, sir, they were expecting to sleep through this speech."

"The troops?"

"The media, Mr. President. I, uh, well, when I saw your first draft, I told them there wouldn't be anything earthshaking."

Haines grinned. "They may be a little annoyed at you. I noticed the network White House regulars were on the plane. Will there be camera coverage?"

"I assume so, sir. By their Miami affiliates."

"Live?"

"No, sir. Uh, I suppose that's my fault. I shouldn't have played down the speech."

Haines smiled again, and for a fleeting second, Dillman saw a look of long-gone youth faintly visible through the prominent fatigue lines. "No matter. My speeches have been rather dull lately." The grin grew broader. "But from now on, Mr. Press Secretary, I don't think that's going to be one of our problems."

Two hours later, having delivered the required compliments on the statesmanship and legislative brilliance of Senator Benjamin Shub, President Jeremy Haines dropped the bomb.

"Farsighted leaders like Senator Shub share my concern over the crisis facing Medicare," he declared. "It is a major and immediate crisis, demanding major and immediate action. We owe it to millions of concerned senior citizens not to let this crumbling and rapidly deteriorating system of medical protection go down the drain of indifference and inaction."

He paused, then continued, "I am therefore proposing to the Congress that it enact legislation authorizing the establishment of a national lottery, with the proceeds used to finance Medicare and save it from the brink of oblivion."

Haines waited for the gasps, followed by waves of applause, to subside. "I can tell you tonight that I already have received from the nation's largest insurance companies their pledges to underwrite this lottery during its initial stages so that Medicare benefits, endangered to the point of extinction, will continue without interruption during the period the national lottery is being organized."

A mob of suddenly stirred reporters bolted for the nearest telephones.

The President turned to Ben Shub and winked.

And on the return flight to Washington the next morning, in the inviolate seclusion of the 747's upper lounge, Jeremy Haines once again faced the ghost of Franklin Delano Roosevelt.

"An excellent speech," FDR declared. "Absolutely thrilling."

"I wasn't sure you could hear it," Haines remarked with that touch of sarcasm he felt was fair replacement for skepticism.

"Let's just say I was aware of what you said. And how did the good Senator Shub react?"

"I figured you already knew."

"I can't stand being around that man, Jeremy. He reminds me of a few Senators I positively detested."

"Initially, he thought I was out of my mind. But I talked with him at length after the dinner and he came around. He even said he'd co-sponsor the bill in the Senate."

"And our friends of the press?"

"Too early to tell. The CBS correspondent wanted to bet me it won't go through Congress. But Malcolm Jones of IPS is all excited—of course, Jonesey's always on my side. He's my favorite in the press."

"As Merriman Smith was mine," the ghost said soberly. "Grand person, Merriman. Like the majority of his colleagues, I know he liked me. It was always a point of personal pride with me, that I got along so well with people who covered my administrations, even though 85 percent of the papers they worked for opposed me."

"Things have changed, Mr. President," Haines

said, conscious of how natural it was to use that formal salutation. "The media is far more adversary than it was in your time. You didn't have to contend with hostile television reporters who can scarcely hide their contempt for a President they don't really respect."

"Oh, I had my share of obstreperous journalists, especially the reactionary ones. That fellow John O'Donnell of the *New York Daily News*. Walter Trohan of the *Chicago Tribune*. And Drew Pearson could be an awful pain in the neck at times. The thing is, Jeremy, I don't think the newspapermen—I guess I should say newspaper people because May Craig covered the White House with those funny hats of hers and the equally funny questions she loved to ask—well, I was going to say that they didn't appreciate the way I made myself accessible to them. Did you know that until Teddy Roosevelt became President, reporters weren't even allowed into the White House? And I went a lot farther than my illustrious cousin did. Before the war, I used to average one news conference a week. In twelve years, I met with the press exactly nine hundred and ninety-eight times! God, how I loved to match wits with those fellows."

"There were those who said your press conferences were more like lectures," Haines said, smiling.

"True," FDR chortled. "And some of the boys needed a lecture now and then. I remember the time I told O'Donnell to put on a dunce cap and go stand in the corner. My God, his face was the color of a tomato." Roosevelt caught Haines shaking his head in resigned disdain and hastily changed course. "Well, I'm absolutely delighted at how things are going."

"Congress still has to approve," the President reminded him. "I don't enjoy the luxury of what you had in your first term—a rubber-stamp legislature. The House is solidly Democratic and we have only a five-vote margin in the Senate."

"I assure you, Jeremy, they won't turn this down. I'm so completely positive that I believe it's time to discuss some other problems. Let's talk about unemployment. I have some ideas . . ."

FIVE

"I'm sorry, Mr. President, but this proposal is totally unacceptable to every God-fearing, right-thinking American with any sense of true Christian moral ethics! And I believe I speak for the majority of the people."

Jeremy Haines stared down the long conference table in the Cabinet Room at the speaker, Secretary of the Interior T. Wellman Agee, a hawk-faced man with the personality of an unctuous undertaker. The President's stare had to traverse the entire distance of the table, a wooden runway on which the evenly spaced ashtrays in front of each cabinet member resembled a row of landing lights; the Secretary of the Interior, as the most junior cabinet officer, was at the far end.

Haines would have preferred the large oval table

that normally graced the room, providing more intimacy and an easier means of conversing, but this more practical piece of furniture was being refurbished and the elongated, oblong Chippendale was the only available substitute. Probably just as well on this occasion, Haines mused; T. Wellman Agee irritated him like an unscratchable itch.

The Interior Secretary, nominated and confirmed only five months before, was far from the President's own choice; Agee had been forced on him by conservatives in the party and Haines, too weary to endure any more internal strife, caved in. As his stare hardened into a look that came close to a glare, he was conscious that his anger symbolized the change in him since he first met the ghost. At previous cabinet meetings, he had treated Agee with some deference even though he could not deny the revulsion he felt—toward himself and this self-righteous glob of pomposity.

"Wellman," the President said in a tone that seemed to have steel slivers embedded in every syllable, "if you're trying to tell us gambling goes against your personal grain, then say it. But don't give me any crap about your feelings representing those of most Christians—or anyone else!"

Someone halfway down the table gasped—Haines could not tell who it was—and he could almost feel the room stir. Agee, his face red and flustered, managed to sputter, "There are more Americans opposed to gambling than you apparently believe. And that's all a lottery is—gambling in the most pernicious, evil form of all because it hides under the mask of official sanction."

"Thirty-seven states now have some kind of lottery," Haines observed, "and most of them were approved by the voters themselves. Lotteries are about as morally unacceptable as church bingo games."

"If Catholics prefer hypocrisy to the dictates of their own religion, that's their business," Agee retorted, and then immediately knew he had blunderered when he intercepted the angry, bulldog countenance of Secretary of State James Sharkey, one of three Catholics in the cabinet. Sharkey was the cabinet member closest to Jeremy Haines; he was the only one who knew where the President really was the night Air Force One crashed, and he had kept quiet simply because Haines had requested his silence. That Sharkey was the lone Democrat in the cabinet was immaterial to either himself or to the President. Despite their political differences, they saw eye-to-eye on foreign affairs, and Haines trusted him implicitly. Sharkey wanted to retaliate at Agee but he had, instead, a curious but delicious impulse to sit back and watch Haines dismantle the Secretary of the Interior. He didn't have to wait long.

"There are three Catholics in this room," the President said sharply, "and on behalf of all three I'd suggest an apology is in order."

"I certainly meant no disrespect to their religious beliefs," Agee said smoothly, "although what I said doesn't seem to call for an apology. I was merely pointing out that . . ."

"You will either apologize or leave this meeting," the President said with ominous calm. Sharkey, not bothering to hide the smile that walked on to his face, felt like cheering.

Agee's lower lip trembled. "If I've said anything to offend anyone, I'm sorry," he muttered.

"Fine," Haines snapped. "Now, I've heard one objection to the lottery based on moral grounds that I consider invalid. I'm not going to defend gambling as one of man's nobler activities, but unless carried to an extreme, when it becomes a disease, it's something in which most of us indulge to varying degrees. Gambling is a way of life, from playing the stock market to a friendly game of poker. All I'm suggesting is that we tap into this enormous revenue potential and direct the money toward a Medicare system that's about ready to go over the cliff. Mary, I'd welcome your views inasmuch as Medicare financing problems are right in your backyard."

Mary Jackson, head of the social security system, was a handsome black woman with upswept gray hair and a soft, lilting voice, Jamaican in its cadence. "I have no real objections, Mr. President, merely some concern, or perhaps *caution* would be a better word. And that's the temptation many people would feel to spend too much on lottery tickets instead of basic family needs—food, for example."

"There's always that risk," Haines conceded, "but I was reading in *Newsweek* the other day that state lotteries haven't encountered that problem to any large extent. There have been instances, of course, but nothing close to serious proportions. I share your concerns though, Mary, and if we get this program under way, I think it should be accompanied by some kind of advertising or publicity campaign urging people not to go overboard. Does this allay your fears?"

Mary Jackson nodded. "You've eased them," she said, smiling, "even though you haven't erased them. Actually, Mr. President, I'm rather excited. Medicare will be totally out of funds inside of three months. Without some kind of fresh financing, the only alternative would be to reduce social security benefits, which is robbing Peter to pay Paul."

"Exactly," Haines said. "Bill, what's the Secretary of the Treasury have to say?"

William Lagos, a burly man of Greek extraction, scowled unhappily. "Theoretically, I'm not opposed to this lottery, but that's the trouble—so far I've heard nothing but theory. How much is it supposed to raise? Will it be a weekly affair, monthly, or what? What will tickets cost? Damnit, Mr. President, ideas are fine but ideas have to be executed."

Haines smiled to himself. In about the same language, those were the questions he had put to Roosevelt when the ghost presented his grandiose scheme for a national lottery in intriguing but vague terms. Haines had pressed him for more details, but FDR simply dismissed the request with a wave of his arm, nonchalantly remarking: "Oh, you have plenty of experts to work this out. Y'know, I've always said that to accomplish anything worthwhile, there must be a compromise between the ideal and the practical. I supply the former and expect someone else to supply the latter."

That cavalier attitude toward execution and implementation, the President knew, was typical of Roosevelt, a simultaneous virtue and fault. It reminded Haines of Harold Laski's description of Roosevelt as "a broker of ideas rather than an architect of systems." Only too true, the President realized, yet apparently he had been an intuitive broker. "We should be able to sell a hundred million dollars' worth of tickets every month," FDR had predicted confidently.

"Where did you get that figure?" Haines had asked.

The ghost had tapped his head. "Right here. You must remember, Jeremy, that when we were rearming for World War Two and I went to Congress and said we were going to build a hundred thousand planes and seventy-five thousand tanks a year, everyone thought I was crazy. Herman Goering told Hitler those figures were impossible, pure propaganda. Even Harry Hopkins warned me I was being grossly overoptimistic. Well, I wasn't crazy, was I? I just have an instinct for that kind of thing. Figures never bothered me. I got them off the west wall and let other people worry about making them stand up. Why, in 1933, when I raised the price of gold to twenty-one cents, Henry Morgenthau wanted to know where I got that amount. I told him twenty-one was just a lucky number—three times seven. Ha!"

It made Haines shudder to have any President treat important figures with such debonair indifference. Yet when he had talked to one of the insurance executives the afternoon of the Miami speech and asked for an estimate of a national lottery's probable revenue, this prestigious gentleman had cited a figure only slightly below FDR's.

"I appreciate your need for a firm outline, Bill," he told the Secretary of the Treasury, "and I promise you one as soon as possible. Incidentally, when I meet with the insurance people this afternoon, I'd like you present and you, too, Mary and Don"—the last name was directed toward the Secretary of Health, Education and Welfare. "All I can give any of you right now is the skeleton of this thing. The lottery will be monthly, and we're estimating gross proceeds of around ninety million a month, with about ten million going out in prizes. That'll net us approximately eighty million per month that we'll add to Medicare tax revenues. Now, it may take some time to get this through Congress and all set up, so what the insurance companies have promised to do is underwrite Medicare for thirty to sixty days if it goes broke before the lottery's under way. They'll be paid back from lottery revenues over an agreed-on period. They've also offered to help establish a lottery commission, using some of their own personnel and with government input—I hope from your department, Mary, and Bill's, too—that will run the damned thing. Oh yes, I almost forgot. Sunday night I talked to Bob Boyer, head of the Advertising Council, which represents the major ad agencies. Boyer has agreed to contribute an advertising and promotional campaign at no cost to the government, and all three networks will give this campaign free television spots for the month preceding the lottery's start and for another month after it gets going. Now, as I said, this is the skeleton, the bare bones, so to speak. I'll welcome questions but with the admonition that I probably won't have many answers until after today's meeting with the insurance people."

"I've got one," Commerce Secretary Edward Silverman said. Haines liked and respected this gamin-faced Jewish industrialist, who had served in the cabinet from the day of Haines's first inauguration. His wit had enlivened more than one cabinet meeting, largely because it came at unexpected times. Silverman was famous for never opening his mouth during long discussions until he got bored.

"I'm always afraid when you decide to comment," the President drawled. "But go ahead."

"What will a national lottery do to those thirty-seven state lotteries you mentioned earlier? Seems to me you'll be cutting into their respective territories, particularly if the national prizes are bigger than what any state can offer. You'll be in direct competition for the public's dollar, and I don't have to remind you, Mr. President, in this recession there may not be enough dollars around to support all lotteries."

"A good point, Ed, and one raised when I met with Congressional leaders earlier today. It may be a problem, but I don't think so. I believe people will simply buy tickets in both lotteries, the government's and their individual state's. And if we get some flak from the states, all I can do is point to Medicare's imminent collapse and ask them if they'd like to take over its financing. Matter of fact, I've already sent telegrams to the directors of those thirty-seven lotteries asking them to come to Washington next week to discuss the whole thing with me. I believe I can convince them we haven't any other choice, and it may be we can work out some kind of revenue-sharing program if the national lottery is as successful as I'm confident it will be."

"What about ticket distribution?" Don Nickels wanted to know.

"Probably through post offices, at least for the time being. Later we may be able to set up some kind of mailing system or utilize retail outlets as the state lotteries do."

"Sell 'em at internal revenue offices," Lagos murmured, and everyone laughed.

Mary Jackson asked, "What was the reaction of Congressional leaders this morning, Mr. President?"

"I think I'd like the Vice President to answer that. Geoff was present and his appraisal of the atmosphere may be a bit more objective than mine. Geoff, how do *you* feel our friends from the Hill reacted?"

Vice President Geoffrey Mitchell, a lean, leathery-faced Westerner who might have stepped right out of a Marlboro ad, rubbed his jaw in contemplation. "Some doubts, some cynicism, a lot of questions similar to the ones you've raised here. But in general, a realization that something has to be done. Just before I came to this meeting, Mr. President, I was on the phone to some of the leaders who were present this morning. I'm happy to report that bills will be introduced in both houses as soon as you can provide a detailed plan."

"And that," Haines said, "will be forthcoming shortly. Any more questions?"

It was Silverman who summed up the session. "This program undoubtedly has many faults and loopholes and may well turn out to be a failure, but at least we're trying. We're taking action, doing something. I must compliment you, Mr. President, on this novel if risky approach. I just wish we could do something equally dramatic to help solve unemployment."

"Maybe we will," Haines said enigmatically; and Jim Sharkey stared at him. After the President adjourned the meeting, Sharkey lingered behind.

"Thanks for sitting on that asshole Agee, Jeremy," he said.

"No thanks necessary. Next time he opens his yap like he did today, I'll cut off his balls. You were right,

Jim. I should have told the National Committee he was unacceptable to me as a cabinet nominee. I wanted to name Dan Stone, even if he was too liberal for those mossbacks on the committee."

Sharkey inspected the President with new interest and not a little curiosity. Haines's eyes were bright, alive, and alert. Even the shoulders seemed less stooped, and he had handled the cabinet session with an aggressive confidence Sharkey hadn't seen for months.

"What's gotten into you lately?" he asked. "Taking pep pills or something?"

The President's smile, pleasant yet devoid of humor, was unfathomable. "Just feeling better these days, Jim. Picked myself off the floor by my bootstraps, you might say."

Sharkey eyed him with a suspicion he could not explain. "Where the hell did you get that national lottery idea? Not from Frank Donnelli, I'll bet—your esteemed top administrative assistant hasn't had a constructive thought since he married that ex-hooker. He spends half his time in the sack and the other half wishing he was back in it."

Haines laughed. He had a private notion that James Sharkey, a widower like himself, envied Donnelli for that red-haired, vivacious wife. "She wasn't a hooker, she was a chorus girl," he corrected.

"Same thing," Sharkey grumbled. "Anyway, I'd still like to know who thought up that lottery. It sure as hell didn't come out of thin air."

"You might say it practically did," Haines said cryptically, and laughed to himself.

"In other words," the Secretary of State deduced,

"you thought it up yourself. Figures. Jeremy, you're virtually running a one-man show in this Godforsaken mausoleum. You always have. Every President from Franklin Roosevelt on down has had a corps of good advisers he could rely on, capable staff people to assume most of the routine burdens and some of the big ones as well. About all you've got is that sex-starved Donnelli and Wayne Dillman. One half-assed aide and a press secretary! Christ, you don't even have a full-time speechwriter. No wonder you've been coming apart at the seams."

The Presidential eyebrows lifted. "Oh? I just heard you ask me if I'm taking pep pills."

Sharkey shook his head as if the gesture could dislodge his memories of a fatigued, dispirited chief executive. "So I did. You were like a new man at that cabinet meeting. The old take-charge Jeremy Haines comes to life again. Frankly, I can't believe it."

"Jim," said the President of the United States, "you ain't seen nothin' yet."

Air Force One droned toward Omaha, Nebraska. The ghost watched almost wistfully as Haines mixed himself a Scotch and soda before sitting down to once more face him.

"I always hated funerals," the ghost commented, "including my own."

"You remember yours?"

"Oh, my, yes. I got a grand sendoff. Plenty of tears, including those of the crocodile variety from a fair-size proportion of your Republican ancestors. Reminds me of the time a Senate delegation visited Woodrow Wilson on his sickbed in the White House, and one of the Senators told the President, 'The Senate is praying for you.' Wilson looked him right in the eye and asked, 'Which way?' Ha-ha! Anyway, there's too much hypocrisy connected with funerals. The one you're going to in Omaha—that man was no friend of yours. Nothing but another one of those reactionary Republicans. He would have voted against a resolution wishing you a happy birthday."

"Senator Frandsen was a very sincere person who had the courage of his convictions. Attending his funeral is simply a mark of respect—and also a means of mending a few political fences. I need all the support I can get from my party."

The ghost laughed. "You're as devious as I, Jeremy. And just as hypocritical, using a funeral for political gain. Not that I blame you, my friend. I probably would have done the same thing myself except I tried to avoid funerals—used my, ah, physical affirmity as an excuse. Of course, when someone close to me died, I attended. Like Pa Watson, my military aide. He passed away on the *Quincy* coming back from Yalta. Great shock to me. Pa's death seemed to bring home my own vulnerability to the inevitable. Actually, I'm delighted this funeral gives us a chance to chat again. I want you to know I think you handled yourself splendidly at the cabinet meeting."

"Thank you," Haines said gravely. "It sounds bizarre, but you seem to have restored my energy, even my self-confidence. I actually feel like taking on people like Agee."

"And Congress has just passed the lottery bill. An

absolutely thrilling development, Jeremy. Not that I had any doubts. Of course, the positively disgraceful show that fellow Agee put on! One of your own cabinet members testifying before Congress against the lottery. You can't afford to have feuds within your official family, my friend. I think we should fire that man."

Haines said dryly, "I seem to recall you allowed a few battles in your own official family. Ickes-versus-Hopkins, Hull, and Morgenthau, and so on."

Roosevelt dismissed this with a good-natured shrug. "They fought among themselves, remember. They weren't disloyal to me, although old Cordell had some rather heady political aspirations of his own. He was no Harry Hopkins, certainly, or a Sam Rosenman. Now there was a grand fellow, completely loyal. Reminds me of your Ed Silverman. That's one thing I'm proud of, Jeremy—I was never an anti-Semite. Sidney Hillman and I were always very close, even though I do believe he let too many radicals into his CIO. He loved to play power politics, that Sidney. Do you realize that Harry Truman never would have become President if it hadn't been for Hillman? The party bosses wanted Jimmy Byrnes to run with me in 1944 and were ready to dump Henry Wallace, and Sidney got into the act. He didn't want Byrnes but he knew Henry would cost ,e votes, so he and Bob Hannegan agreed on either Bill Douglas or Truman. I was about to send a telegram to the convention saying I'd be happy to run with Douglas or Truman but Hannegan asked me to change the order of names, so the telegram finally read that I'd accept Truman or Douglas. Sidney was really calling some of the shots. He was smart, a lot smarter than that labor dinosaur, Bill Green of the AFL. Green actually had the temerity to oppose my plan for the Civilian Conservation Corps, to get poor kids out of the slums and put them to work in a healthy environment. The old goat told a Congressional committee that CCC was a combination of socialism, fascism, and communism, and was simply a device to obtain cheap, nonunion labor. He had some strange bedfellows in his opposition—the Communists were claiming it was forced labor. Even my own Committee on Unemployment was against it, but I . . ."

"Perhaps we should discuss the present instead of the past," Haines said, with a show of impatience. It was fascinating to hear FDR talk, but garrulousness could also be as irritating in this specter as the talkative Roosevelt had been in life. Yet what really disturbed the President—even frightened him—was the way he had come to regard the apparition as someone so real that he looked forward to each encounter. He knew that it actually hadn't been essential for him to fly to Omaha; the political advantages were merely a rationale for a desire to visit with the ghost again, a desire so great that it effectively overcame the lingering suspicion of hallucinating insanity.

"I'm not really digressing this time," Roosevelt was saying. "The last time we met, we discussed your unemployment problems in general. Now I'm ready to get down to a few specifics and that's why I mentioned the CCC. I believe we can revive that marvelous idea in a somewhat more modern form."

Haines shook his head. "We don't have the money for any large-scale social experiments. We're still running an annual deficit of some two hundred fifty billion dollars. The only way we can solve the unemployment problem is to turn the economy around."

"I'm ashamed of you," FDR scolded. "That kind of talk is right out of Ronald Reagan's mouth."

"But it's also coming from the mouths of every economist I've talked to, including Democratic economists. We don't have the financial wherewithal for your old pump-priming solutions, as you used to call them. Besides, we have some five million unemployed youths, most of them black. A new CCC to get them out of the slums would cost a fortune. Your own conservation corps was on a relatively small scale."

"It definitely was not!" the ghost retorted. "We started with three hundred thousand just the first year, and by the time the program ended, we had enrolled more than two and a half million boys—half a million in 1935 alone. Louie Howe, God rest his soul, developed the program. I just gave him a few general ideas and he put the whole thing into effect."

"But as I recall," Haines said, "the Army ran the corps."

"It did. And very effectively, too. Do you know who organized seventeen highly successful camps in the Southeast? A colonel named George Catlett Marshall. Amazing fellow, Marshall. Allergic to shellfish. Used to faint if he just tasted a piece of shrimp. He had more integrity in his little finger than Doug MacArthur had in his whole body. I remember once I asked Marshall not to send out to the troops an issue of a news magazine containing a libelous article about me. I sent Harry Hopkins over to see him; it was a mistake.

Marshall told Harry, 'I won't obey that order unless I get it in writing and if I do, it will come back with my resignation as chief of staff.' A foolish error on my part. Marshall was a great American. I almost named him Supreme Commander in Europe instead of Eisenhower. But I needed him here in Washington, and I also had the feeling that Ike wouldn't have been the right man to run the Pentagon. Unquestionably, I made the right choice because Winston Churchill disliked Marshall and they would have been at each other's throats. Of course, that was one of Winston's failings—he had some terrible prejudices about people. Almost as big a fault as his propensity to talk too much. But Marshall wasn't the easiest man to get along with—rather stiff-necked, if you know what I mean. I used to hint I'd like to call him George, but he told me that would be out of character for him. Ha-ha! He would have made a great President but he never could have gotten elected—he simply detested politicians, excluding myself, of course. Yet . . ."

Diplomatically and adroitly, Haines steered him back on course. "Mr. President, your experience with the CCC intrigues me. If we could find some means of financing such a program on an even larger scale, it has definite possibilities. I'm not sure the Army should run it, however."

"Probably not," FDR agreed. "In 1933, the Army didn't have much else to do. "The important thing, Jeremy, is to develop a general concept and put some good people to work executing it. Now, about funding this idea of mine. These figures are off the top of my hat . . ."

* * *

The following story appeared on page one of the *Washington Post* one week after Haines returned from Omaha, under a banner headline:

PRESIDENT UNWRAPS SURPRISE
YOUTH EMPLOYMENT PLAN

President Haines yesterday asked Congress to approve a dramatic new program aimed at putting unemployed youths to work on new highway projects and on refurbishing the entire national parks system.

The plan, reminiscent of the New Deal's Civilian Conservation Corps in the 1930s, would establish a Young America Recovery Corps (YARC) that Haines said would enroll 500,000 youths in the first six months and up to 3 million over the two-year period the program is expected to be in effect.

To fund the massive attack on one of the nation's most pressing problems—the high rate of unemployment among the young in virtually every urban area—Mr. Haines proposed:

1. A two-year special tax of five cents a gallon on gasoline used by private automobiles and trucks.

2. A two-year, 15 percent cut in all federal salaries from the President's on down, including those of members of Congress and their staffs.

3. A two-year, 1 percent surtax on incomes, both individual and corporate.

The President emphasized that YARC

> was conceived not only to reduce unemployment "but also the urban crime rate, which has reached dangerous and unacceptable proportions . . ."

Duane Collison walked into the quiet Georgetown bar, his eyes adjusting from the bright sunlight outside. It was mid-afternoon, and The Rendezvous was almost deserted. Izzy, the proprietor, a man with the fearsome physique of a gorilla and a heart the size of a Pratt & Whitney jet engine, was tending bar himself. He smiled happily at the sight of the general—Duane Collison had been coming there since the day he made colonel.

"Hi, General," Izzy greeted him, with a jerk of his head toward the rear of the saloon. "Your guy's back there."

"Thanks, Izzy." Collison peered ahead of him and finally spotted his target. "I'll take a Miller's Lite on tap."

"Comin' right up. That Peter Frain waiting for you?"

"The same."

"How about that! The Post's most distinguished columnist. This joint's getting positively respectable."

Collison approached Frain's table, carrying his beer—Izzy didn't mind tending bar, but he drew the line at being his own waiter. Frain stood up as the general approached the plain wooden table.

"Good to see you, Duane," he greeted. His voice held a kind of cultured, sardonic drawl unmatched to his physical appearance. The columnist was a rumpled man, with shaggy gray hair and the sartorial taste of an unemployed lumberjack. As usual, he was wearing a suit that apparently hadn't seen the inside of a dry cleaners for a year. The jacket was studded with three pipe burns, and its herringbone tweed clashed starkly with a loud striped tie that Frain must have selected in the pre-dawn. Only his sleepy eyes, set in a moon-crater face, were incongruously youthful.

But in this case, as Collison well knew, clothes did not make the man. Peter Frain was one of the most influential and respected political writers in Washington, with a column syndicated to more than five hundred newspapers and a reputation of tough yet fair conservatism. In truth, his ideology was hard to pin down, for occasionally he espoused opinions that were anathema to his right-wing readers, such as his pro-abortion stand and vitriolic attacks on anti-abortion forces. Unpredictability was the word that described him best; he was a journalistic sniper with a habit of firing at unexpected targets—including the *Post* itself, which ran his column three days a week and spent an inordinate amount of time answering Frain's attacks on its own editorials.

Like virtually every Washington columnist, he had his pet causes and pet officials, and Duane Collison was one of the latter. Peter Frain's most consistent trait was his hatred of the Soviet Union. "Peter pours acid on his typewriter keys whenever he writes about Russia," a colleague once remarked, and this was an accurate appraisal. It went a long way toward explaining why Frain, once one of the President Haines's staunchest supporters, had lately been devoting two columns a month to attacking him. It also explained why the slovenly columnist and the fastidious general had become friends—ideological beliefs are worn inside a person.

"That was one hell of a piece you wrote this morning," Collison began. "Calling Haines 'that wimp in the White House'—you probably ruined his breakfast."

Peter Frain grunted unhappily and took a meditative sip of the rum and Coke he always drank. "I almost wish I hadn't used that phrase. First the national lottery and then this goddamned YARC business—I wrote the column before he announced that boondoggling brainstorm. The trouble is, Duane, all of a sudden he's not acting like a wimp. I'll give you odds that by the end of the week the *Post* will be running letters accusing me of inconsistency—which is worse than calling me a liar."

Collison said heatedly, "There was nothing inconsistent about your column. You criticized him for his do-nothing attitude toward Russia. That's the only real issue. It's immaterial what he does domestically. His Achilles' heel is foreign policy and in that area he deserves everything you throw at him. You praised the lottery. No one could accuse you of being biased."

Frain nodded, a sour expression on his face, as if his drink had been laced with concentrated lemon juice. "The lottery was one thing. It's imaginative and gutsy. But that YARC crap—Jesus, he got that one right out of Franklin Roosevelt's textbook. I'll bet that old hypocrite is doing a war dance in his grave."

Collison chuckled; Peter Frain's hatred of FDR was well known and only slightly less intense than the late Westbrook Pegler's detestation of the whole Roosevelt family. Haines's praise of FDR in his Harvard speech, in fact, had prompted a Frain column wondering "why Mr. Haines chooses as a model leader, to be adored and emulated, the most devious, politically motivated, and prevaricating President ever to occupy the White House."

The general said, "Pete, after I read your column this morning, I decided I needed your help."

"I was wondering why this mid-afternoon summit conference."

"I've got something to tell you, Pete—off the record, for the time being."

"The phrase *off the record* should be stricken by law from the vocabulary of every bureaucrat and politician. It's frustrating, insulting, and invites temptation. But go ahead—you're no bureaucrat and you're no politician."

"I appreciate your confidence. Pete, Operation Umbrella's ready to roll. Within a month, two at the most."

Frain said nothing at first. He took a worn briar out of his breast pocket and began filling it with tobacco, although it was so caked with carbon there wasn't much room for anything but a few flakes. He lit the pipe and stared at Collison a few seconds before speaking.

"I knew it was in the works, but that timetable surprises me. Haines said in California they were making progress but that we were a long way from the goal line."

"Pure window dressing. We're this close." Collison held up a thumb and forefinger with only an inch between them.

Frain puffed out instead of in, and a burning ash fell on his pants leg. The columnist swatted at the tiny conflagration with an open palm, murmured, "Shit," and looked at the general again. "Okay, what kind of help do you need from me? You just told me this is off the record."

"Let's say I'd like a slow leak."

"Meaning what?"

"As soon as possible, even tomorrow, a column stating that Umbrella is closer to reality than the administration professes, and that the nation should understand the implications of this enormous technological success. What's off the record is that timetable I gave you. I don't want people to know how close we are."

"And just what *are* the implications?" Frain asked mildly.

"Good God, man, do I have to draw you a diagram? Umbrella gives us the greatest opportunity of our lifetime! Our invulnerability against their vulnerability. The perfect equation."

The pipe had gone out, but Frain kept it clenched in his teeth. "By *opportunity,* I take you to mean that we should clobber them."

Collison hesitated, trying to judge from the columnist's enigmatic expression whether he was shocked, revolted, or intrigued. He finally decided to be honest. "In the end, it may have to come to that. It might be possible to turn Umbrella into a sword of Damocles, ready to drop on their heads if they don't reverse their course of aggression. Frankly, I don't think threats will achieve this goal, but at least I'd be willing to try."

Frain took the pipe out of his mouth. "It seems to

me that nobody would give a damn whether Duane Collison's willing to try. More to the point is whether Haines would be willing. Which, if his miserable performance of the past two years is any indication, I seriously doubt."

"Exactly. He has to be prodded, pushed, and forced into taking a more aggressive stand—by journalists like yourself, people who can mold public opinion. He could never justify a continuation of his vacillating policy once Umbrella is operational."

"A journalist," Frain said with a grin, "has been defined as a newspaperman who wears spats. However, this particular newspaperman sees your point, although I don't think it's very well taken."

"Why not?"

"Because Siberia will be like Miami Beach before Jeremy Haines tries blackmail on the Soviet Union. The bastard hasn't got the guts—and, for that matter, neither does Congress nor the public. The large hole in your admirable thesis, Duane, is that our commie pals may well call our bluff. We could threaten 'em from here to doomsday behind Umbrella and they'd probably tell us to go stuff it up our butts. Then what do we do—push the buttons, and good-bye Kremlin? Not me nor a thousand other columnists could ever sell the American people on a preventative war. Not that it isn't a damned good idea, mind you. I wish to hell we had a President with the moxie to do it on his own."

"So do I," Collison breathed, anger edging into his voice.

Frain stared at him. The columnist said softly, "I'll write that column, chum. But it won't do a hell of a lot of good. What you need—shit, what *we* need—is another guy in the White House."

"That won't happen for another two years. By that time, the Soviets will have their own anti-missile system and our chance will be gone. I shouldn't say this, Pete, but so help me God, I wish Haines would have a heart attack. Anything to get him out of office ahead of schedule."

"Do you think Geoff Mitchell would be an improvement? Hell, that Arizona cowboy's nothing but Jeremy Haines with a ten-gallon hat. He's not a Vice President—he's a clone."

"He could be persuaded," Collison insisted.

"Maybe, but barring your devoutly wished-for coronary, you won't get the chance. Too bad Haines keeps his skirts so clean. What we really could use is a nice, juicy scandal—something that would effectively discredit Mr. Haines."

Collison said, "Not likely, I'm afraid. Well, Pete, I'll leave it to your discretion as to how much you can say in your column. At least we'll get people thinking about what's at stake."

"Sure thing. I'll bat out something for tomorrow morning. Haines is holding a news conference at ten. If the column's already in print, maybe somebody will ask him about it. Duane, quit frowning—frowns beget ulcers."

Collison sighed, "I was just fantasizing about what you said. A nice juicy scandal—of gargantuan proportions . . ."

SIX

Following is an extract from the transcript of President Haines's sixty-seventh news conference:

The President: Good morning, ladies and gentlemen. I have no prepared announcements or statements, except on a somewhat personal level. This is the first news conference I've held in the past two months, and I'm sorry to have waited so long. We met frequently during my first term, and frankly, I enjoyed those sessions even when you were asking me have-you-stopped-beating-your-wife questions. [*Laughter.*] I consider the Presidential press conference an example of democracy in action. The questions you ask as reporters, to me, are the same ones the average American citizen would ask if he or she were given this opportunity to meet with their President face-to-face. By the same token, of course, my answers are not only directed to you and the media you represent, but to the people of this nation. I realize that through the years, over virtually every administration since Franklin Roosevelt's, an adversary relationship has developed between the press and the President. Every chief executive has felt that too often you people are out to get him, to embarrass or to entrap him, to pin him down on issues that sometimes can't be covered with a simple yes or no. But I also realize that every conscientious reporter resents evasiveness, distortion, or dishonesty. There have been times when I've had to resort to evasiveness, and it's going to happen again—when I feel that a direct answer is impossible in a situation that is neither all black nor all white. I'll always try to be honest with you, but honesty doesn't mean I can speak with complete freedom and conviction. I'm going to try to meet with you more frequently from now on, perhaps every two weeks. It may even develop into a weekly news conference, if you don't get tired of me, and vice versa. [*Laughter.*] Franklin Roosevelt used to hold weekly press conferences, so the precedent, while ignored for many years, has been set. Now, having gotten that off my chest, I'll entertain your questions.

Q. Mr. President, Peter Frain's column in the *Washington Post* this morning claimed that our anti-missile system is a lot closer to completion than your administration has suggested. You said in California we had a long way to go.

A. The exact status is that it's still under development. I wouldn't want to comment beyond that. I'm sure our friends in the Kremlin would like to have an exact status report.

Q. But Frain quotes a high administration source to the effect that Umbrella is almost ready for a full-scale operational test—and that if it's successful, to all intent and purposes Operation Umbrella will be in existence.

A. Is Mr. Frain with us today?

Q. I'm here, Mr. President.

A. You wouldn't care to divulge the name of your high administration source, would you? [*Laughter.*]

Q. No, sir, I would not. But I can tell you I regard him as an unimpeachable source.

A. If I had a dollar for every unimpeachable source you people quote, I could donate my salary to charity. [*Laughter.*] Peter, I read your column this morning. For those of you who may have missed it—even though Mr. Frain seems to be required reading in this town [*laughter*]—he suggests that Operation Umbrella will afford us the golden opportunity to make the Russians see the error of their ways. That may well be, and I certainly hope so. But let me state unequivocally that Umbrella is a system of defense, not a terrorist weapon allowing nuclear blackmail against any nation vulnerable to nuclear attack. Even to hint at such blackmail is monstrous. It would serve merely to increase tension and perhaps invite further Soviet aggression before we get our shield up. I repeat that Operation Umbrella has yet to be tested under realistic attack conditions, and any suggestion that it might be used as a kind of diplomatic club is not only premature but stupidly dangerous. I'd like to change the subject, if you please.

Q. Mr. President, all I was saying . . .

A. Peter, you've said enough. Next question.

Q. Mr. President, could you give us any hint as to when Umbrella will be tested under, as you put it, realistic attack conditions?

A. I said I prefer to change the subject. But in

answer to your question, no, I can't give you any hint. It might not be for another year. It also could be in a few months—I don't know, and if I did have an exact date in mind, I wouldn't tell you.

Q. Does this mean that no coverage of the test will be allowed?

A. It means exactly that. Come on, now, Jules, you don't honestly expect open coverage of such a highly classified test, do you?

Q. One can hope, Mr. President. [*Laughter.*]

A. Well, I'm sorry to disappoint you, but Umbrella represents the biggest technological development since the first atomic bomb was tested in New Mexico. When we know it's a success, we'll let you in on the good news. It also could be a complete failure, and that's something I wouldn't want our Russian friends to know.

Q. May I remind the President that a pool reporter was permitted to witness that A-bomb test? And that he honored the embargo until the government said it was okay to publish?

A. I don't have to be reminded. In my opinion, the circumstances were different then. The outcome of the war didn't rest on whether or not the bomb was a success. The stakes are higher this time, so high that we cannot afford the slightest leak of either success or failure. I'm sorry, but I won't entertain any more questions concerning Operation Umbrella . . .

Congress passed the national lottery bill only two weeks after the President first proposed it and, less than a month later, enacted a measure establishing the

Young America Recovery Corps—two pieces of legislation, *The New York Times* noted, "approved with the speed reminiscent of the rubber-stamp activities of Franklin Roosevelt's mesmerized Seventy-third Congress."

Both the *Times* and the *Washington Post* were ambivalent toward both bills, endorsing their goals but questioning the wisdom of their revenue-raising features. Yet what surprised not only the pontifical editorial writers but the entire news establishment was the public's reaction to both the lottery and YARC—an avalanche of mail descending on Congress supporting both plans. A typical letter was sent to Vice President Mitchell from Colette Jackson, the wife of a Tucson resort ranch owner. "I don't mind paying more for gas and a few more dollars in income taxes," she wrote, "so long as Congress also pays its own fair share toward getting us out of the youth crime and unemployment mess."

Eight days after YARC's passage, Jeremy Haines flew to Atlanta and addressed the AFL-CIO annual convention. The delegates expected the usual I-Love-Labor platitudes and got instead a Presidential suggestion that hit every front page and led every newcast in the country. Haines called for a two-year, no-strike pledge by labor and elimination of all work rules inhibiting productivity in exchange for industry-wide profit-sharing plans and a no-layoff policy for all unionized employes with five or more years seniority.

The AFL-CIO president said the idea was "absolutely unworkable" and the president of the National Manufacturers Association said it was "absolutely unthinkable," but two weeks later they were both sitting in the Oval Office at 1600 Pennsylvania Avenue, along with the heads of the six largest industrial unions, the U.S. Chamber of Commerce, and the chief executives of two big steel companies, four automobile manufacturers, and seven giant aerospace firms.

They all were there for two reasons: The President of the United States had invited them, and by the time they received the invitation they were well aware that every public-opinion poll showed four out of five Americans favoring the idea, and union members themselves supporting it by an eight-to-one ratio. So they listened not only politely but attentively when Haines urged establishment of a joint labor-industry committee to work out a general agreement.

"I'll give you thirty days from this date," he declared. "And don't tell me it can't be done. The precedent was established throughout the airline industry several years ago."

After the meeting, most of those present told reporters they had never seen the President display such determination and forcefulness. "He patted us hard on our rumps and told us to be good," one guest commented ruefully. But privately, the president of the Ford Motor Company remarked to Boeing's chairman of the board: "Something's bothering him. Something very deep inside, like a man harboring a terrible secret he can't even talk about."

The Boeing official shook his head. "God, I didn't get that impression. Just the opposite. He was lecturing us like a schoolteacher getting tough with a class of unruly kids. Lately he's been acting like a man possessed."

"Possessed by what?" the other murmured.

The president of the Ford Motor Company had no way of knowing that one hour before the White House meeting, Jeremy Haines had come from the office of Captain Catlin Baxter, who had worriedly advised him to consult with a psychiatrist named Jessica Sarazin.

SEVEN

Dr. Jessica Sarazin pushed the off button on the tape recorder, removed the cartridge, and inserted a new tape. She scribbled something on the label of the used cartridge; the President cleared his throat.

She looked up. "Sir?"

"I was just wondering how you're labeling those tapes. *Side One—Crazy President?*"

"Nothing like that. You're completely anonymous. Here, see for yourself."

She handed him the tape. On one side she had inscribed X-1 and on the other X-2. Haines handed back the cartridge. "I'm afraid I'm getting paranoid as well as subject to hallucinations."

Jessica hit the on button and leaned back in her

chair, arms behind her head. "You really believe you've hallucinated?"

"No. I was being facetious. And that's what has begun to scare the hell out of me. The ghost's become a part of my life. I look forward to seeing him. I rely on him, to such an extent that I went out of my way to manufacture the last two trips on Air Force One. One of them involved a speaking engagement, an invitation I had no intention of accepting until I realized it would give me a chance to meet Roosevelt again. The other was a vacation flight to Palm Springs that I had no right to take—not with the schedule I've been following and all the fireworks I've been setting off."

"Or the fireworks the ghost has been setting off. I try to keep up with current events, Mr. President. And I read history, too. Even before you walked into this office, I had found myself comparing your activities of the past four months with the first hundred days of the New Deal. There are uncanny parallels. Not necessarily in content but in the speed and impact of your actions. You differ from Roosevelt on specifics, but you're remarkably alike in methods. Just as he did, you've put Congress almost totally on the defensive. You've captured FDR's sense of drama, of urgency. And"—she grinned slyly—"you're even speaking more effectively. I heard your speech to the AFL-CIO convention last week. You were never better."

"Thank you. We, uh, seem to work well together. He gives me a general outline of what I should say and I go on from there." The matter-of-fact tone Haines used chilled her.

"Has the ghost suggested everything you've been

doing?" Jessica asked. "You told me about the lottery and YARC. How about the other proposals you've been making? Such as that little bomb you dropped at the labor convention—another example of collaboration?"

Haines nodded. "It followed our pattern. We agreed that we needed more productivity in American industry, but that management had to give something in return for labor's concessions. The profit-sharing gimmick was FDR's idea. Incidentally, that discussion led to a little argument."

"An argument?"

"If you'll recall the speech, I said that if labor and management didn't agree on a peace pact along the lines I suggested, I might as well wish a plague on both their houses. Roosevelt insisted I use that phrase. He said it was a line he used when he was castigating both John L. Lewis and the coal industry and that it was about the best line he ever wrote. I agreed it was a great phrase but that it wasn't his—it came out of *Romeo and Juliet*. We must have argued about it for an hour before he finally conceded that I might be right. He's a fascinating person, Roosevelt. Tremendous ego yet curiously sensitive. Told me Shakespeare may have originated the phrase but nobody had ever used it as effectively as he. Then he lowered his eyes and said, 'I'm sorry, Jeremy, but I'm afraid I'm a rather vain person.'"

Jessica took a deep breath. "Your inconsistency bothers me. At various times during this session you've expressed the fear that you're insane, that you're hallucinating. Yet you seem convinced you've been seeing and talking to a ghost, one so vividly real that you've accepted it, or him, as a factual, living influence. Usually you even refer to the apparition as Roosevelt, not as *it* or *the ghost.*"

"I think," Haines said slowly, "I'm more bewildered and confused than inconsistent. My logic is in conflict with what I see and hear. The unreality of the situation collides head-on with the evidence of my own senses. I submit to you, Doctor, the dilemma of a man who has witnessed the impossible become fact. And telling me it's just in my own mind doesn't do me one damned bit of good."

"I've never said it was just in your mind. I indicated this was a possibility, but I also conceded the possibility that you've been in contact with a legitimate ghost."

"Well, how would you vote on the issue?"

"Sir?"

"Ghost or insanity?"

"Mr. President, your phraseology is unfair. Hallucinating is not necessarily insanity."

"It's abnormal. You're quibbling, Doctor. I realize there are degrees of mental illness—somewhere I've heard or read that all of us have a little bit of paranoia, schizophrenia, or manic depression. The deciding factor is the degree of affliction and our ability to control it or compensate for it. Isn't that right?"

"Essentially, yes. But let's paraphrase that old chestnut about lawyers defending themselves—a person who tries to psychoanalyze himself has a fool for a patient."

A tiny smile curled the corners of the President's mouth. "Okay, then answer my question."

"I can't answer it at this stage. I'm in somewhat the same position as you are—I'm leaning slightly toward the ghost, but logic tells me to go in the other direction—which simply means I haven't reached a firm diagnosis. Nor did I expect to, on the basis of one session. I can reassure you on one point, however. If you *are* hallucinating, you're also exhibiting the most controlled, sanest response I've ever encountered. No sign of hysteria, not one iota of debilitating panic, not a single indication that it's affecting you adversely in other areas. Your medical record, for example, is generally good except for poor sleeping habits. You have no trouble communicating with others, and in every respect except for this persistent form of hallucination—if that's what it is—you're a completely normal, rational person. And I must emphasize that word *rational*. It is highly unlikely that a rational person can also be suffering from a serious mental disorder, certainly not to the point of disorientation or inability to function normally. A hallucination in itself can respresent dissociation from reality, but such dissociation usually laps over into other facets of behavior. That's not true in your case, at least as far as I can tell from what you've told me or from what I glean from the medical data."

A silence hung between them like an invisible curtain, providing them with the privacy of their own thoughts. It was Haines who spoke first.

"I take it, then, that this is not the only session we'll be having."

"That's up to you, or perhaps to Captain Baxter. But I must caution you, whether I see you again once or twenty times, I can't guarantee results. If we really do have a ghost to deal with, exorcism is out of my bailiwick. And if hallucination is the answer, we have to dig for the source."

Haines muttered, "You won't have to dig very far. My long-standing interest in Franklin Roosevelt seems to have become an obsession, and I suppose stress turned an obsession into this delusion, this mirage with a voice."

Sarazin laughed—it was almost a giggle—and shook her head disapprovingly. "What did I just tell you about not psychoanalyzing yourself? Leave that to the experts like me."

The President refilled his pipe and, before lighting it, examined her with a look that mixed curiosity with admiration. "You've acquired the rank of expert at a relatively early age, Dr. Sarazin. I'd be surprised if you've celebrated thirty-five birthdays."

"I'm over forty," she said promptly, and he warmed to her disdain of coyness.

"Married?"

"Divorced. No children, fortunately. We were married only a year before we both agreed we had made a mistake. Do you have any more personal questions?"

"I'm sorry. I shouldn't be prying." But the amused twinkle in her eyes told him the apology hadn't been necessary. The twinkle worked its way down to her mouth and emerged as a full-fledged smile that encouraged him to probe further.

"Was he a medical student?" he guessed.

"We met in school and married after graduation,

when we both went into psychiatry—which turned out to be all we had in common. I wanted us to go into practice together, which made a lot of sense financially, but he insisted on his own office. After four or five months, my dashing and ardent young med student had turned into a cold and pompous ass. I married Doctor Jekyll and wound up with Mr. Hyde. My married name was Sarazin and I've retained it professionally, not for sentimental reasons but because at the time of the divorce I was too broke to print up new office stationery. Does that satisfy your curiosity, Mr. President?"

He eyed her warily, looking for some sign that she had taken offense, but she still was smiling. "No. Except I now have to ask when I'm supposed to see you again."

Jessica consulted her appointment pad. "How about a week from today, at the same time?"

Haines frowned. "Look, this situation is too delicate for me to be traipsing around when any of your neighbors or a passerby might recognize me. I trust the Secret Service without reservation, but it still makes me uncomfortable to have anyone—including the agents—know that I'm coming to a psychiatrist's office on a regular basis. Those guys are loyal, but they don't make a hell of a lot of money and even loyalty has its price. As a matter of fact, I told those two agents waiting outside you're a specialist on migraine headaches."

Jessica said, "I understand. Does this mean you'd prefer not to continue our talks?"

"No. It means I'd like you to come to the White House. In the evening, a week from tonight, if you have no other plans. We can have a bite to eat and then talk."

"I'd like that very much. Do I just drive in and give my name to the guard at the gate?"

"I'll send a car for you. The gate guards will be told to expect a Jessica Sarazin—I'd prefer your not being identified as a doctor, not for the present, at least. In this town, even a sphinx would leak information. My press secretary will probably get a call from some columnist the next day asking who's Jessica Sarazin and what was she doing in the White House at ten o'clock at night?"

"Tell him I'm a call girl," Jessica suggested, and Haines laughed.

"That would probably do me less political harm than an admission I'm seeing a psychiatrist. I appreciate your taking the time to see me, Doctor, and I *would* like to talk to you again. Telling someone I trust and respect is a form of therapy, I suppose—I hope so, anyway. About next week—we'll make it eight o'clock if that's satisfactory. The car will pick you up at seven-thirty. The driver, incidentally, will be a Secret Service agent. I'm not being paranoid, I assure you. Merely prudent."

"I understand. And seven-thirty will be fine. By the way, Mr. President, do you have any more trips scheduled in the near future?"

"Phoenix next Tuesday. I'm addressing the American Bankers Association. Why do you ask?"

"I thought you might take along a camera, a Polaroid if possible. Maybe our ghost would pose for us."

"Knowing FDR, he'll probably complain that I didn't give him advance warning so he could change shirts."

Haines expected her to smile, at least, but there

was no mirth even in her voice. "I never did ask you if he wears the same clothes at every appearance."

"Always. That cape and a dark blue suit with a Harvard-red tie. He told me once he wore that tie because he wanted a touch of color in the portrait he was sitting for. Funny."

"Funny that he wore a red tie?"

"No, I just remembered something else he mentioned. We were talking about the day he died. While he was sitting for the portrait, he was playing with his stamp collection, and he tossed some duplicate stamps he didn't need into a wastebasket. Then he threw in something he had taken from his wallet. His draft card."

"Draft card? The President of the United States had a draft card?"

"Every male had a draft card in World War Two. What was hard to understand was why he suddenly decided to throw it away, at that particular moment and for no good reason. I asked him if he knew why he did it and he looked at me with a strange, almost pained expression. He said, 'Jeremy, all of a sudden I had the feeling I simply wouldn't need it anymore.'"

For a long moment, they stared at each other until Jessica shut off the tape recorder. They rose simultaneously, like puppets tied to the same strings, and she held out her hand. Haines took it and with an impulsive, courtly, Old World grace that surprised him almost as much as it did her, he kissed it.

He turned and walked out. She heard him say, "Okay, boys, let's go home," and waited for the sound of the outer door closing before she sat down again.

She idly fingered the recorder as if its contents could be absorbed by touch instead of sound. After several minutes, she reached for the phone on her desk and dialed a number. It rang only once before a gruff voice answered.

"Baxter here."

"Dr. Sarazin, Captain. I apologize for calling you on your private line but I wanted to make sure nobody else might be listening."

"That's what I told you to do, so don't apologize." His tone, as usual, was brusque; it always gave Jessica the impression that he would be curt even if someone called and told him he had just won a million-dollar sweepstakes. But she also realized it was pure window dressing—she had met Catlin Baxter at a medical seminar and had found out there was a thick layer of old-fashioned sentiment under the barnacles.

She said cautiously, "I've been talking to him for well over two hours. He's a remarkable person, and he tells a remarkable story."

"Hell, I knew that before I sent him to you. What I'd like to know is whether you've formed an opinion."

"I have an opinion but it's far from conviction."

"I'd still like to hear it."

"You understand this is very tentative."

"Of course it's tentative! I didn't expect you to come up with cause and cure in one goddamned session."

Jessica Sarazin took a deep breath. "All right. I think he's hallucinating."

TWO

EIGHT

"Lovely town, Phoenix," the ghost was saying. "In my days, it was practically the Wild West. Now it's a sophisticated, progressive community."

Jeremy Haines sighed. "Arizona's always been a favorite state of mine. When I leave office, I think I'd like to live out here, around Tucson, rather than Phoenix—the climate's better. Barry Goldwater introduced me to this area. I spent a few days with him at his home and fell in love with the desert."

"For a liberal Republican," Roosevelt chided, "you've kept some bad company. That Goldwater fellow—terrible reactionary."

"Conservative, not reactionary. And one of the most honest men I've ever known. He never compromised his convictions for political reasons—a rare virtue in politics, wouldn't you say?"

"Rare, and usually foolish. Politics is the art of compromise, and compromise is the only way to get elected. Now you take my first campaign, Jeremy, back in 1932. I won votes by attacking the Republicans for wasteful, extravagant spending and I even demanded a balanced federal budget. Nobody in their right mind could have foreseen what I'd do when I got into office. If I had tipped my hand during the campaign as to what the New Deal was going to involve, Hoover might have beaten me. Y'know, I had nothing but unvarnished contempt for Herbert Hoover at first. I considered him coldblooded and insensitive, a slave to big business. A slave he was, of course, but not coldblooded or insensitive. Just a frustrated, unhappy prisoner of his own economic and political beliefs. He had neither the will nor the imagination to compromise those beliefs, and in the end, that's what defeated him. I dare say Hoover was always jealous of my success. After all, I did what he should have done—acted boldly, as you're doing now, Jeremy. I'm still not entirely happy with the proposal you put to those bankers, but I've never argued with you about our goals—just the means."

Haines gave the ghost a baleful look. "You called me an economic royalist—one of your favorite epithets, I seem to recall." Ghosts, he assumed, could not blush but he could swear Roosevelt seemed embarrassed.

"Nothing personal," FDR said hastily. "I simply felt that your new tax plan came right out of the Republican elephant's trunk. The fact that the bankers ate it up merely proved my point. Those Louis the Fourteenth Bourbons have been trying to eliminate the income tax for generations."

"I'm not trying to eliminate it," the President said patiently. "I'm trying to reduce it without loss of revenue."

"Benefiting the few at the expense of the many," the ghost said a bit testily. Then he flashed that 250-watt smile and held up his hand. "Forgive me, my friend—I keep forgetting who's the President around here. I should keep my task always in mind. To help you, to counsel you, to advise you, but never to dictate to you. Which, I think you'll agree, is rather difficult for a fellow of my personality."

"I'm trying to, uh, cooperate," Haines said gravely.

"And you are, Jeremy, you are! Your attitude has been perfectly splendid, considering the rather unusual circumstances."

Haines could not resist asking the question that had popped into his mind. "Are you aware I've seen a psychiatrist?"

"I am. Very attractive young lady, by the way. I love her black hair. You should cultivate her friendship. You've been a hermit and celibate too long."

The President burst out laughing. "I'll ignore your romantic advice. Frankly, I thought you might be offended."

"Offended? At what?"

"My going to a shrink."

"Why on earth should I be offended? I fully realize this relationship of ours is unique, one that calls for a certain amount of skepticism on your part. The important thing is not your occasional and perfectly natural lapses into self-doubt but the fact that we're working so well together. Incidentally, did you bring the camera, as she suggested?"

Haines was startled momentarily. "It's in my overnight bag, in my stateroom. I'll go get it."

Roosevelt motioned him to sit down. "Don't bother, Jeremy. My likeness won't appear on any piece of film."

Haines remembered Jessica's accounts of photographed ghosts. "It's been done before, Mr. President."

"But not in this case. Besides"—Roosevelt's voice turned sulky—"I don't like having my picture taken. I look now like I did in 1945 just before I died—old and tired. That was bad enough but those damned newspaper photographers absolutely delighted in catching me in an unflattering pose, when I looked even older and more ailing than I really was. They used those shots all the way through the 1944 campaign, deliberately giving the impression that Dewey was running against a sick man."

"You *were* a sick man," Haines said gently.

FDR looked surprised, as if Haines had just revealed something he hadn't realized. "Well, that was at the end, of course. I assure you I was perfectly fine when I ran for a fourth term." The golden voice dropped an octave. "The Yalta trip took an awful lot out of me. Pa Watson dying. Churchill driving me crazy trying to protect that anachronism known as the British Empire."

"I've read that Stalin was shocked at your physical appearance and was very solicitous," Haines said.

FDR nodded. "He said if he had realized how fatigued I was, he wouldn't have insisted that we had to meet on Russian soil. Y'know, he was a ruthless person but I couldn't help liking him. You Republicans have claimed for years that Stalin hoodwinked me because I couldn't see him for the monster he really was. I give you my word, Jeremy, I went to Yalta with my eyes wide open. I already had seen examples of Soviet paranoia, that inbred suspicion of theirs that makes them so hard to deal with. I thought at first it was just Stalin's but now I realize it's a trait of communism itself, the ultimate consequence of a monolithic police state that doesn't trust anybody, including its own people."

The President said, "Every night I pray for the only real solution. That the Russians themselves will rise up and throw out their oppressors. But I don't think it will happen in my lifetime." He paused. "I've often wondered, and so have many others, what would have happened to Soviet-American relations if you had lived longer. If Stalin respected anyone, it was you."

The ghost wore a pensive expression. "I did get along with him surprisingly well, better than I did with Churchill."

"Stalin trusted you up to a point," Haines observed. "It didn't keep him from a lot of double-dealing and double-crossing. Historians still claim you gave away more than you had to at Yalta, primarily because you took him at his word."

"As I said before, historians have the advantage of hindsight, though it's sometimes hindsight with a touch of astigmatism," Roosevelt retorted. "I admit I made some unnecessary concessions, mostly to guarantee Russia's entry into the war against Japan. I had no way of knowing that two atomic bombs would knock out the

Japs—I didn't even know if the bomb would work. I needed Stalin's promise to declare war on Japan in order to tie up the Japanese army in Manchuria. The Pentagon was warning me we'd take a million casualties if we had to invade the Japanese homeland—a million casualties, mind you, even if that very sizable Manchurian force stayed where it was. Now let me tell you something, my friend, people have forgotten what I *didn't* give Stalin.

"He wanted to leave France out in the cold when it came to control of postwar Germany. I absolutely refused. He demanded impossibly cruel and excessive German war reparations, and I held firm. I got him to accept virtually every one of my suggestions regarding the formation of the United Nations. I stopped him from getting the leeway he wanted for all his political shenanigans in the liberated areas. Why, I . . ."

"They wound up controlling most of those areas anyway," Haines interrupted.

"Poland and the Balkans, yes. But the Russian army already was occupying Poland. As for the Balkan countries, it was Churchill who gave away the store, not me. Even before Yalta, he and Stalin had a cozy little meeting in Moscow where they divided up the spoils. Winston gave Stalin carte blanche in Hungary, Bulgaria, and Rumania, and handed him a 50 percent share in Yugoslavia, all in return for British control of Greece. Now I had great affection and admiration for Winston, but he was far more guilty than I when it came to making deals with Uncle Joe."

The ghost fell silent for a moment and then, more agitated than Haines had even seen him, resumed. "My enemies love to spread the canard that I was too sick and too feeble to stand up to the Russians. Balderdash! I wasn't up to snuff, but I was far from feeble. I know my hands shook a little when I signed papers or lit a cig, but that was natural for a man of my age after twelve years in the White House."

"I'm tired after six years," the President said soberly. "It wouldn't be so hard if all I had to worry about were domestic matters. But Soviet aggression and all the ramifications of a nuclear war—well, I wish I could sleep at night. As you did, from what I understand."

"True. Babs used to marvel at the way I could sleep, no matter how difficult the day had been or the next day promised to be. The only sleepless nights I had were due to interruptions, not insomnia. But I can understand your being kept awake, Jeremy. Today's Russian leaders are just as dangerous as Hitler, and it took a global war to destroy the Nazis. They know we'd never start World War Three, so they wage aggression with their overwhelming superiority in manpower and conventional arms. A frightening dilemma, my friend. We're afraid to fight a nuclear war and we can't win a conventional one."

"There are times when I wish you had never given the go-ahead for the atomic bomb project," Haines said.

"Now that's absolutely ridiculous," FDR scolded. "I had to, y'understand. Positively had to. I was warned the Germans were trying to develop an A-bomb and I had no other choice. I acted, you might say, for defensive reasons."

"If defense was your motive, would you have used the A-bomb against Japan, as Truman did?"

Roosevelt answered unhesitatingly. "Probably. Harry ordered the Hiroshima mission after the military told him what an invasion of Japan would cost in terms of lives. I suppose I would have reached the same conclusion—by weighing a million American casualties against the thousands who'd be killed by an atomic bomb. It was a terrible decision to make, and I'm glad I didn't have to make it."

"Somehow," Haines commented wryly, "I have to doubt that. You loved to make decisions, particularly the tough ones."

"Just as you do now," Roosevelt said with the air of a proud father. "A man of action. A man of decisiveness. Y'know, Jeremy, you're getting more and more like me every day, even if you are a Republican. Now, tell me, why that pained expression?"

"I was thinking of a few traits of yours I wouldn't want to emulate."

The ghost smiled, but rather tentatively, Haines thought. "Well, I know I wasn't perfect. Name some."

"I'll cite what I and others who've admired you believe was a principal fault. Your inability, or perhaps reluctance, to tell a man to his face that you totally disagreed with him. Time after time, someone would walk into the Oval Office and try to sell you his point of view on some issue. Invariably, he'd leave with the definite impression you agreed with his view—only to find out later you completely disagreed. Such instances have been well documented, and I don't think it's necessary to mention individuals. You seemed to have a penchant for avoiding face-to-face unpleasantness. Oh, you could lose that Dutch temper of yours, but seldom in any personal confrontation with people you really despised. Hence, your reputation for deviousness. For example, you hated to fire anybody. You let others do that dirty work while you allowed the victim to believe he had your support and friendship. John Gunther once interviewed a government official who told him that when six people with different views on the same issue left the White House after a meeting with you, and all six went away happy, you could be damned sure somebody was going to get his throat cut. Am I being too critical?"

"No, I'm afraid you're not. Excessive affability was one of my worst faults. I had a natural desire to be liked by everyone, but I carried this trait to extremes. I admired candor in others, but I didn't always practice it myself."

Haines grinned. "Of late I've demonstrated somewhat the same weakness."

"I don't quite follow you."

"I let myself be talked into appointing some people who don't belong in my administration. I've put up with incompetents, because I didn't have the energy or guts to fire them. Now that you seem to have turned me into a man of decisive action, as you put it, I'm finally going to do something about my past mistakes. Such as canning my leading dissident, General Collision."

The President was surprised to see a look of startled concern cloud the ghost's face. "I would advise against such hasty action," Roosevelt said.

"For God's sake, why? Duane Collison is disloyal

and disrespectful. Truman fired MacArthur for the same reasons."

"And came close to making a martyr out of him. You'd be playing right into Collison's hands. I beg of you, Jeremy, wait a little while. You and I can work out something to solve this Russian problem and we'll pull the rug out from under him."

Haines gave him a stare coated with doubt. "I don't get it. What possible advantage would there be in not firing the bastard? He's done nothing but harm."

Roosevelt nodded sympathetically. "I know, Jeremy, I know. But we must think in terms of long-range strategy, not of a personal vendetta that would give you immediate emotional satisfaction with no lasting benefits. Listen to me carefully. If you fire Collison now, you'll be sending the Soviets an untimely message. One that says in effect, 'Look, gentlemen, I've dismissed the severest critic of my policy toward you. You may now rest assured I'm going to be just as weak-kneed and spineless as I have in the past.'"

"Whose side are you on?" Haines demanded angrily. "You're using the same adjectives Collison . . ."

FDR stopped him with a wave of the hand. "Calm down, Jeremy. I'm just stating facts, and don't let vanity get in the way of judgment. You *have* been weak and vacillating toward the Soviet Union. In that respect, the general has been accurate. You and I know that's going to change, but until we can formulate some positive methods to contain Russia, this is no time to confirm Collision's charges, and firing him would do just that. Furthermore, by eliminating him from your administration, you invite even more strident accusations and dissension. When our plans jell, you may even find him an effective and articulate ally."

The caped figure leaned back in his seat, a smugly satisfied look on his face—one planted there by the President's own disconcerted expression. Haines seemed shaken.

"Exactly what do you have up your sleeve?" he finally asked.

"At the present moment, absolutely nothing. Oh, a few vague ideas, some very tentative thoughts and one or two rather wispy notions. I need more time to think things out but in the end, Jeremy, I'll suggest to you a very workable plan. Foreign affairs were always my forte, right?"

"So was secrecy—and your love of surprises," Haines said in a tone of mild reproach. "I think there's more in your mind than a few wispy notions."

"I give you my word, I have no specific plan or plans. Not yet. You have to trust me, my friend. I haven't let you down yet, have I?"

"You win," the President sighed, and the ghost of Franklin Delano Roosevelt smiled broadly.

Thomas Patrick Rafferty, Speaker of the House, inspected the gloomy countenances of his two colleagues and shook his head in disgust.

"Come on, boys!" he boomed, in his bass drum voice. "Get your asses off the floor and start thinking!"

It was, perhaps, inevitable that the pair sitting in the Speaker's private quarters seemed to snap to attention in the manner of two rookie Marines caught sulking by a drill sergeant. Tom Rafferty was a smallish

Irishman with thinning red hair and a pinkish complexion that deepened into varying shades of crimson in direct proportion to the decibels of his voice. Coming from one so diminutive, it was like hearing a toy poodle bark like a Great Dane.

Bob Ballman, House Majority Leader, gauged Rafferty's complexion as being only one notch below maximum intensity and winced inwardly. He shared with about 85 percent of the House membership a fear of the Speaker that no one admitted publicly; Rafferty could be a vindictive tyrant at times, a man who demanded unyielding party loyalty and whose grudges had the longevity of a sea turtle.

"If your constituent mail is anything like mine," Ballman ventured, "you'd be as frustrated as I am. Opposing Jeremy Haines right now is like coming out four-square in favor of sin. Let's face it, Tom, the country's behind him."

Sitting next to Winston, nodding in glum agreement, was the Senate Minority Leader, Jordan Caldwell, a dark-haired man whose handsome features were marred by a perpetual bristle. "I have to agree with Bob. I know damned well the President has the Senate in his hip pocket—we're not only in a slight minority to begin with, but I can't stop party defections any more than I could hold back a charging bull. What the hell, Tom, you haven't done much better in the House and you've got a fairly solid Democratic majority. They've been bolting the same as my people."

"Not to the extent they have in the Senate," Rafferty growled. "I've kept most of 'em in line."

"Not in sufficient numbers to keep Haines from

getting what he wants," Caldwell said sharply. He was unafraid of the Speaker, whose influence stopped at the borders of the lower chamber.

Rafferty glowered, but his momentary silence was a grudging admission that Jordan Caldwell was right. "He's flushing this country right down the toilet," he muttered sourly, "and Congress is pulling the chain."

"I'm not so sure," the Senator said. "Maybe some of these half-assed ideas of his won't work, but at least he's doing *something*. He's providing leadership, and people are responding. We had a chance to supply leadership and we blew it. All we've been offering is the same shopworn crap—more welfare benefits, higher taxes, and invectives about greedy big business. That spend-and-tax philosophy of ours is not only obsolete but it has let Haines take the initiative."

Rafferty's face went to the color of blood. "What the hell do you think that fucking wimp in the White House is doing but spend and tax? Gas taxes, sales taxes, income taxes—all of 'em taking the skin off the poor and the middle class. For Christ's sake, Jordan, his goddamned lottery's nothing but a hidden tax!"

"The point is, it's a painless tax—and so is every damned tax he's proposed. Look what he came up with in that Phoenix speech to the bankers—a permanent 5 percent national sales tax with a corresponding 25 percent income tax reduction. My God, the people are eating it up! Why? Because they'll wind up paying just about the same taxes as they do now, probably even more, but in bits and pieces and dribbles instead of tearing big chunks out of paychecks and that April fifteenth annual bloodletting. Painless, Tom. Painless—and it'll win elections."

House Majority Leader Ballman had been listening to this exchange, his mind a pair of eyes watching a tennis match. "Well, constitutionally he can't run for a third term," he pointed out, "no matter how popular he is now."

"A popular outgoing President," Caldwell said unhappily, "can name the party's next ticket, and even if he picked a chimpanzee, he'd get elected. William Howard Taft couldn't have won a dog catcher's post if Teddy Roosevelt hadn't named him his heir-apparent."

"Two years is a long time," Rafferty mused darkly. "A lot can happen. He might fall flat on his face with these programs of his."

Senator Caldwell snorted. "Maybe, but don't count on it. At last reports, they've had almost a million applications for those YARC camps. What you don't seem to have grasped, Tom, is the undeniable fact that Haines has suddenly emerged as a real, live, fire-breathing leader with guts, imagination, and charisma. And that, Mr. Speaker, spells trouble for our side. A friend of mine at ABC tipped me that a Gallup poll to be released next week shows his popularity has jumped 23 percent in the past three months."

"He still has his weak spots," Rafferty insisted. "He's still a wimp in foreign affairs."

Ballman, leaping with alacrity to agree with the Speaker, bobbed his head. "Did you happen to see Duane Collison on *Crossfire* the other night? He really tore Haines apart. Said the President is abdicating world leadership to the Russians by default—'criminal inaction and cruel indifference' were the words he used."

Rafferty stared at the House Majority Leader as if he had just uttered a holy revelation. "I didn't see the show, but he sure as hell expressed my sentiments. Maybe I should cultivate that guy."

"What for?" Caldwell demanded. "He's a political eunuch and always has been. Nobody even knows what party he belongs to—probably none."

"I don't give a damn if he's a socialist. His most eminent qualification is that he hates Jeremy Haines's guts and isn't afraid to say so."

The Senator's face was almost as red as Rafferty's. "Tom, if we get the Democratic Party into bed with that guy, we'll be juggling dynamite. Collison's a hawk, pure and simple."

The Speaker grinned. "Hawks are more politically digestible these days. Why the hell do you think Haines's popularity went down in the first place, before he started all these Alice-in-Wonderland schemes? You know why, Jordan. He was consistently demonstrating a mealymouthed, do-nothing policy toward the Soviets, and he still is. I seem to remember you've made a few speeches on that subject yourself."

Caldwell said dourly, "I've got enough trouble holding my troops together in the Senate without inviting a trigger-happy fanatic like Duane Collison into the fold. I've been told on good authority that he's Peter Frain's favorite pipeline, and Frain's been launching trial balloons all over the place. Have you been reading him lately?"

Rafferty lit a cigar and puffed away meditatively. "Yeah, I've been reading him. He makes sense. If that anti-missile system is as close to reality as he claims, we could tell those Kremlin cocksuckers to go to hell.

And now that you've mentioned trial balloons, what's wrong with that? This town's seen more trial balloons than pigeons. They're a very effective way of gauging public opinion on some controversial proposal, and I haven't heard any loud, anguished cries directed toward our Mr. Frain."

Caldwell said, "He's just one columnist."

"And a goddamned influential one, with a nationwide audience, not just Washington. You say Collison's his pipeline?"

The Senator nodded. "They're close friends."

"Well, maybe I oughta get together with Pete Frain and his pipeline. I think we could make good use of them."

"They're both hawks," Jordan Caldwell warned. "You can't commit our party to support of their position."

"What position?" the Speaker demanded. "All they're saying is that when Umbrella's activated, we should tell Russia to piss or get off the pot. And believe you me, Jordan, there are about a hundred million Americans who'd say amen to that kind of talk. They haven't heard it for two years."

Jordan Caldwell fired one final shot, even though he knew it would miss. "There are more than a hundred million Americans who don't want war. The war Collison would have us start if all the tough talk didn't work."

Rafferty's homely mouth hardened. "I can control guys like Duane Collison. I'll just plant a few seeds of political ambition under his so-called eunuch skin. And they'll sprout like weeds in a rain."

Caldwell said suspiciously, "Are you talking about *Presidential* ambition?"

"I sure as hell am."

"You're crazy. The voters won't buy a military man."

"They elected Eisenhower, didn't they? Twice."

"But he was a war hero with a personality that invited trust. Collison's just another general."

"Duane Collison," Rafferty said emphatically, "is a smart, articulate, and persuasive guy. Even the President respects him. Now just a second, Jordan"—Caldwell had started to say something—"I said Haines *respects* him. Shit, I know he doesn't like him. He's even a little afraid of him, and well he might be. Collison's a very effective man in front of an audience. And the more he lambastes Haines, the better it is for us. He isn't gonna get us into any war—not with those visions of Presidential sugarplums dancing around in his head."

Senator Caldwell shook his head sadly. "Don't underestimate him, Tom. He doesn't have your motives—he has his own. You just want to get rid of Jeremy Haines. Duane Collison wants to get rid of Russia."

* * *

Approximately one mile from the House Office Building, where the Speaker was holding court, a black Lincoln slid noiselessly up to the east gate of 1600 Pennsylvania Avenue. The driver rolled down his window as a White House policeman came out of the guard shack, nodded in recognition, and peered at the woman in the back seat.

"Jessica Sarazin," the driver said. "She's on your list."

"Right," the guard acknowledged and waved the Lincoln through. As he watched the red taillights disappear in the darkness, he scratched his head.

"Who the hell is Jessica Sarazin?" he wondered aloud to a second policeman, standing by the sentry box. "Good-looking dame."

"You don't suppose the old man imported a call girl for the evening?" his companion suggested with a grin.

"Naw. Not Haines. Not that I wouldn't blame him, all alone in that big house and with all his troubles. He must go crazy at times."

"Maybe she's a lady psychiatrist."

They both laughed.

NINE

Jessica sipped her cream sherry and looked around the President's private sitting room on the second floor of the White House.

The furnishings were early American, the style achieving a marriage of the past to the present; it had the quality of making a twentieth-century person still feel at home in an eighteenth-century room. Sitting on a surprisingly comfortable divan—she had always considered Colonial furniture a bit awkward for the human body—the psychiatrist let her eyes roam around the room and return to Jeremy Haines, slouched languidly in an upholstered rocking chair across from her.

"I can understand why someone called the White House a place of lonely splendor," she commented.

"And the Presidency a life of splendid misery," Haines said, with a dryness that managed to escape outright cynicism. He was drinking one of his inevitable Scotch and sodas while studying her calm, chiseled face. "I must say, however, that perversely I've been having more fun of late."

"Why do you say *perversely?*"

He laughed shortly. "Come now, Doctor. Isn't it perverse to feel better and stronger and more capable just because I've spent the last four months with a ghost as my most trusted adviser?"

"Extremely unusual," she conceded, "but I wouldn't say *perverse*. A lot of your renewed energy and confidence is self-generated. It's coming from within you. The experience actually seems to have tapped your own dormant abilities."

He looked at her suspiciously. "Is that a psychiatrist's way of telling me it's all in my mind?"

"That's always a possibility. At this point, I can't say."

The Scotch tasted strong, and Haines stirred the tumbler unhygienically with a forefinger—a gesture, Jessica thought, that made him seem quaintly mortal. She still had not quite adjusted to the heady experience of dining alone with the President of the United States.

Away from the professional sanctity of her office, Jessica felt unsure of herself, almost as if the role of dominance and authority she enjoyed as the doctor had suddenly been transferred to the patient. And she could not deny that the role reversal also made her feel more like a woman than a doctor. Before dinner, he had taken her for a guided tour of the Executive Mansion and gallantly attempted to make light talk to dissipate her obvious awe in these surroundings.

He took her into the Oval Office. She had seen pictures of it, but no photograph really captured the room's size and splendor, with its twelve-foot French windows and the Great Seal of the United States of America woven into the huge, grayish-green carpeting. The massive Presidential desk caught her eye instantly; even in so large an office it dominated the room and gave her the impression that she was looking at a giant wooden heart connected to the arteries of a nation. Behind it, on gold stands, were the Stars and Stripes and the purple and gold flag bearing the Presidential seal.

She examined the desk's ornate carving and peeked at the few personal items on the polished top. A combined pipe stand and tobacco humidor. A picture of an attractive woman and another photograph of a smiling youth in an Army uniform. "My wife Barbara and my son," Haines explained. "Kevin was killed in Vietnam."

She smiled at another item on the desk top, a small plaque reading THE BUCK STOPS HERE.

"Very appropriate," Jessica remarked. "It describes your job."

"It describes the job of every President," Haines

said soberly. "Harry Truman put that little sign on the desk and no subsequent President has ever removed it. Seems to fit right in with that telephone console." He was pointing to the eighteen-button communications console on one side of the desk and saw her eyes widen.

"It would take too much time to explain all those buttons," he told her. "I'm not sure I remember all of them myself. But the blue one is the maximum security line—it scrambles my voice so the person being called hears nothing but gibberish unless he has an unscrambling device at his end. The red button is hooked to the War Room at the Pentagon, so I can talk to any military base in the world. The amber one is a direct line to an Army switchboard that connects me instantly to any cabinet member and the heads of certain key agencies. Impressed?"

"Very. But most of all by the desk itself. It must be seven feet long."

"Just about. There's an interesting story behind it. It's made from the timbers of an old British warship. When the ship was scrapped, Queen Victoria had some of the hull wood made into this desk and sent it as a gift to Rutherford Hayes. Every President used it until FDR, who, for some reason, didn't like it and ordered it put in storage. Jackie Kennedy found it hidden under a hunk of canvas on the ground floor and had it moved to this wing. Originally it was in the Lincoln Room on the second floor, when that room was used as a Presidential study." He chuckled.

Jessica's eyebrows lifted. "Did I miss something amusing?" she asked.

"No. I was just thinking I should ask Roosevelt what there was about that desk he didn't like."

That bothered her. He was talking about the apparition again, an indication that it was on his mind constantly, and with the same taken-for-granted attitude he would display toward a living person. As if he had so totally accepted the ghost's existence that he could no longer distinguish it from a real human being. Yet somehow, she realized, his very matter-of-factness added credibility to the incredible. He followed his joking remark about FDR by taking her arm and steering her down a short corridor into the Presidential study, a room possessing an easy intimacy that the Oval Office lacked.

She complimented him on the study's furnishings—two big maroon-leather armchairs, several marine landscape oils on the walnut-paneled walls, a stand-mounted illuminated globe next to a black mahogany desk, and a wooden bookcase along one wall. With the typical curiosity of a book-lover, Jessica could not resist examining his choice of literature.

She noted with a professional interest his absorption with naval history. The entire works of C. S. Forester, including every Horatio Hornblower novel. The complete Captain Bolitho series by Alexander Kent. The Time-Life "Seafarers" volumes. Many books on World War II naval operations. There also were a number of Sinclair Lewis novels and most of Herman Wouk's works, plus various political biographies and a number of books on American history.

Jessica turned from her inspection to remark, "You weren't a naval officer, were you?"

"My dream was to go to Annapolis but I couldn't hack the required math," he confided. "So I read about naval history—something I have in common with Mr. Roosevelt."

She was still mentally masticating that second reference to FDR and his preoccupation with the subject throughout dinner and afterward, as she drank her sherry. She was having increasing difficulty differentiating between this considerate, totally compatible man and someone who quite possibly could be mentally ill.

Jessica cleared her throat nervously. "That shrimp salad was delicious," she said, conscious that she was indulging in some unprofessional small talk.

"I'm glad you liked it." He eyed her sagely. "You're uneasy, aren't you?"

"Yes."

"I don't have to ask why. This place has a sobering effect on the most blasé and cynical. It's built out of two hundred years of history, and its very permanence gives every occupant a feeling of his own impermanence. I live with more ghosts than just one. So I understand why you feel ill at ease. Please don't."

"It isn't just the White House."

"Oh? That leaves only your dinner companion to blame."

Jessica smiled. "It's very disconcerting to feel I'm more of a date than a doctor. After all, this is supposed to be a professional visit, not a social evening."

The President returned her smile. "Up to now, it has been social—and very enjoyable. But if it will make you feel better, we can return to the subject of my friend Franklin."

"Not entirely social," Dr. Sarazin said. "The psychiatrist in me never seems to rest. I've been observing you, even through dinner. You're a fascinating, very personable, and confident man, but I've also gotten the impression you're a little ill at ease yourself. It makes me curious."

"Is it the woman who's curious or the psychiatrist?"

Jessica laughed. "Both, I guess."

"I think my answer would be identical for either species. I'm not, well, not accustomed to female companionship. I must confess that I've looked forward to this evening, but not from a medical angle. The psychiatrist in you scares the hell out of me. I like the woman better. Yet if I'm ill at ease, it's just as much because of the latter."

Jessica said slowly, "I would prefer your being comfortable in either case. Are you afraid of psychiatrists in general or does the fact that I'm a female psychiatrist concern you?"

"Not in the slightest. Dr. Sarazin, I've named more women to high government posts than any other President in history. A chauvinist I'm not. However, you're an easy person to talk to and I find it difficult to tell at what level we're communicating. At times, over that shrimp salad, I kept wondering whether I was unburdening myself to a doctor or to an attractive woman. Either way, it seemed to be excellent therapy."

"The therapy is more important than how you perceive me," Jessica said. "Provided, of course, that you really need therapy. I didn't use the word—you did. I find it far more likely that you merely needed someone to talk to."

"Someone more real than a ghost, is that it?" Haines said in a self-chiding tone that made her smile in return. He rose to replenish their drinks and, his back to her, said unexpectedly, "By the way, Mr. Roosevelt knows about you."

Jessica gulped. "Oh?"

Haines handed her a second sherry and dropped his lean body into the rocking chair. "I asked him if he was aware I've seen a psychiatrist. He was not only aware but he even mentioned the color of your hair."

"He seems to get around," she said with false lightness. All her training, her carefully acquired faculty of detachment, was suddenly threatened. If Roosevelt's ghost really existed, it was probably in this very room, and she could almost hear the pounding of her heart.

"I wish he'd materialize right now," the President said laconically. "Proof of the pudding. Or maybe it would send *you* racing into therapy. Do psychiatrists go to other psychiatrists?"

Dr. Sarazin ignored his attempt at wit. "Did you ever try to take his picture?"

"I brought up the subject. He made it clear he didn't want to pose, and he told me even if he did, it wouldn't do any good."

"I wish you had tried anyway."

"I would have been photographing an empty seat. Remember, he makes rapid exits."

"What was his reaction to your seeing a psychiatrist?"

"He said he didn't blame me. He also urged me to cultivate your friendship—more along romantic lines than medical. In fact, he came out four-square against my continued voluntary celibacy."

Jessica was not quite sure whether to laugh or frown, and settled for an enigmatic smile. "Why is your celibacy voluntary?" she asked calmly.

"Are you asking as a psychiatrist or as a woman?"

She answered in a sharp tone that seemed to snap. "As a psychiatrist, of course. And I'm asking for purely clinical reasons. Total abstinence in a healthy man of your age is not exactly the norm."

"Are you kidding? I'm a widower with all the privacy of a goldfish."

"I'm sorry, Mr. President, but that won't wash. Some of your predecessors managed to have extracurricular affairs even when they were in the White House. Harding was one, and reportedly Kennedy. Franklin Roosevelt had a clandestine relationship with Lucy Rutherford for years. I'm not advocating an immediate plunge into bed with somebody, and if you prefer celibacy, that's your prerogative. But remember, a psychiatrist looks for departures from the norm and the reasons or motives behind them. They're part of the total clinical picture, because a person's sex life or lack of a sex life may reveal some factors related to overall behavior."

Haines's laugh was brittle. "Sounds like you're telling me a horny man is more likely to see ghosts."

"You know that's not what I meant," she said in a patient tone. "Sexual tensions can lead to other tensions. If this ghost exists only in your own mind, I have to look for causes before I find a cure. A psychiatrist has to dig, to pry, and to probe. I have no prurient interest in your sex life, Mr. President, other than to determine if your self-imposed celibacy is having any subconscious harmful effects."

Even as she spoke, she realized how pontifical this jargon must sound. But Jeremy Haines merely lit one of his ubiquitous pipes and smiled at her.

"I suppose," he said gently, "my lack of sexual desire is related to my job—the constant stresses, the demands on my time, and the inhibiting atmosphere of the White House itself. I'll admit to occasional stirrings, but I'm not about to ask the Secret Service to go find me a call girl who can keep her mouth shut. I won't argue your point that total abstinence isn't normal, but I must remind you that the life of a widower President isn't normal, either. I find it difficult to conduct conventional social relationships with women, and I'm sure you can appreciate why. So if you think celibacy is related to my friend the ghost, you're grasping at air."

"I didn't say I think so," Jessica said. "I meant I have to consider all possibilities." She was admitting to herself that her analytical pendulum had swung away suddenly from the "all-in-his-mind" theory. She still favored it as the most logical explanation, but she was impressed by his logical responses, his sincerity, his acute perceptions. That brief excursion down the path of possible sexual connotations had been a blunder—it was a blind path from which he had adroitly steered her away. Maybe Jeremy Haines was conjuring up a ghost, but never in her career had she encountered a supposedly mentally disturbed patient who exhibited such complete rationality. And while her psychiatric training told her there still must be something wrong, the parapsychologist in her was resisting that conviction.

They talked for another hour, not about Franklin Roosevelt but about Jeremy Haines—his childhood, his family background, his youth, and his eventual marriage. He held back nothing.

"Barbara was a passionate woman," he said at one point. "When you've been married to someone like that—so responsive, so giving—well, a man can live on such memories."

"You're fortunate to have them," Jessica said, "but it shouldn't preclude your finding those qualities in someone else."

"I don't have the time to look," the President grunted unhappily. "At least not until I leave office. A day of rejoicing, I might add. Maybe I'll depart this godforsaken place with a feeling of some accomplishment. I know I won't leave it with any regrets."

Jessica asked, "Do you really hate your job? This life?"

Haines downed the last of a drink he had been nursing for the past half-hour. "At times I do. Oh, I've enjoyed the Presidential perks. The ego-massaging experience of being called 'Mr. President'—I have a very human appreciation of that. But glory carries a steep price tag. I once kept track of the number of documents I had to sign in a twenty-four-hour period. Five hundred and seven pieces of paper. Petty routine is one thing, perpetual crisis is another, and even worse, there are no time-outs between solutions. Crisis follows crisis with the inevitability of thunder following lightning. And that, Jessica, is why I've been talking and listening so insanely to a goddamned ghost—because he's helping me, and the only decent, satisfying thing I can take out of this mausoleum of memories is a feeling that I've done something for my country."

The unexpected use of her first name surprised Jessica, even startled her—she hadn't been aware he even knew it; instantly she began to interpret it. Inadvertent, perhaps, maybe presumptuously familiar—yet that would not be like him, for he carried a kind of natural dignity. No, she sensed, the *Jessica* had emerged from a need for a friendship too long denied him. It was an interpretation that somehow flustered her, for it dawned on her that she, too, needed such a friendship. Decidedly unprofessional, she chastised herself, but she could not prevent herself from looking into those expressive gray eyes—eyes that mirrored a tortured, sick mind, she wondered, or simply a lonely, warmly human man.

His voice broke the silence.

"Do you think we've accomplished anything tonight?"

It was the psychiatrist who answered briskly. "Yes, although I'd hate to be pinned down on specifics. I think I've gotten to know you better. I've gotten some insight into the kind of person you are and the kind of existence you lead. Understanding you is vital, and in that respect we *have* accomplished something."

What the woman said was to herself. A disturbing realization that her objectivity was crumbling. That she was being inexorably drawn to him in a subjective way—a sliver of emotional metal propelled toward a magnet.

And a few minutes later, on the porch overlooking the Executive Mansion's circular driveway, she held out her hand and said quietly, "Thank you, Jeremy. I'll see you here next Friday after your Dallas trip."

General Duane Collison, though he towered over Tom Rafferty like a carrier dwarfing a destroyer, was deferential out of respect, not obsequiousness. The Speaker of the House was one of those small men so dynamic that his personality seemed giant. People always felt they were looking up at Rafferty even as they looked down.

The Speaker and the general were seated in the oak-paneled library of the former's Potomac, Maryland, home, Rafferty studying his guest intently over the rim of a glass filled with straight hundred-proof bourbon. He liked what he saw. Most high-ranking military men seemed strangely subdued in civilian clothes, as if their air of authority and power had somehow disappeared along with the uniform. Not Collison, Rafferty thought. He wore an aura of command as naturally as a suit of well-fitted clothes, and it made no difference whether the garment was a uniform or a business suit. It was mostly his eyes, Rafferty decided; they looked through you instead of just at you.

He rumbled, "I appreciate your coming all the way out here, General. I know we could have talked downtown, either in your office or mine, but as I explained on the phone this morning, I didn't want a lot of interruptions in a conversation that has to be private and confidential."

Collison said smoothly, "And I appreciate this

chance to finally meet you on a one-to-one basis. I've seen you at various social functions, of course, but that's not the same." He took a sip of the dry martini Rafferty had mixed and sat back in the armchair, one long leg draped over the other, waiting for the Speaker to make the first move. Frain had forewarned him, "When you dance with Thomas Patrick Rafferty, you never, *but never,* try to lead."

Even as Collison thought of the columnist, Rafferty seemed to be reading his mind. He growled, "I thought of asking Pete Frain to this little confab, but I decided against it. I know he's your friend, but I just don't trust any newspaperman, even when I agree with what he writes."

Collison said a little huffily. "*I* trust him. I've never known him to violate a confidence. However, it was your prerogative."

"Good. Now we can talk business. First, I like what you've been saying about that spineless creep in the White House. Second, I called you this morning as soon as I read the item in Jack Anderson's column—that Haines sent you a personal note a couple of days ago telling you in effect to keep your mouth shut or get fired. Is that true?"

"It's true, but I'd like to know where Anderson got it. That note was hand-delivered to me personally by a White House courier and marked Confidential."

"You mean you didn't leak it yourself?"

"I did not. I wouldn't give Jack Anderson a week-old weather report. If I had told anyone, it would have been Frain. Matter of fact, he's upset that I didn't."

"Well," Rafferty barked triumphantly, "that means

the White House did the leaking. I'll be a son of a bitch! That goddamned Haines is smarter than I thought. He's trying to make like the tough guy he really ain't. That phony new image of a fearless leader! Okay, General, what are you going to do about it? Lie down and let the bastard kick you in the nuts?"

"I . . . I haven't decided whether to do anything. That letter came as a surprise."

"I'll just bet it did!" the Speaker snapped. "You've been attacking a pussycat and all of a sudden a tiger jumps down your throat. And just how long do you think you can afford to think it over? The whole town's talking about it."

Duane Collison suppressed the urge to snap back. He had the military man's inherent and frequently justified suspicion of the politician, suspicion that could easily stray across the border of disdain. But he also was aware of Rafferty's clout. A strong Speaker of the House in his own way was as powerful as the President.

"In West Point and throughout my military career," he said quietly, "I learned to follow the orders of my superiors. The National Security Council is part of the executive branch and Mr. Haines, regardless of how I feel about his policies, is my immediate superior. My only alternative is to resign and that I don't want to do."

"Why not, for Christ's sake? He just cut off your balls."

Duane Collison gave the Speaker a contemptuous look, so intense that Rafferty squirmed. Seldom if ever could the Speaker be intimidated by any mortal being, but this time he sensed the strength of will behind those cold eyes, challenging him and defying him.

"No offense, General," he said with rare equanimity. "Hell, I can understand discipline. That's the way I run the goddamned House. But damn it, if he shuts you up, he eliminates the only effective opposition we've got. The rest of us are just baying at the moon. We don't have your stature. We criticize and it's called partisan politics. You criticize and it's from the horse's mouth. There are millions of Americans who have the same opinion of Jeremy Haines as you do. You're their spokesman, their only real hope. You let the President get away with that gag order, you'll lose all the respect you've built up throughout the whole country."

"I don't intend to keep the gag on forever," Collison said with a softness that somehow imparted resolve.

Rafferty's eyes narrowed into half-slits. "Keep talking."

"You asked me how long I could afford to think this over. I want you to understand something, Mr. Speaker. I've been asking myself how I can afford to *leave* the Security Council. The answer is simple—I can't, no matter how much humiliation and anger I feel. As NSC chairman, I'm privy to information denied even to you. Outside the council, I'm just another retired Air Force officer who can only read the newspapers. Inside the council, I know what's going on."

"And exactly what *is* going on?"

"Coyness doesn't become you, Mr. Speaker. You know I'm talking about Operation Umbrella."

"Frain's first column was right? It's almost ready?"

"I was the source of that column. I told him what I'm telling you now—Umbrella's on the verge of becoming operational."

Rafferty tried to hide with a snort the fact that he was impressed. "It still has to be tested, of course."

Collison's cold eyes narrowed. "Is this conversation between just the two of us?"

The Speaker chuckled. "I'll admit that most Congressmen couldn't keep a secret longer than a nympho can hang onto her virginity, but that doesn't include yours truly. Yeah, this conversation is completely off the record—I give you my word."

"And I'll accept your word." Collison leaned forward, almost as if Rafferty were hard of hearing. "Actually, there is no test as such. There's no real way to judge its effectiveness without putting the whole damned system into orbit—which means several hundred laser beam satellites and all the other hardware involved in a supposedly foolproof anti-missile defense. When those satellites are launched, they'll be tested against almost five hundred dummy missiles fired from nuclear submarines and from Alaskan missile bases. Umbrella's mission will be to destroy every one of them. If it doesn't, we've got a hundred billion dollars worth of flying white elephants in orbit."

Rafferty poured himself another straight shot. "Well, do you think it'll work?"

Collison nodded slowly. "If Umbrella doesn't do the job, I'll be the most surprised man in the world. Anything can go wrong with a system that complex, of course, but we've got backups and redundancy in every crucial area. Frankly, I'm not worried about failure. I'm worried about success."

"Now what the hell's that supposed to mean?"

"Simply that Operation Umbrella gives the President a chance to redeem himself completely—and I hope he does. But if he fails to take advantage, he will not only disgrace himself but endanger this country. I am deeply concerned, Mr. Speaker, that the latter is more than a distinct possibility. Mr. Haines lacks the courage to recognize the greatest opportunity any President has ever been granted."

Rafferty eyed him shrewdly. "It's said that you favor an attack on the Soviet Union from behind Umbrella's protection. Is that true?"

Collison composed his answer with the care of a man walking over hot coals. He said in a soft but firm voice, "No sane man wants an atomic war. Yet no sane man who believes in freedom can tolerate a collection of ruthless gangsters trying to shape the world in their own twisted image. Yes, assuming Umbrella is successful, I would attack Russia, but only if her leaders refused to listen to reason. I'm talking about an ultimatum. The demands in that ultimatum would not be mine to determine—pulling out of certain Iron Curtain nations, for example, or allowing free elections in countries like Poland. If they refuse, then bang!" With the last word, Collison slammed one fist into an open palm so hard that Rafferty jumped at the sound.

He looked into the general's eyes and saw not fanaticism but cold, determined logic of almost hypnotic force; Rafferty, both frightened and moved, settled for a weak, "Well, you've raised some interesting possibilities, to say the least."

"I realize that, sir. Life and death possibilities. I won't go into the philosophical justifications for what I feel should be done, except to say that communism is a cancer that must be excised before it becomes terminal. America is the patient; we are the doctors who must make the decision."

Rafferty shook his head. "General, I have to question whether Congress or the majority of the public would favor a declaration of war against Russia, unless we were provoked beyond endurance."

Collison said promptly, "In my view, we've already been provoked to that extent. But I agree, debating this issue in Congress would be futile—it's not a subject for debate, nor is it something any legislature should vote on or have the people decide. The policy decision has to be made at the executive level."

"Meaning the President."

"Precisely. The ultimatum should be presented in absolute secrecy, and if that fails the attack should be made without warning. Any other course would result in a war of words, both in this country and elsewhere, and the more talk there is, the less chance of bold, decisive action."

Rafferty rasped, "If you want to keep this whole affair top secret, then why the hell are you using guys like Peter Frain to spread your gospel? You're inviting debate."

"Frankly, I don't care how much debate we stir up, so long as the decisions aren't made via a referendum. You asked me an excellent question, Mr.

Speaker. My motive in enlisting Frain's support was simply to start people thinking about what's at stake, to prepare them mentally and emotionally for what might have to be done. When and if it happens, they will understand *why* it had to be done."

"It won't happen with *this* President," Rafferty said.

"Unfortunately, you've arrived at the crux of the problem: Mr. Haines and his namby-pamby turning of his back on destiny. It's possible that by my bringing the issue to light through people like Frain, he could be forced to understand the justification for what amounts to a holy war."

"I wonder if he could be forced to do anything," Rafferty grumbled. "Up until a few weeks ago, I figured Haines would sway in whatever direction the wind was blowing. Now I'm not that sure. All of a sudden he's Mr. Tough Guy."

"But not when it comes to the Soviets," Collison said quickly. "If we have to assume the President is an immovable object, he must be discredited in some fashion—made to look as feeble and ineffective as the appeasement road he follows."

"A tall order," Rafferty said. "How do you propose to accomplish this?"

"I don't know," Duane Collison replied, "but every man has weaknesses and I'm going to do my damnedest to find out his."

The Speaker's sigh came out in the form of a rasp. "Duane, I can't tell whether you're the biggest damned fool in the world or the smartest. But I'll say this much—while I can't quite buy this holy war concept, I have to admit it's something to think about. And when it's all over, you might wind up being President yourself."

The general laughed with polite deprecation. "I'm no politician, Mr. Speaker. I don't even belong to any political party."

A tight little grin curled the corners of Rafferty's mouth, and almost on impulse, he tossed out the seeds.

"Neither did Dwight Eisenhower," he murmured.

But after Collison left, Speaker of the House Thomas Patrick Rafferty wondered to himself if he hated Jeremy Haines so much that he could be swayed by a man proposing Armageddon.

"I still think," Jeremy Haines said grouchily to Franklin Roosevelt, "I should have fired him instead of giving him an option."

"Compromise, my boy, is the lifeblood of politics. With one bold stroke, you have effectively neutralized an able opponent without divesting yourself of his services. I'm proud of you for accepting my suggestion. Jeremy, do you realize how much you've grown since we met? The extent to which you've matured and gained not only self-confidence but stature? We've accomplished much in these few weeks. And the nation has benefited accordingly."

A thought skipped through the President's mind; he gave the ghost a quizzical look. "I don't want to sound ungrateful, but just how long are you planning to be around? Until I leave office?"

FDR chuckled. "Getting tired of me?"

Haines put the question on his mental scales. Yes,

he was a little fed up with this implausible, unreal travesty of common sense; this crazy reliance on an apparition for guidance and even companionship. It was almost frightening and degrading to admit how much he looked forward to every Air Force One trip, eagerly anticipating the ghostly manifestation and the subsequent give-and-take repartee. There was even something uncomfortably illicit about its clandestine nature, as if he were an unfaithful husband sneaking off for a rendezvous with a mistress. And above all else, he could not rid himself of the fear that no sane man could be experiencing all this.

Yet, did he really wish these encounters would end? Dr. Sarazin herself had admitted the possibility that they were not the product of hallucination. And if this were true, he was enjoying a rare privilege—visual and verbal contact with one of history's greatest and most colorful leaders, a continuing relationship that was coming close to friendship. The ghost not only liked him but seemed to respect him—Haines had no sense of being dominated or manipulated. Maybe it was rationalization, but the President felt he was increasingly capable of standing up to Roosevelt's powerful personality; sometimes when they argued, it was more like the duel of two skillful swordsmen. And suppose he was insane? It still was the illogic and irrational spawning logic and rationality. It was madness creating fresh and innovative ideas. It was the bright fire of positive action emerging from the blackness of mental disorder. The scales in his mind tipped.

"No," he answered, "I'm not getting tired of you. But my own question still stands."

"And one deserving of an honest answer. I'm going to hang around until I feel you no longer need me. Does that seem fair to you?"

The President smiled grimly. "I would prefer that you hang around until *I* feel I don't need you."

Back went the aristocratic head and out boomed the infectious laugh. "By golly, you're getting positively obstreperous! Tell you what, Jeremy, we'll make another compromise. I'll bow out when we *both* agree it's time I go." The grin shrank to a small smile. "However, I trust we haven't reached the point where the matter requires immediate discussion. We still have much to do. We've just begun to make a dent in the unemployment problem. All those alphabet agencies of mine—the Public Works Administration and Works Progress Administration, for example—I've been wondering if we couldn't come up with some modern variations. Why, the PWA alone took a million men off the relief rolls and the WPA put three million people to work. Oh, I know there were abuses and scandals, but by and large, these were honest, fruitful jobs. My God, Jeremy, do you realize how many dams, post offices, bridges, airports, and schools were built?"

"I do, indeed. I also know what it cost. I can't pump a dry well, Mr. President. There's no way in which we could finance a program on the scope of your old PWA."

FDR nodded thoughtfully. "Perhaps give industry some kind of incentive?"

"I suppose so. But in what form? A tax-credit program would be one answer, but we're back to robbing Peter again. We can't absorb any losses in tax revenues. Not with the size of that national debt."

The ghost was staring out the lounge window; a shaft of sunlight silhouetted the handsome profile, set in repose as motionless as a painting. "Pump priming at the source," Roosevelt mused aloud. "Aim it at heavy industry, automobiles, large appliances like refrigerators, stoves, and radios. Give these manufacturers tax credits in exchange for providing new jobs. Then put a special tax on the products they make—high enough to offset what we lose from those credits, but no so high as to discourage people from buying those products."

"A value added tax," Haines said, his face alive with interest.

"I beg your pardon?"

"Value added tax. A kind of selective sales tax. More than one economist has proposed it in lieu of raising the income tax. Like our national sales tax plan, it would be more palatable because the doses are smaller and, in effect, voluntary. You don't pay a value added tax unless you buy the product on which it's been levied. It's not a bad idea, Mr. President. I think I can work out something along those lines. Frankly, I'm rather surprised you suggested it. Your initial reaction to a sales tax was negative, to say the least."

Franklin Roosevelt sighed. "A man has to be flexible. Flexibility is what keeps a truly great leader from becoming stale, jaded, or even despotic. Times and circumstances change, and if we don't recognize this, we can get into trouble. That's why generals lose battles—they try to fight today's wars with yesterday's strategy. It's true that the problems you face are similar to the ones I faced, but that doesn't mean the solutions must be identical. Yours is a far more complex society than mine, just from the technological standpoint. It was relatively easy for me to stand up to the Axis powers, confident that we could outproduce them in conventional weapons. I don't envy the choice you must make—defying the Soviets, knowing that the ultimate defiance could destroy civilization. Technology has carried a terrible price tag."

"It has also carried mixed blessings," Haines said. "The same technology that could wipe us out in seconds carried man to the moon." He eyed the ghost with wry amusement. "I'm almost afraid to ask if you know about Neil Armstrong and Apollo 11."

"Of course I know about it," FDR said in a tone of mild indignation. "An absolutely glorious achievement! And not just the mission, mind you, but the fact that the whole world could witness it on television. To me, that was as significant as the landing itself. It's mind-boggling to realize how far we've come in the field of communications. Why, a few minutes ago I think I cited radios as primary items for taxation. Shows what an old-fashioned fellow I really am!"

He sighed again, then gave Haines a sly look. "Y'know, my friend, if television had been around in my day and I could have stayed healthy, I'll wager I could have run for a fifth term. Ha-ha! Now, tell me what you're going to say about crime in this Dallas speech. I have some ideas . . ."

At almost the same moment that Air Force One began its letdown to the Dallas/Fort Worth Airport, the Premier of the Union of Soviet Socialist Republics was glowering across a desk at the chief of the Russian Air Force, General Dimitri Balenov.

Andrei Magoyan was a tall, beefy, heavily jowled man in his early sixties who seldom smiled; it was said, albeit always behind his back, that it was just as well because a Magoyan smile was something to fear, resembling the visage of a guard dog about to attack. The Premier was, indeed, humorless and bad-tempered, and one of his rare smiles was usually a prelude to a tirade.

He was not smiling now. Magoyan laid down a letter that he had just read for the third time, a communication from the Soviet ambassador to the United States. He threw it across the desk instead of handing it to the general.

"Read it, Comrade General. Then let me know what you think of it."

Balenov complied, perusing the contents quickly with his doe-like eyes, imbedded incongruously in moon-cratered features. Unlike so many senior Russian military officers, he was ramrod-lean and flat-bellied, with battleship-gray hair and a grudging admiration for Americans that he discreetly kept to himself. He handed the letter back. "It seems as if their timid President is now a man of action," he commented.

The Premier nodded. "Exactly. As our ambassador reports, Mr. Haines has suddenly developed into a leader of men, a creator of innovative ideas and new policies. The question is, how will this newfound initiative of his affect his attitude toward us?"

Balenov hesitated; Magoyan invariably asked questions in a tone suggesting that the answer had better agree with the Premier's way of thinking. The general said cautiously, "Well, the very fact that Ambassador Granski saw fit to send this letter would indicate some concern on his part."

"The letter expressed no concern, merely a summary of the American President's recent activities—all of them in the field of domestic problems."

"Concern may be implied, Excellency."

Much to Balenov's relief, the Premier nodded. "I agree. There's nothing in his report I wasn't already aware of. The Tass people have been following these Haines activities faithfully—which is interesting in itself. Our journalists describe his recent actions as moves of desperation, last-ditch efforts to prevent that damnably rotten capitalistic system from collapsing. Much as the American President Roosevelt did so many years ago, a point that Granski makes in his letter. A rather alarming point, don't you think?"

"I'm not sure I quite follow His Excellency," the general said uncertainly.

"Too bad. That's the trouble with you military people—you don't study history. So let me give you a quick lesson, Balenov. This Roosevelt was a very smart man and, I must admit, a good friend of the Soviet Union. He committed himself to Hitler's defeat even though he was up against his own country's cowardly apathy toward any direct military involvement. But he schemed, manipulated, and even lied when he had to, until eventually he brought the United States into the war."

Balenov answered stiffly. "It could also be said that Japan's attack on Pearl Harbor pushed him into it. And it was Germany who declared war on the United States, not the other way around."

"American participation was inevitable. Japan merely gave Roosevelt the excuse he needed. What I'm getting at, Comrade General, is the parallel Ambassador Granski draws between a ruthless leader like Roosevelt and President Haines. The latter seems to have become a dangerous clone."

Balenov looked bewildered. "But Roosevelt was a friend of the USSR. You said that yourself. I fail to . . ."

"A friend to us, but ruthless when it came to his enemies. Americans now regard *us* as enemies, with a despicably blind hatred no less intense than what Roosevelt displayed toward Hitler. Haines, for all his attempts at conciliation and fortunately weak-kneed reactions to our endeavors, is as guilty of anti-Soviet prejudice as the rest of his countrymen. And *that*, Balenov, is what worries me."

The Premier fingered a small-scale model of a Soviet missile that rested on his desk. "This so-called Operation Umbrella, the American anti-missile system—it's about ready, isn't it?"

"So I'm told," the general said.

"How close are we?"

"At least a year, probably longer. There has been no significant change in the status of our project since I last reported to you, two months ago."

"And at that time, I was informed we could destroy at least 75 percent of any attacking force, both manned bombers and missiles—which, as you know, is totally unacceptable. The remaining 25 percent could wipe us out. And even 75 percent may be over-optimistic—on more than one occasion the military promised me more than it eventually delivered."

Balenov did not point out that such over-optimism

stemmed largely from fear—Magoyan didn't always want to hear the truth. The general settled for frankness that managed to fall short of argumentativeness. "For that matter, Excellency, even 95 percent might be categorized as over-optimistic. Five percent of a thousand nuclear warheads could destroy us."

Magoyan sighed; coming from his barrel chest and thick neck, it was more the rumble of far-off thunder. "Is it your professional opinion that this Operation Umbrella of theirs will have 100 percent defensive capability?"

"To assume otherwise would be foolhardy. I have never been one to underestimate American technology." He had managed to avoid an accusatory tone, but he quailed inwardly at the Premier's frown. Magoyan, however, added a nod to his grim expression and said calmly, "I'm afraid in this case you're right. Which is why we must move very cautiously during the coming months. For the next year, those bastards will hold the balance of power."

The officer's eyebrows shot up to full staff. "Balance of power means nothing unless the holder wants to use it. Are you saying the Americans would attack us?"

"We must consider such a possibility."

"Sir, it makes no sense. I'm convinced that, basically, their President is a man of peace."

"Then you're a fool. When good intentions collide with opportunity and temptation, it is a one-sided contest. A man who is apparently mimicking the leadership qualities of the legendary Mr. Roosevelt is capable of anything."

"I cannot believe he is capable of starting a nuclear war," Balenov said.

"You don't? Not even from behind an impervious missile defense?"

"No, Excellency, I don't."

That deadly smile cracked the Premier's broad Slavic features, like a fissure suddenly splitting the earth. "I don't see why not. *I* would."

General Duane Collison seldom made luncheon appointments. Invariably he ate his noonday meal at the Army–Navy Club, where he was virtually assured of running into some old military crony or cronies. Today, he walked into the club's handsome foyer and, as usual, looked around for some convivial acquaintance. At first he saw no one, and he was about to reconnoiter the dining room when a meaty hand thumped his back, and simultaneously his ears were assaulted by a gravelly voice.

"Well, if it isn't flyboy Collison! Eating alone?"

Collison turned and inwardly groaned. Far down on the list of desired luncheon companions was the owner of both hand and voice, Vice-Admiral Virgil "Rhino" Robertson, USN (Ret.), until recently deputy chief of staff for Naval Air Operations. The nickname fitted the potbellied admiral far better than his uniforms—Rhino, in a naval career spanning almost forty years, had walked away from seventeen crashes and collected almost as many reprimands as medals. He was feared for his temper, revered for his fairness, respected for his ability, and enshrined in the Navy's annals for his idiosyncrasies. These included wearing his old Navy football helmet and monogramed *N* sweater on the bridge of every ship he commanded, which gave him the appearance of a college student who had somehow wandered accidently into a combat zone.

Collison knew the admiral mainly by reputation and considered him a loud-mouthed boor. Yet when their paths had crossed occasionally at the Pentagon, Collison had found him capable and an articulate advocate of the Navy's defense role. There was no other luncheon prospect in sight at the club, and the general, who hated to eat by himself, bowed to the inevitable.

"Just popped in for a quick sandwich," he said with false cordiality. "Why don't you join me?"

It wasn't as bad as Collison had feared. Rhino was a bit too bombastic for the general's taste and decidedly opinionated, but he had a quick wit and was nobody's fool. Besides, he shared Collison's conviction that President Haines's last two budgets had called for military spending cuts of alarming proportions.

"Not just foolhardy but insane," Collison was saying. "The man's an absolute lunatic if he thinks we can reduce defense expenditures and still stand up to the communists."

Robertson admired Haines even though he didn't always agree with him. "He means well, General. Hell, you know as well as I do the Pentagon wastes too much dough."

"Are you defending that last cut? Seventeen percent?"

"The budget the Pentagon submitted contained at least 20 percent fat. The trouble was that Haines didn't go after the fat—he zeroed in on specific projects, including some we really needed. I should know. He torpedoed one of my own pets—that experimental aluminum carrier. I really wanted that baby. A sixty-five knot flattop! Christ, I went all the way up to the old man to plead my case."

"The old man? You mean Haines?"

"Yep, the President himself. Three weeks before I retired, I spent a half-hour trying to sell him on that project. He really surprised me—he's a naval history buff. We talked for ten minutes about Leyte Gulf and the way Bull Halsey fell for that Jap decoy fleet. Haines actually defended Halsey, can you imagine that? Anyway, I didn't get to first base with my aluminum carrier. I was disappointed and I still think he was wrong, but I couldn't help feeling sorry for him. Here I was, on the eve of retirement, full of piss and vinegar, and he looked like an accident going someplace to happen."

Collison snorted. "He looks like the jellyfish he really is."

Rhino's eyes glinted. "He's been no jellyfish lately. You should know—he told you to shape up or ship out. Or was that Jack Anderson tidbit just a lot of bilgewater?"

Collison didn't answer at first, then said cautiously, "I'm trying to be a loyal subordinate, Admiral, but considering the spineless anatomy of my immediate superior, it's rather difficult."

"What the hell do you want him to do—push the button and blow up the world?"

"I have my own theories as to what should be done," the general said huffily, "and when I consider the time opportune, I'll make Haines put up or shut up."

Rhino Robertson felt a throb of dislike. He said curtly, "After what's been happening the past few weeks, I'd say you have a pretty good chance of getting your tits caught in the wringer. Haines sure as hell isn't the same guy I talked to at the White House or at Navy Medical only a few weeks ago."

Duane Collison's growing boredom with Admiral Robertson suddenly evaporated. "You saw the President at the medical center? What was he doing there?"

"How the hell should I know? Routine checkup, I suppose. I was visiting an old shipmate in there for a prostate operation and I bumped into the President when he was coming out of Cat Baxter's office. Damned if he didn't stop me to say hello. Even told me he had met someone who'd be interested in my aluminum carrier idea. I got curious, but he just laughed and said his friend was just another navy buff like himself. He seemed a little distracted, even worried, but I figured . . ."

"Who," Collison interrupted, "is Cat Baxter? A doctor? Some kind of specialist?"

"Chief of psychiatry at Bethesda. Nice guy. Something of an expert on combat fatigue. Say, Collison, you've had some engineering background. I'd like to show you a rough sketch of the hull design I had in mind for my carrier. Lemme see if I've got some scratch paper . . ."

"Some other time, Admiral. Have to get back to the shop. Nice seeing you again."

After he left, two things dawned on Rhino Robertson. First, the general had stuck him with the check. Second, he wished he had not mentioned Catlin Baxter. There was nothing wrong in the President seeing old Cat—certainly it couldn't have been for medical reasons, so mentioning Baxter to Collison couldn't have done any harm.

But there remained in the mind of Admiral Rhino Robertson the nagging suspicion that he had made a mistake.

TEN

Jessica Sarazin had become professionally ensnared and emotionally entangled.

She admitted this to herself reluctantly. The President represented the most fascinating, challenging case of parapsychology she had ever encountered. But Jeremy Haines himself represented the most fascinating, challenging man she had ever met. She was honest enough to deplore the obvious conflict of interest, yet not strong enought to resolve it. Neither the psychiatrist nor the woman wanted to let go.

So she set a course that merely temporized, seeing the President with increasing frequency, rationalizing that personal involvement was the price to be paid for scientific observation and study. They always met in the White House at night, the gate guards and Secret Service detail alike having been advised that a Dr. Sarazin was treating the President for chronic backaches. Haines had suggested this subterfuge; after all, a woman physician, Janet Travell, had often administered to John F. Kennedy for a similar ailment. Jessica even resorted to the camouflage of bringing along her old medical bag, something she hadn't used since her internship days; she placed it on the right front seat of her red Mustang, in plain view of the gate guards. They only checked the contents once, the first time she drove her own car to the White House.

"A little embarrassing," she had confessed to Haines.

"Why? They're supposed to check such things." He chuckled. "You might have had a gun inside."

"That's not what I meant. My stethoscope belongs in a museum and the blood-pressure kit was thirdhand when I was in med school. They must have thought I was indigent."

"But if your gear had looked new, they might have suspected you of posing as a doctor. Aren't worn medical instruments a sign of experience? Doc Phillips had a bag so old that I once accused him of treating Lincoln for his gunshot wound."

"He was White House physician during your first term, wasn't he?"

Haines's eyes had clouded. "He was killed on Air Force One that night. One of those innocent people I sent to their deaths." He paused, for his voice had choked slightly. "Let's change the subject, Jessica."

But she made him talk about it, then and on subsequent occasions. Still groping for causal factors if the ghost was the product of hallucination, she was intrigued by the strong guilt Haines felt over that crash. Yet Jessica became convinced that she was following a false trail; there was evidence of deep guilt but not to the extent of trauma. She also reasoned that it would have made more sense if the ghost Haines kept seeing were that of someone who had been on the ill-fated plane. Such a manifestation would have been a logical psychiatric residue and far easier to explain than the appearance of a historical figure like FDR.

In her constant diagnostic tug-of-war between mental aberrations and a psychic phenomenon, she now found herself gradually leaning toward the latter. It was a shift she kept from Catlin Baxter, and for a very good reason—she had a real fear that if he knew the extent of the President's involvement with a ghost, he would feel it his duty to declare Haines at least temporarily mentally unfit to hold office.

Her periodic reports to the Navy psychiatrist were deliberately optimistic and slickly evasive. The President was in full control of his mental faculties. Yes, there had been sporadic recurrences of the psychic experiences or hallucinations—she still was unable to determine the exact cause or origin—but she was confident she was on the right track and that Haines, a most cooperative patient, evinced no clinical sign of mental disease.

She herself felt no guilt at keeping the whole truth from Baxter. Jessica Sarazin had been observing with fascination and mostly approval the President's recent blizzard of legislative proposals and administrative orders. They were dramatic, controversial, and shrewdly aimed at mustering public support—Haines had become an expert on what might intrigue the average American even though it might infuriate the average Congressman.

Three of his recommendations involved constitutional amendments. He urged the establishment of four-year, instead of two-year, terms for House members. "We'll have more effective lawmakers if they don't have to start running for reelection the day they're sworn in," he declared, in submitting the legislation. He asked for an amendment giving the President line-item veto authority—the power to veto specific provisions in a bill without killing the entire measure. And he proposed a third amendment exposing child pornography dealers to prosecution by removing them from protection under the First Amendment.

He asked for mandatory death sentences for child molesters convicted of murdering their victims. He broadened his previous tax programs by setting up a special, one-year commission to study the feasibility of a flat 10 percent income tax, with elimination of all deductions except a percentage of mortgage interest. And he appointed a second commission on Pentagon procurement policies, telling Defense Secretary John Hammond, "Whatever those guys recommend I want put into effect immediately—no more five-hundred-dollar expenditures for a screw we can buy in a hardware store for five cents."

Hammond had protested, "You're giving the commission a blank check."

"You're damned right I am. On that commission

are industrialists who know the score and military men who know what we really need. I've already told them the gouging has to stop or I'll order every goddamned Pentagon contract in existence renegotiated. Every penny we save on this crap can go into legitimate weaponry and military pay incentives."

The conversation with Hammond was one of many he found himself relating to Jessica, for their relationship was evolving into one of shared confidences—mostly, it must be admitted, on his part. Not since Barbara Haines's death had he encountered the priceless asset of a woman who could be sounding board, critic, or sympathetic supporter, assuming whatever role she felt was required. Whether she responded from her psychiatric training or from womanly intuition was of no importance—she didn't even try to differentiate between the two but reacted instinctively. She had quickly recognized his motivation: the inherent need of a man at the end of the day to talk things over with a wife.

They continued to discuss the ghost, almost routinely, as if both accepted it as the catalyst that had brought them together, but not to the point of excluding all other, far more normal subjects. Yet it continued to disturb Jessica that Haines had come to regard FDR as totally real, whereas she could never stop treating the apparition as a potentially alarming element.

One night he was telling her that several cabinet members were complaining that the President was acting first and consulting them later. "I suppose they're justified in feeling that way," he remarked. "Roosevelt usually gives me his ideas when we're en route to some speech. They go into the speech itself, and on the way back to Washington, we talk about future plans. I don't seem to have the time to brief my cabinet in advance."

"Or don't really want to," Jessica ventured.

Haines stared at her. "Why would you say that?"

"Aren't you afraid the cabinet might try to talk you out of something Mr. Roosevelt has proposed? You're a couple of grand conspirators, gleefully concocting all these schemes—most of which, I've noticed, seem to be aimed at embarrassing the legislative branch." She swallowed hard before continuing, for she knew what she was about to say would seem harsh. "It's as if you subconsciously hate Congress and want the public to feel the same contempt you do. And, not incidentally, the same contempt Roosevelt consistently demonstrated. Very interesting, Jeremy. Almost a clinical pattern."

"That," Haines remarked, "sounds very much like a clinical diagnosis."

"It worries me. I see more and more evidence that you're assuming Roosevelt's beliefs and prejudices, his absolute conviction that if necessary, he could go over the heads of Congress and take his case to the people. I've followed your recent activities most carefully. You're taunting Congress, daring them to defy you, and almost hoping they will, so you can show them who's really running the country. Am I being unfair?"

"Maybe not unfair but historically inaccurate. Roosevelt was very circumspect in his relations with Congress. He always treated the legislature with courtesy."

"Precisely my point. His public deference masked his private opinion—especially his belief that if Congress thwarted him, all he had to do was hold a press conference or go on the radio and muster public support. It was no secret that many Republicans didn't dare vote against the legislation he demanded simply because the mail from home was so pro-Roosevelt. Tell me something, Jeremy, do you and Roosevelt discuss your feelings toward Congress—or his? I can't believe you haven't."

"We have," he admitted. "Quite recently, as a matter of fact. My line-item veto proposal stemmed from what he was telling me about his troubles with Congress. He said the practice of attaching mischievous, irrelevant riders to bills was nothing but legislative blackmail. It was something that had plagued him and every other president who has been forced to accept such riders or to defeat the original purpose of the measure itself. We agreed something should be done."

Jessica frowned. "So line-item veto was as much his idea as yours. It caused such an uproar in Congress that your child-molestation bill almost didn't get through the House. It shouldn't have been that close, Jeremy, and you know it."

He gave her an amused glance. "Are you handing me psychiatric advice or political?" he asked gently.

She had the grace to blush, uncomfortably aware that she had been scolding the President of the United States. Yet while she realized her presumptuousness, she knew her sharpness merely reflected how close their relationship had become. If she had descended from the lofty, detached level of his psychiatrist, he had allowed her to climb right back up to the equal level of his confidante.

She said in an intense voice, "I am trying to point out the danger of your overreliance on this . . . this being."

"Does this mean you've accepted its existence?"

This time, her voice dropped an octave. "It means, Jeremy, I care about what is happening to you, about the craziest thing anyone could imagine—a President almost totally dominated by someone who may very well be the ghost of a great man. Franklin Roosevelt and Jeremy Haines apparently are becoming or may already have become one and the same person."

The President shook his head slowly, a motion that was both wonderment and denial. "I think you're wrong. I'm not being dominated nor manipulated. I've told you that none of my recent actions have been dictated by Roosevelt. They were products of mutual agreement, of give-and-take discussion and compromise. We have had numerous differences of opinion, and in the end it was *my* judgment that prevailed, not his. I remember telling you how violently he opposed the idea of a national sales tax. We're a team, Jessica. A partnership. Nothing more, nothing less."

Jessica smiled tightly. "Not bad. Not bad at all. A very persuasive and logical answer. But you're evading the real issue. Roosevelt is still supplying the form, while you provide the substance. He creates the concept, and you come up with the execution. Don't you see? That was the way FDR operated during the entire twelve years he was in office."

The President mixed himself a fresh drink. He said nothing until he returned his chair, facing the divan where she sat. He gave her a long, inquisitive look that seemed to flow from a well of inner pain.

He said, "Perhaps, then, it boils down to the end justifying the means. In which case, I still fail to see any inherent danger."

"You don't?"

"No."

"Then let me spell it out. Eventually, you may be asked to do something you know is wrong, and you won't have the strength or will to resist."

"If that day ever comes," he said quietly, "I'll ask you to have me committed."

Jessica looked at his solemn face and wondered if the pledge was sincerity or bravado. Maybe a little of both, she decided, for she had come to know him as a man of great pride tempered by a sense of responsibility to his office. He would want to do the honorable thing, but what constitutes honor is subjective, and might become false pride. More than ever, she wished she had never become involved—knowing that in the end, it would be mostly Dr. Jessica Sarazin's medical opinion that could force Haines out of office. And yet, while she feared the ghost's persuasive influence, she kept wishing the apparition was real and that Haines was perfectly sane.

She said, with a forced offhandedness, "I don't think it will come to that. I'm only trying to warn you that self-delusion can be an insidious byproduct of manipulation, and it takes a strong person to realize when it's happening."

"And you don't think I'm strong enough?" He asked the question with a flimsy smile.

Jessica said promptly, "You're one of the strongest individuals I've ever known. You're trapped in a situation where you are very sanely questioning your sanity, and that takes strength. Conversely, if the ghost truly exists, you've reacted to an incredible development with admirable calmness—a lesser man might have collapsed at the prospect of seeing the impossible become fact. No, Jeremy, you're strong, but it remains to be seen *how* strong. I keep up with the news, and I know you're under terrible pressure from this Operation Umbrella business."

The President laughed, but she did not miss the brittleness of that laugh. "I take it you've been reading Peter Frain."

"I have. Until a few weeks ago, he was my favorite columnist. I enjoyed him even when I didn't agree with him."

"And what changed your mind?"

"He scares me, that's what changed my mind. He keeps writing about threatening Russia to be good or else, because we've got something they don't have. Jeremy, are we really that close to perfecting an antimissile system?"

"We are."

"We could attack them without fear of retaliation?"

"The Soviets could retaliate, but with comparative ineffectiveness. Their defeat would be inevitable. Our first-strike capability would be enormous, and if Umbrella's as good as we think it is, the first strike would be virtually unanswerable."

"Then isn't there some logic to what Frain says—use Umbrella as a bargaining weapon?"

The President sighed. "Et tu, Brute?"

"I didn't say I bought Frain's argument. I'm playing kind of devil's advocate."

A note of grimness seeped into Haines's voice. "Yes, there's logic, a cruelly oversimplified brand of logic that ignores too many factors. The question of morality, for one thing. Whether any nation has the right to threaten anyone with nuclear destruction if it can't get what it wants through diplomatic means. Whether any President has the right to threaten millions of innocent civilians with mass murder because their government is a collection of aggressive hoods. When you come right down to it, Jessica, an actual attack is no more immoral than a threat. The threat itself is a commitment unless you're bluffing."

She digested this reasoning. "Frain says the Soviet Union would be threatening us if they had an Umbrella," she said.

"He's right. They probably would."

"Well," she declared with devastating positiveness, "we're not the Russians—it's as simple as that."

Haines smiled sadly. "I wish that *were* the case. There are a great many Americans who would like to destroy Russia once and for all. I've been told that since Frain wrote that first column, the *Post* has received more letters from readers than they've ever gotten on a single issue—and almost half were in favor of an ultimatum."

Jessica said, "I'm curious to know what Roosevelt would have to say about an ultimatum."

"I assume he'd be against it."

"That's quite an assumption. Suppose he was for it?"

The President snapped, "Then I'd have to tell him he was wrong—abysmally, criminally wrong. No one in this world could convince me we'd be justified in attacking Russia."

"No one in this world," she repeated. "But ghosts, whether real or in your mind, are not of this world."

General Duane Collison was looking for a Trojan horse.

More precisely, he was trying to find out why the President of the United States had found it necessary to see the Navy's chief psychiatric officer. He knew he was fishing in deep water with precious little bait; all he had was a chance, offhand remark by Rhino Robertson, and his own acute intuition that warned him something didn't smell right. His inherent sense of suspicion occasionally led him astray, but there were other times when it guided him like unerring radar toward some unsuspecting target.

A few discreet inquiries as to the personality of one Catlin Baxter convinced Collison he could get absolutely no information from that source. Like most career military officers, however, the general had connections in all branches of service. One of them was an Army psychiatrist, Lieutenant Colonel Ralph Sutliff, assigned to the Walter Reed Army Medical Center. Collison arranged to have a drink with him at Izzy's late one afternoon.

"I have a delicate problem," Collison began. "I have reason to believe that a certain high-ranking naval officer has been seeking psychiatric help. Now, Ralph, you might say this is really none of my business except that this particular officer has been involved in some extremely sensitive security matters. I know that he has consulted with Baxter at Navy Medical. I'd like to find out the nature of his illness and to what extent it may effect security."

Sutliff, a pale-faced man sporting a gray-sprinkled beard, shook his head disapprovingly. "You're invading a doctor–patient relationship, Duane. A sacrosanct relationship, especially in the field of psychiatry. In plain words, you're playing with dynamite."

"I realize that. But when I say this matter involves security, I mean *national* security. And I'm making this confidential inquiry in my official capacity as chairman of the National Security Council." He paused to add dramatic effect. "I may be playing with dynamite, Ralph, but so is the officer in question."

"If it's that serious, why the hell don't you just ask Cat Baxter?"

Collison gave him a don't-be-foolish shrug. "I've been led to believe that Captain Baxter would, uh, be uncooperative."

"Wouldn't be surprised," Sutliff chuckled. "Well, how do you want me to help you? I'm sure not gonna beard old Baxter in his den, not even for you."

"I thought you might suggest some subordinate of Baxter I could talk to. An officer of great integrity and highest patriotic leanings, and one who would put his country's welfare above . . . above, well, so-called medical ethics."

"Those medical ethics aren't exactly *so-called,*" Sutliff said rather sharply. "What you're asking for is a kind of spy with no particular ethics of his own."

Collison's voice could have been wrapped in the American flag. "I assure you," he said with great earnestness, "that I would not ask any officer to do anything other than his solemn duty. And in this case, Ralph, duty to one's country supersedes allegiance to any medical code. You know me well, and you know how I feel about the grave dangers facing us. We are an embattled island in a hostile ocean of communism, and when our very security is threatened, I think a doctor–patient relationship must be viewed in its proper context."

Sutliff frowned unhappily. Collison had picked his pigeon shrewdly. Ralph Sutliff owed the general a very great favor, a debt stemming from an incident involving the psychiatrist's son when the latter was an enlisted man in the Air Force and Collison was chief of staff. The boy had been brought up on charges of homosexuality, and Collison had arranged to have him honorably discharged for medical reasons. Now, Sutliff knew, the general was calling in the note.

He sighed. "Well, there is one guy in Baxter's shop who might be able to help you."

Eight days later, Commander Grant Loving, a heavyset man with a tomato-red complexion and snow-white hair, sat in the office of General Duane Collison and delivered his report, having already been told far more than Sutliff was.

"You understand," he began in a ready voice, "that I have not been able to find any direct reference to the President as Captain Baxter's patient. Even if there were documents, reports, correspondence, or any other written evidence that he had consulted Baxter professionally, I would have no access to them. It's no secret that Mr. Haines paid a visit to Captain Baxter around the time you suggested, but what happened at that meeting is either locked up in my superior's mind or—equally inaccessible—in his personal files. To break into those files would be a court-martial offense, not to mention a breach of medical ethics, transcending the great admiration I have for you."

"I understand how hard it is to get the information," Collison said smoothly, "but did you find some indirect clue?"

"What I've found, General, is an interesting coincidence. It may be nothing more than that—a mere coincidence. I'll tell you about it, but I'm afraid I'll have to leave the interpretation to you. Is that understood, sir?"

"Perfectly."

"Captain Baxter went on leave for a few days last week, leaving me in charge. I took the opportunity of examining his appointment schedule for the past two months, and also the record he keeps of outgoing and incoming phone calls—a very precise, organized person, Captain Baxter. Actually, I was looking for some factual indication of Presidential visits other than the one we know about. I found nothing. But I did stumble on several references to a Dr. Sarazin."

"Who," Collison asked, "is Dr. Sarazin?"

"I'm getting to that. In Baxter's notes, there were a number of reminders to call a Dr. Sarazin, or that Sarazin had phoned him and asked him to return the call. The most recent was three days ago, a message asking Baxter to contact Dr. Sarazin as soon as he returned from leave. I checked around for Sarazin's identity and found the answer in the physicians' directory of the telephone book. Under the listings for practitioners of psychiatric medicine is a Dr. Jessica Sarazin, the only Sarazin so listed. Frankly, the name already had sounded vaguely familiar; indeed, I had heard of her before. She is a psychiatrist with excellent qualifications and an impeccable reputation. She also happens to be a parapsychologist."

"A what?"

"Parapsychologist. Parapsychology is the study of psychic phenomena. In other words, ghosts, ESP, and so forth."

"Continue," Collison murmured.

"We come now to the coincidence I mentioned. Last Monday, a gossip columnist in the *Washington Times* ran a small item to the effect that, over the weekend, President Haines took a little trip down the Potomac aboard a cabin cruiser owned by his brother, Senator Bert Haines. Accompanying him was the Senator, his wife, and a woman the columnist referred to as an old friend of the Senator's wife, from somewhere in Ohio."

"I fail to see the coincidence," the general said.

"The *Times* item referred to her as Jessica Vaughn, and the name rang a bell."

"Having the same first name isn't much of a coincidence," Collison said in an annoyed tone.

"I'm coming to that. When I was looking up Dr. Sarazin's credentials in *The American Directory of Psychiatry,* her biography listed her maiden name. It was Vaughn."

ELEVEN

The cruise had been the President's idea, the product of sheer impatience. He was weary of the charade that involved Jessica Sarazin and his growing fondness for her.

"I'd like to introduce you to my friends," he told her. "I'm tired of these secret visits, I want to spend time with you in a normal environment."

"To have a normal environment you have to have a normal relationship," she reminded him. "I'm your psychiatrist as well as your friend, and we can't escape that fact. You said yourself it would be politically more damaging to be seen publicly with a psychiatrist than a prostitute. That's why you made these arrangements in the first place."

"Hoist by my own petard," Haines muttered. "Look, Jessica, maybe it would be smarter to bring our friendship out in the open. Let's be seen together in public. No one would suspect that you're playing a dual role. If I were dating a woman surgeon, people wouldn't assume I had cancer. So dating a female psychiatrist doesn't mean I'm being treated for a mental disorder."

Jessica threw him an unhappy look. "In our case,

people would be far more likely to jump to the worst conclusion. Jeremy, I honestly think it's best to play it safe."

In the end, he acquiesced and the suggested cruise was a compromise. Jessica agreed, keeping her doubts to herself. She recognized the President's insistence for what it was—the natural desire of a man to show off his lady—even as she was painfully cognizant of its dangers.

She liked Bert and Ruth Haines. The President's brother was two years older than Jeremy and, like many siblings, so totally unlike him that it seemed questionable whether they had emerged from the same parental genes. She had read enough about Bert Haines to know that he did not have the close family, political, and intellectual ties with Jeremy that the Kennedys, for example, had enjoyed as brothers. Bert's impulsiveness, loudness, and earthiness were in direct contrast to the President's innate dignity. Liberal out of fashionable convenience rather than conviction, Senator Haines often regarded compromise as an acceptable excuse for surrendering a principle.

Yet Jessica found Bert friendly and entertaining; being around Jeremy seemed to keep his bombastic tendencies under control. More important, she sensed his concern and affection for Jeremy and his pride and admiration, which he could not quite keep hidden under his backslapping personality. More than once she had caught him eyeing her with an almost wistful curiosity, as if trying to gauge what she meant to his brother and what Jeremy meant to her.

Only one Secret Service agent, Mike McNulty,

was aboard, although a Coast Guard cutter carrying other agents preceded the Senator's boat at a respectful but still protective distance. Jessica had already grasped that McNulty was the President's favorite among the White House detail, and she could see why—he obviously worshipped his boss and showed it in his attitude toward her. Once McNulty had fetched a sweater from her stateroom, and as she thanked him, they heard the President laughing at something Bert Haines had said. McNulty sighed and looked at her with admiration in his eyes.

"I haven't heard him laugh like that for months," he marveled. "You've sure been good for him, Doctor."

"Beats all what back therapy will do," Jessica murmured demurely, wondering at the same time if McNulty had ever really swallowed the osteopathic story. Not that it mattered; she was convinced that even if McNulty knew about her actual medical assignment, he would have stayed unfalteringly loyal and convinced that Haines was sane. It amused Jessica that McNulty, in Haines's presence, always referred to him as Mr. President, but to others called him the Boss. Most agents, she learned from McNulty, used that sobriquet but he imbued it with a special meaning of its own—he made *the Boss* sound like *His Majesty*.

She learned something else from McNulty; if there was one thing on earth he disliked and even feared, it was water. On the return trip, he mentioned how glad he'd be when when they reached the shore.

"Heavy date, Mike?" she asked.

"No, I just hate boats."

"Then why did you accept this assignment?"

"Because I hate it even worse when the Boss is out of my sight," he explained.

She asked, curiosity mixed with dread, "Mike, there isn't an awful lot the Secret Service could do if somebody really wanted to assassinate the President, is there?"

"Not much to prevent a nut from firing at him, particularly from a distance. Think of Kennedy in Dallas. All we can pray for is a glimpse of the bastard just before he pulls the trigger."

"So you can get him before he shoots?"

"Nope. So we can step in front of the bullet." His answer was so devastatingly simple that she shuddered. For the first time, she understood the heroism of men like Michael McNulty and why the lack of privacy that chafed Haines so was a necessary evil. She wondered if McNulty ever could have seen something unusual aboard Air Force One, anything out of the ordinary that might add credence to the ghost's existence.

She tiptoed her way into that area. "When you travel with the President, are you ever with him in the upper lounge?"

"Not unless he asks me to be there. The Boss, well, he likes his privacy. My job is to make sure nobody disturbs him when he wants to be by himself. Outside of his own quarters in the White House, that 747 lounge is about his only refuge. Personally, I wish he'd let me stay up there with him. I don't like it when he's alone."

"Why? Certainly you can trust the crew."

"Oh, I trust 'em all right. That Colonel Cardella,

he wouldn't let his own mother aboard Air Force One without a security clearance." He hesitated, frowning uncertainly, wanting to say more and yet reluctant. He inspected her face, and evidently something told him she, too, was devoted to Jeremy Haines.

"The thing is, Doctor, I don't think a man should be alone as much as the Boss. Sometimes . . . sometimes, well, I swear he talks to himself."

"Talks to himself? You've heard him?"

"I've heard voices coming from that lounge, when I know he's alone. Or supposed to be alone. I guess he's rehearsing his speeches up there. Or maybe talking to Cardella or some other crew member. Couple of times, I heard him laugh. Figured he must have been reading something that struck him funny. Only thing is, though . . ." McNulty hesitated again.

"Only what, Mike?"

"Well, it just didn't sound like his laugh."

"Did it sound like anyone you know? Such as Colonel Cardella?"

The agent grinned. "If Cardella laughed, the whole crew would faint." He paused. "Do you ever watch old movies?"

"Many times."

"There was an actor named Edward Arnold. He had a very distinctive laugh. Deep, like it came more from his stomach than his throat, if you know what I mean. That was the kind of laugh I heard."

Jessica nodded thoughtfully. She remembered the Arnold laugh. She took a deep mental breath because she was almost afraid to ask the next question and led into it with a deliberate offhand detour.

"I wouldn't be surprised if the President sounded like Edward Arnold at times. He's prone to slight lung congestion. I have to wonder if that airplane of his isn't at fault. Could he be exposed to some kind of draft when he's flying?"

"Not likely," McNulty assured her. Then he frowned again, as a certain recollection crossed his mind. "One time, though, I thought I felt a draft of cold air coming from the lounge. It was on the flight down to Miami a few months ago. Lasted only a couple of seconds. Probably came from a ventilation duct."

"Probably," Jessica agreed in a matter-of-fact tone that successfully hid a surge of interest. If McNulty had sensed something unusual on that plane, so could a person like herself—a trained parapsychologist, sensitive to psychic stimuli and uniquely capable of interpreting it objectively. She found herself wishing fervently there was some way for her to travel on Air Force One.

She broached the subject to Haines a few hours before they docked at the Alexandria, Virginia, marina where the Senator kept his cruiser. They were sitting in aft deck chairs, McNulty just out of earshot a few feet away, his back to them and his alert eyes scanning the shoreline and the river traffic.

"When are you planning to fly again?" she asked.

"Early Wednesday morning, to Denver, and back that night. I'm speaking at the Air Force Academy in the afternoon." He sensed it was not an idle question and took a guess. "I have this feeling you'd like to come along."

"I would. For purely scientific reasons."

"And for purely prudent reasons, I have to say no.

I realize you'd like to be in the upper cabin just in case he shows up. Unfortunately, there will be a press pool aboard—at least a half-dozen reporters from the wire services and networks. I can't afford to have them see you go up that staircase into my private quarters. Poor Wayne Dillman would go crazy trying to explain your presence. And not even McNulty could smuggle you up there unnoticed."

"For a man insisting he'd like to be seen with me in public, you seem to have done an about-face."

The President smiled. "Touché. Except there's considerable difference being seen with you, say, in a restaurant or at a public reception, and having the cream of the press corps watch you go up those stairs unaccompanied by anything but their dirty minds."

Jessica was groping. "You could tell them I was a reporter getting an exclusive interview."

"That," Haines laughed, "would set them off like a pack of wolves. They'd badger Dillman on who you worked for, and there'd go your cover."

Jessica, watching McNulty's broad back, thought of their conversation and got a sudden inspiration. "Maybe he could smuggle me," she said, nodding in the agent's direction. "*Before* anyone else boards. I'd stay in the upper cabin the whole trip and nobody would even know I was there, except the crew, perhaps. And you could pass me off to them as anyone who sounded logical—Dr. Sarazin, specialist in curing backaches, for example."

Haines looked at her sharply. "I'm afraid as a ghost-hunting expedition, it would be a waste of time. Roosevelt only appears when I'm alone. You already know that from our first session. And I've told you how he disappears if anyone comes into the upper cabin. Cardella, Collison, Dillman—I don't think you'd be an exception." The President grinned mischievously and added, "Even if he was a bit of a lecher in his day."

She said stubbornly, "I'd still like to try. Remember, I'm a parapsychologist. I might be able to sense something out of the ordinary." Her voice softened. "Would it embarrass you, my being on the plane? I mean, if no one other than the Secret Service and the crew knew I was there?"

"No," he answered promptly. "And incidentally, I'm grateful to you for having come along today. It's the first time I've relaxed in months."

"I've had fun, too. I like your brother and his wife. They made me feel as if I were part of the family."

"You passed inspection," Haines chuckled. "I wasn't worried about Bert—he'd like any pretty face—but my sister-in-law is a mite protective. She worshipped Barbara, and when she accepted you, that was the Good Housekeeping Seal of Approval. McNulty seems taken with you, too. I've noticed you've been talking to him."

"Jealous?" she couldn't help asking.

"Never of Mike. He's happily married to an airline stewardess. Which reminds me—Mike!"

The agent turned around. "Yes, sir?"

"Dr. Sarazin will be going to Denver with us, strictly on the Q.T., by the way. I want her to board at least an hour before anyone else gets there, including me. She'll be in the upper cabin, away from the press, and she'll stay there the entire flight. Same procedures on the return trip. Clear this with Colonel Cardella and explain the arrangements. Pick up the doctor at her office Wednesday and phone Cardella just before you leave for Andrews. Tell him I don't want any of his security people around that plane when she arrives. She's to be boarded as surreptitiously as possible."

"How about at Denver, Mr. President?"

"She'll have to stay in the lounge the entire time I'm at the Academy. Your assignment is to make sure nobody gets into the upper cabin area while we're on the ground in Denver, so park yourself at the foot of the staircase and look menacing—as you do for me. All understood?"

"Yes, sir. Am I to assume you don't want the other agents to know about the doctor?"

"You assume correctly. And thanks, Mike."

"You're welcome, Mr. President."

He walked away and resumed his sentry duties.

"Thanks, Jeremy," Jessica whispered.

"I still think you're wasting your time. I know he won't show up, and sitting alone in that plane for hours is going to be pure essence of boredom."

"I'll bring along a good book," she assured him. "Besides, even if he doesn't appear, flying on Air Force One will be an experience in itself. Not to mention being with you."

Their hands entwined, a contact of flesh possessing the intimacy of a caress.

It occurred to Jeremy Haines that sneaking a woman aboard the Presidential aircraft, with the connivance of a Secret Service agent and the mandatory acquiescence of the crew, could be the height of folly if something went wrong. At best, it would result in ugly gossip; at worst, in embarrassment to Jessica that might ruin their relationship.

He didn't give a damn. She was going with him, and it made no difference whether she saw the ghost or not.

It occurred to Jessica Sarazin that her professional curiosity could mean political trouble for the President if her presence on that plane were to be leaked. It would be difficult to explain away, and she suspected that Haines probably was right—the ghost wouldn't appear. Hers had been a foolish and potentially dangerous request.

She still didn't give a damn. Even if there was no psychic manifestation, she was going with him and on the flight itself they would be alone with a chance to talk and share . . .

It was an unhappy President who saw the *Times* item. Wayne Dillman had brought it to his attention.

"Some friend of the columnist spotted you at the marina and called the paper," the press secretary explained. "Naturally, they wanted to know who the mystery woman was. I identified her just the way you told me to if anyone saw her, as Jessica Vaughn, an old friend of Ruth Haines's from Ohio. I'm sorry, sir."

"Wasn't your fault," Haines grumbled. "Damn those press Peeping Toms. I never dreamed she'd be seen. Jessica isn't going to like this."

Jessica didn't.

"Jeremy, maybe I shouldn't go to Denver with you."

"That's nonsense. Seeing us at the marina was a fluke. Nobody's going to know you're on Air Force One, McNulty will see to that."

So she went to Denver, relaxing as she witnessed McNulty's quiet efficiency in boarding her unnoticed by anyone but Colonel Cardella. Air Force One's commander was the sole person in the huge hangar when her White House car, driven by McNulty, pulled up outside.

Cardella treated her with a deference that surprised her. "Welcome to Air Force One, Doctor," he greeted her as she climbed out of the black Mercury. He was formal yet friendly, and Jessica got the impression he was delivering a verbal salute. He insisted on showing her through the magnificent aircraft with a pride that touched her. He did not, she noticed, take her into the communications area that Haines had described to her. But he did introduce her to his crew, one by one, as they boarded, "This is Dr. Sarazin, the President's medical consultant." Each man acknowledged the introduction with flawless circumspection. The formalities were so routine that McNulty remarked about it to Flight Engineer Curtis.

"I would have been polite to a visiting Russian spy if Cardella ordered it," Curtis explained in a rather awed tone. "He told us at preflight briefing that the first guy he caught even thinking out of line would be flying cargo to the Antarctic on his next mission." It dawned on McNulty that the colonel was as loyal to the President as he was himself.

The upper lounge was the last stop on Jessica's tour.

"The President's helicopter will be here in a few

minutes," Cardella announced, "so you sit down and make yourself comfortable. The Air Force stewards won't be allowed up here during the trip, so I've taken the liberty of brewing some fresh coffee in that little galley over there. There's also juice and danish pastry. When we get to Denver and the President has left for Colorado Springs, one of the crew will bring you some lunch from the lower-deck galley."

"Where does the President usually sit?" she asked, glancing around the luxurious quarters.

"In one of those two armchairs over there, usually the one on the left. Either will do. Here, let me show you how they swivel, Doctor. Just pull this lever here for whatever position you want. Now, is there anything I can do for you before I go to work?"

"Nothing, Colonel. I appreciate your making me feel so welcome. And I enjoyed meeting your crew."

Cardella allowed himself a small grin. "They enjoyed meeting you, too, ma'am. Lady visitors are rare on Air Force One."

As Cardella's stocky frame marched to the cockpit, Jessica sat down in the same chair Haines had told her the ghost always occupied. She did it with a strange uneasiness, as if she were somehow intruding. The feeling persisted even after the President boarded and they were en route to Denver. When she remarked to Haines about it, he suggested she use the big divan across the aisle and they both waited expectantly, albeit nervously, for what they hoped would happen.

There was no sign of Franklin Roosevelt.

After Haines left by helicopter for the Air Force Academy, she had a light lunch that Cardella himself brought her. She tried reading a medical journal until her eyes drooped and finally moved from the divan over to the President's chair, still facing the ghost's, and let her eyes rove over the ominously quiet lounge. She had heard the crew depart the aircraft. Only McNulty was aboard, standing his silent, patient guard at the foot of the spiral staircase. The 747 itself had been towed into an empty United hangar, the airline's personnel having been warned not to approach it. Not even the most curious would have attempted it, for two Air Police guards sporting sub-machine guns were stationed outside the huge plane.

It was rather warm in the upper cabin, even though an outside auxiliary power unit provided air-conditioning and lights. At McNulty's request, Cardella had sent Curtis back into the Presidential quarters to close all upper lounge window shades; but even with the lights on, the lounge seemed forbiddingly gloomy, like a dimly lit old house—a haunted house, Jessica thought morosely, and then chastised herself for such childish notions. Yet the very incongruity of something from the grave taking possession of this antiseptic, upholstered splendor was what tantalized her. With the perverseness of a teenager wanting to be scared by a horror movie, she kept wishing the ghost would materialize even as she dreaded its appearance.

The cabin was oppressively, ominously still; the only sound was the barely perceptible hum of the power unit outside. She was wearing a black suit with a white blouse underneath the jacket; feeling stifled, she removed the jacket and turned around to fold it over the headrest of her chair.

It was then, with her back still to where Haines had told her the ghost had always sat, that she felt the chill.

It did not fit the President's description—"Like a damp fog, only colder . . . fog you can't see but can feel," she remembered him saying. It was nothing like that—more like a sudden draft of winter air coming from an open window in a hot room. More contrast than clammy, she decided analytically with a calmness that belied her thudding heart.

She turned back toward the empty chair and stared at it mesmerized, fear wrestling with curiosity.

The intensity of the draft lessened markedly, the cold lingering for just a few seconds and then fading, as though a freezer had been opened briefly, then closed.

She could not take her eyes off the chair, staring at it unblinkingly.

Her throat constricted.

Just above the seat cushion, the air seemed to shimmer.

Jessica swallowed hard, unaware that her hands were gripping the armrests, knuckles five hard ridges of bone and flesh.

Something was rising from the floor and swirling slowly around the empty chair. Something with the vague contours of smoke, its gossamer tendrils weaving thin, curling paths that danced before her horrified eyes.

From Jessica's half-open mouth came a gasp, and she sensed rather than felt the sweat forming not just on her forehead but over her entire body.

The wispy ballet shimmered, and began to dissolve into nothingness. "No, no," she whispered. "Don't go. Talk to me . . ."

The tendrils were gone and she saw nothing but the chair, mockingly empty. She leaned back, shaken and trembling. So close, she thought. So damned close . . .

". . . Dr. Sarazin?" Agent McNulty's voice shattered the silence, and Jessica heard his heavy steps on the spiral staircase. Through half-closed eyes, she saw him emerge into the lounge and come toward her, concern on his face.

"Everything okay?" he asked worriedly. "I thought I heard you cry out."

She managed to put composure into her voice. "I'm fine, Mike. I dozed off and must have had a bad dream."

He looked at her doubtfully and she guessed, correctly, she must be pale. "I'm fine, really," she repeated.

He glanced at his wristwatch. "They won't be back for another hour or so. Wish I could keep you company up here, but the Boss said to stay put at the foot of those stairs. Call me if you need anything."

He had turned to leave when Jessica stopped him. "Mike, did you happen to feel a draft a few minutes ago? From this cabin?"

His expression was puzzled. "Matter of fact, yes. I almost came up but it only lasted a minute. This airplane must have some bugs in the ventilation system. That's the second time it's happened. I think I'll tell Cardella about it."

Jessica refrained from saying that she doubted

whether Cardella could do much about it. A few minutes later, however, Air Force One's commander puffed his way up the stairs and looked around the cabin, frowning as if the aircraft had somehow challenged his authority. He approached her, jerking his head once in what for him passed as a friendly greeting.

"McNulty says you felt a draft up here, ma'am. Can't imagine what it could have been, although these contraptions can come up with some weird ailments. We had a KC-135 once with the damnedest rattle I ever heard. Couldn't figure out the source until we finally took the plane apart and found that some Boeing assembly-line worker had left an empty Coke bottle inside a fuselage panel. This draft, now—did it last long?"

"Only a few seconds."

Cardella nodded. "Happened once to me several months ago. I told Maintenance about it, but they couldn't find anything wrong. I'll report it again when we get back. They'd better take another look at those air ducts. Or it might be that auxiliary power unit—they can do some screwy things."

"This other time you mentioned, Colonel. Was the President with you on that flight?"

Cardella scratched his graying hair. "Well, let's see. We were coming back from California around the end of January and, yes, Mr. Haines was aboard." He looked at her a little suspiciously. "Mind telling me why you asked?"

They were all protective of Jeremy, Jessica realized—alert to every nuance, any hint that was nobody's business but the President's. She said disarmingly, "It's just that the President is susceptible to minor chest colds. Exposure to a draft may kick one off."

Cardella accepted the glib explanation at face value. "I'll have those ducts checked again, along with all thermostats," he assured her. Then, in the tone of a man deciding to share a great secret, he added, "You know, Doctor, there are times when I could swear an airplane's ventilation system must be a breeding ground for gremlins. It can produce some funny effects. There was a British transport plane back in the 1960s—the Viscount, a prop jet with four engines. Well, its air-conditioning system had the damnedest bug I ever heard of. Under certain humidity conditions, it produced air condensation that looked for all the world like smoke. Scared the hell out of a lot of passengers who thought the plane was on fire. The condensation would come up from under their seats, sometimes in clouds, like cold steam. I read about one woman who went into hysterics because she thought a ghost was materializing right before her eyes."

"A ghost," Jessica repeated softly.

"Yeah. I suppose when a person's nervous to begin with, imagination can play tricks with your eyes."

On the way back to Washington, she recounted her experience to Haines.

"It really shook me," she admitted. "I had the feeling something was trying to materialize and either couldn't in front of me, or decided against it. Then Colonel Cardella told me about that air condensation phenomenon on the Viscount and now I'm not sure *what* I saw. Or thought I saw."

"Did you ask him if condensation could occur on a 747?"

"I did. He said he had never heard of it happening

but that it wasn't impossible. He went through a long technical explanation of how it could occur on this airplane. I didn't understand much of it but I gather it would be theoretically possible."

He studied her through narrowed eyes. "So what's your professional opinion as of now? Psychic apparition or mental aberration?"

She took both his hands in hers, and he was surprised to find that her skin felt cold. "I don't know, Jeremy. I *thought* I felt a presence in this lounge when I was alone. Then there was that draft. McNulty felt it, too, on the way to Miami and again today. Cardella had it happen coming back from California, the first time you saw the ghost. I wouldn't call this conclusive evidence, but it's damned intriguing. Yet when I talk to a hard-nosed realist like the colonel, my skepticism returns. People like Cardella believe there are scientific explanations for 99 percent of the world's mysteries. And they're confident that, given enough time, science also could solve the unexplainable 1 percent. Or, if not science, then logic."

"Doesn't parapsychology consider things like ghosts logical?" His face was serious but his tone was mocking.

"It holds that the existence of ghosts would not be illogical, but that doesn't constitute proof."

"And what does this particular parapsychologist believe?"

Most unscientifically, Jessica blurted, "If only the damned thing had shown up!"

"The next time I see him," the President muttered, "I'll ask him why he didn't."

* * *

Duane Collison sipped one of Izzy's martinis and looked across the ramshackle table at the jowly face of Peter Frain.

"I need another favor," he informed the columnist.

Frain chuckled. "Accompanied, I presume, by the usual and deeply resented, 'This is off the record!' "

"It *has* to be off the record. Remember your telling me that what we needed was a juicy scandal involving our beloved President?"

Peter Frain's eyes narrowed. "I remember. Don't tell me you've dug up something."

"I'm not sure what I've got. It could be nothing or it could mean the end of that self-righteous coward. That's why I want your help if it's at all possible. I've dug as deep as I can, and I need a bigger shovel."

Frain stared at him for a long, uncomfortable moment. He finally said, "Tell me something, Duane. Why do you hate him so?"

The question startled Collison and gave him a stab of concern. He couldn't afford to lose the columnist as an ally, and the question indicated a weakening of support. "I don't really hate him," he replied. "In his first term, he was a damn fine President, a true leader. But you've seen yourself how he's changed over the past two years. I've lost all respect for him, even though I now realize it may not be all his fault."

"Now *that's* an enigmatic remark if I ever heard one. Elucidate, please."

"I think he's going off his rocker."

Frain lit his ubiquitous pipe and puffed away languidly, as if they were discussing nothing more momentous than the day's weather. Only his eyes betrayed him—they were alive with interest that flashed like sparks. "I'll agree that lately he's been acting like some left-wing nut, but screwball proposals don't add up to insanity. And some of his ideas aren't that crazy—the national lottery's taking off like a supersonic transport. Exactly what do you have on Mr. Haines?"

Collison outlined his evidence, watching Frain's face while he talked. It seemed frozen in a noncommital expression, but the puffs grew more rapid as if the pipe were recording the columist's blood pressure. When Collison finished, Peter Frain shook his head.

"Pretty flimsy stuff," he said. "Circumstantial evidence at best."

"Exactly. Pete, I have to get a look at Sarazin's files."

Puff-puff went the pipe, spewing ashes. "You're nuttier than Haines. That means a break-in and our circumspect society rather frowns on break-ins. You would be lighting a torch while sitting over an open barrel of hundred octane gasoline. Or do I exaggerate this folly?"

"Not in the slightest," Collison conceded soberly. "But it still has to be done."

"Why?"

"If the evidence I suspect actually exists, it will force his resignation. He would be declared mentally incapacitated."

"And suppose the evidence isn't there?"

The general leaned back, martini glass close to his lips. "I venture to say I've already got enough at least to question his mental competence. If he ignores my advice on how to use Operation Umbrella, I can destroy his credibility with Congress and the public. Nobody will listen to a President who finds it necessary to consult psychiatrists. That fact alone casts doubt on his judgment. Naturally, I prefer to unearth precisely what's wrong with him."

Frain took a long swallow of his rum and Coke. "And just where do I fit in? What's this favor you want?"

"I need someone who can get at those files without being caught. A professional with the right skill and a mouth that can be nailed shut with greenbacks."

"What makes you think I'd know someone like that? Or are you suggesting that *I* perform this little chore myself, thanks to my well-known love of greenbacks? Sorry, but gumshoeing isn't my style."

Collison's laugh was more of a snort. "Come on now, Peter. I know you. Not too many years ago you wrote a book on the Mafia that was called the most objective study of organized crime ever done. In researching that book, you had certain channels of information, certain connections, certain pipelines. In employing them, you achieved the impossible—you turned out an essentially honest book yet you made no enemies among the people you wrote about. That's why I think you can help me."

Frain's laugh mimicked Collison's. "You do your homework, Duane. Yes, I know a guy who could do the job. Expensive, mind you. But good."

"Can you put me in touch with him?"

"Yes, but he isn't the only one you're going to pay off. I don't do favors without adequate compensation."

"You want money?" Collison asked in a tone of disbelief.

"Hell, no! I want a story. Your personal guarantee that I break the news of the President's insanity—provided he's crazy, of course. For that matter, if you don't come up with anything solid in the files, I can still run with what you've already got. I'll simply ask in my column why the President of the United States has been seeing shrinks. A very provocative question that Haines may find extremely embarrassing to answer. Do I get either of those exclusives?"

"You do. Naturally, I trust you not to print anything until I give you permission."

"Naturally," Frain sighed.

"Good. You might as well be advised that only one other person will be aware of all this. House Speaker Rafferty."

The pipe almost dropped from the columnist's mouth. "Rafferty? For Christ's sake, why bring that old goat into it?"

"Because I promised to keep him advised of all, uh, developments. He wants to get Haines as badly as we do, although not for the same motive."

"His only motive is spelled *p-o-l-i-t-i-c-s*. He'd sell his own mother for votes. I don't know why the hell you promised him anything."

Collison's cold blue eyes were almost opaque. "He's the most influental man on Capitol Hill. When we use Umbrella the way it must be used, I'll need his support, more than anyone else's. He can influence others, including Vice President Mitchell, if it should come to that."

Their eyes met in a melding of understanding. Frain took a small notebook out of his pocket, scribbled something on an empty page, and tore it out.

"This is the man you want," he said.

TWELVE

Duane Collison couldn't have chosen a more propitious time to ask for another meeting with Tom Rafferty.

For several weeks the Speaker of the House had been surveying with partisan gloom the administration's growing list of successes. The national lottery was under way, with revenues exceeding all projections. The first YARC camps had been opened, and while there had been sporadic, scattered reports of unpleasant incidents—fights, drinking, and minor thefts—the majority of the camps were running smoothly.

And in Congress itself, Rafferty had seen many in his own party succumb to the volcanic pressures of public opinion and approve legislation about which some had sincere doubts. Party desertions were particularly marked in passage of the national sales tax, three out of five Democrats joining with virtually solid Republican support for the measure. There had been little opposition to the child pornography amendment; strong but slightly weakening opposition to one calling for a four-year Congressional term. Yet Rafferty's own Majority leader in the House warned him, "I don't know if we can keep either from being passed—the mail from home is being read."

The last straw was a Gallup poll showing that Jeremy Haines's popularity had gone up another nineteen points; eight out of ten Americans thought the President was doing an excellent job.

So when Collison phoned the Speaker to disclose "I might have something," Rafferty eagerly invited him to his home. What Rafferty did not know was the extent of the general's lobbying within the highest echelons of the Pentagon, in the cabinet itself, and especially in the direction of Vice President Mitchell.

His gist was simple, sincerity-coated, and persuasively earnest. Typical was his approach to Mitchell.

"All I ask," he pleaded, "is that if Operation Umbrella is successful, you give serious consideration to using it as a diplomatic weapon. Believe me when I tell you the future of mankind, not merely America's own future, will depend on how wisely we use this greatest of technological achievements. I want you to know, Mr. Vice President, I'm not the war-mongering hawk you may have been led to imagine. The import of Umbrella is so enormous that it is difficult to appreciate—not even the President realizes this . . ."

And having planted these seeds in the minds of men Jeremy Haines trusted, Duane Collison marched off to his meeting with the Speaker of the House of Representatives.

* * *

"And that's what I have so far, Mr. Speaker," Duane Collison finished.

Tom Rafferty grunted, whether from disappointment or indecision, Collison could not tell. The gnarled little man downed a large slug of bourbon and squinted at the general.

"Seems rather nebulous," he growled. "All we have is that Haines apparently knows some female psychiatrist well enough to invite her on his brother's boat. Maybe she's just a good piece of ass. Hell, the bastard's only human. His wife's been dead for God knows how many years, and I can't accuse the son of a bitch of being just plain horny."

Collison leaned forward, as if closer proximity added credence to his words. "I think it goes beyond a social or physical relationship. If he's merely sleeping with the woman, then why has she been in contact with Captain Baxter, the Navy's chief psychiatrist? Not just once or twice, but apparently with great frequency. We know Haines has seen Baxter, which in itself is rather unusual. I doubt if there has ever been a President who found it necessary to consult with a Navy shrink. That's not a part of routine physical checkups."

"He could have just stopped in to say hello to Baxter," Rafferty argued. "I wouldn't be surprised if they were friends. Haines has always liked the Navy. That's the only thing he ever had in common with a *real* President, and I'm talking about Franklin Roosevelt."

"If that one visit was all we had to go on," the general pressed, "I'd have to admit we were going down a dead-end street. But put that visit alongside those calls to and from a civilian psychiatrist, and we have to ask ourselves what's going on here. No, sir, Mr. Speaker, there's something behind all this, something that tells me Haines may be a very sick man."

"Let's not have an orgasm yet," Rafferty warned. "Consulting a psychiatrist doesn't mean anyone's mentally ill. A guy could have a hundred reasons for seeing a shrink, all of them minor. For Christ's sake, maybe he's a bedwetter, or he has chronic insomnia. Now I'll concede, general, if Haines has some serious problem, that's a different matter. But there's no way we could find out exactly what it is. That Sarazin dame sure as hell isn't gonna tell anybody and neither will Baxter."

Collison said slowly, "I never knew a psychiatrist who didn't keep voluminous notes or tape-record patient sessions."

Rafferty stared at him. "What are you proposing to do—call her up and ask to borrow her files on Jeremy Haines?"

"No," the general said with a deadly calm, "I propose to obtain them by whatever means possible. The stakes are that high."

"And you," Rafferty said in a voice with a cold, cutting edge, "are out of your goddamned mind. Haven't you ever heard of Watergate? Of the Ellsberg break-in? Or what happened to a guy named Richard Nixon—so humiliated and disgraced that the only way he escaped impeachment was to resign? Jesus, we Democrats fed off Watergate for years. We got Carter elected because of it. And you're suggesting we try the same crap that put most of that Nixon gang in jail."

"I am not unaware of those events, nor their consequences," Collison said stiffly. "However, there's a difference between them and what we face today. There really is no analogy to be drawn, Mr. Speaker."

"The hell there isn't. Let's take the Daniel Ellsberg case. An idealist who leaked Pentagon documents on Vietnam to the press. Somebody found out he was consulting a Los Angeles psychiatrist. To discredit him, a couple of clowns named Howard Hunt and Gordon Liddy arranged to burglarize the doctor's office. When all the smoke cleared, all they got were jail sentences and Ellsberg wound up as a damned folk hero. If that isn't a parallel to what you're apparently suggesting, I don't know what is. What do you want to do, Collison—bring Hunt and Liddy out of retirement and send 'em over to Dr. Sarazin's office?"

The general's voice took on the tone of a teacher trying to explain a math problem to a backward student. "The difference, Mr. Speaker, is *motivation*. The Ellsberg break-in was an attempt to stigmatize the reputation of a man who had deliberately leaked top-secret government documents to the press. The Watergate burglars were after any information from Democratic party files that might be helpful to Nixon's reelection. In the first case, the motivation was primarily revenge. In the second instance, pure politics. Neither of those factors relate to our situation."

The emotional barometer that was Tom Rafferty's complexion was somewhere between pink and red. "And just what *is* our situation, General?" he inquired in a deceptively silky tone. "Or maybe I should ask just what is *your* motivation for proposing another Ellsberg caper, presumably by some blundering amateur who couldn't break into an unlocked outhouse."

Collison's cold blue eyes, glinting like ice caught in a shaft of sunlight, impaled the Speaker, and his voice was verbal barbed wire. "I assure you, sir, that any effort I expend in learning the true nature of the President's mental state will be accomplished in a professional manner, undetected as well as untraceable."

He saw a glimmer of interest on Rafferty's face, even though the Speaker's response was to sputter, "I don't give a shit who it's traceable to so long as it's not me or any other member of my party. As far as I'm concerned, Duane, I never even heard this conversation and I'll lie under oath if it should ever come to that."

It had not escaped Collison that the way Rafferty addressed him was as good an indicator of his mood as those varying shades of complexion. It was back to *Duane* now; Collison knew he had him hooked. "I have a strong hunch," he said with a tight smile, "that the information I hope to obtain will be so devastating that how it was acquired will be a secondary consideration."

Rafferty smiled in return, a crack on the face of a gargoyle. "For the record," he rasped, "let it be said that I advise you not to try anything covert because if you're caught your ass is gonna be in Gordon Liddy's copyrighted sling. And now that I've officially washed my hands of the whole idea, how about answering my question? What the hell's different from the Ellsberg mess or Watergate? You talked about motivation. If something's seriously wrong with Haines, the political fallout would be volcanic. So I have to assume your motivation's political."

The general leaned forward again, one hand cupping his chin. "I told you at our last meeting that Operation Umbrella has the potential to change the history of mankind. I doubt whether a President with severe psychiatric problems has the capacity to recognize this and act accordingly. It's my frank opinion that Haines already has displayed signs of mental illness, what with all his wild schemes and his open contempt for Congress. I need only remind you of his recent hundred-eighty-degree turn in personality—from a faltering, ineffective namby-pamby to a dictatorial despot who on an almost daily basis flaunts, insults, and taunts the legislature. I do not require a degree in psychology to label the President as a victim of probable schizophrenia. You asked me my motivation, sir. It's very simple—to get that man out of office before he can sabotage this country's last real chance for everlasting peace with unsullied honor!"

Rafferty was silent, shaken despite himself by the man's intensity, yet vividly cognizant of what that intensity meant in terms of his own war against Jeremy Haines. Tom Rafferty was not really an evil man, but he was a career politician with the instincts of a hungry wolf salivating at the sight of a crippled deer. And he saw in Duane Collison the instrument for flushing out that helpless victim, exposing him to the kill.

"You understand," he said with a slight hoarseness betraying both eagerness and fear, "that I cannot sanction whatever you're planning to pull. But if you don't have my official approval, you do have my blessing. I don't expect Watergate and Ellsberg to be your conscience, but they should be your guide. If there's the slightest doubt of success, back away."

Collison's expression relaxed slightly, but his eyes

remained fixed on the Speaker; Rafferty could almost feel the chilling resolve behind them. "I assure you, timing, discretion, and caution will be scrupulously observed in this venture."

"Fine," Rafferty growled. "Just between the two of us, how the hell are you gonna pull it off?"

"Realizing your, ah, delicate position, I assume you don't want all the details."

"Christ, no! The less I know the better. Just give me a bare outline."

"First, I've learned from a reliable source that Dr. Sarazin will be attending a five-day meeting of the American Psychiatric Association in Philadelphia about a week from now."

"Without naming names, who's your source? So-called reliable ones are pretty damned rare in this town."

"This particular person happens to be a Navy psychiatrist who works in Baxter's own department. He saw Dr. Sarazin's name on the convention program. She'll be delivering a paper at one opening day seminar and is on a panel discussion the fourth day. In that time span, I'll have everything done that needs to be done."

"By whom?" Rafferty asked. "Some private detective?"

"You requested no names, remember? I'll tell you, however, I've obtained the services of a professional who is no amateur, as you so succinctly put it."

Rafferty inquired suspiciously, "Where'd you dig him up?"

"A friend of mine put me in touch with him."

The Speaker chortled, "I'll bet it was that goddamned Peter Frain!"

Collison remained silent, but Rafferty saw confirmation in his eyes. "I thought so. That son of a bitch. You trust Frain's judgment?"

"I do. I've already contacted the person. His fee is five thousand dollars."

"And who's gonna pay for this professional?"

"I will, out of my own pocket. I consider it a cheap price to pay for saving this nation."

"Good luck, and keep me informed," Rafferty said. But for a long time after Duane Collison left, the Speaker of the House sat in his study, brooding. In the bowels of his conscience was a gnawing ulcer of doubt.

Franklin Roosevelt wore the expression of a Jewish mother trying to look brave in the midst of martyrdom.

"Considering the fact that I had no chance whatsoever to contribute so much as one word or idea," he announced rather peevishly, "I thought your remarks at the Air Force Academy were, ah, interesting and presented with admirable forcefulness."

"In other words," Haines guessed shrewdly, "you didn't quite agree with them."

"I didn't say that. I do feel, however, that rapprochement with communist Cuba may be somewhat premature at this point. Fidel Castro has been dead for only a few months and the dust hasn't settled."

"It's settled to the extent that his successor is also a Marxist. It remains to be seen whether he's an ideological exporter like Castro. I figured it was time to make some kind of conciliatory gesture, however innocuous."

"But why the Air Force Academy as your forum?

Of what possible interest could a trade mission to Cuba be to those cadets?"

"Because those are the kids who may have to fight our next war. I wanted them to know I'd do anything in the cause of peace, even if it's a small step, such as trying to restore normal trade relations with a hostile country such as Cuba." He gave the ghost a sharp look. "You seem to be aware of what I said—I'm surprised you evidently missed the point."

"Oh I didn't miss it," Roosevelt assured him. "I simply didn't agree with the subject matter. Cuba is just a branch office of our real enemy. I thought your speech might better have been aimed in that direction—an assurance of firmness toward the Soviet Union. That's what I would have advised, had I been given the opportunity." Once again, his tone was one of petulance, but the President was more amused than bothered.

"Well, you'd have had an opportunity if you hadn't insisted on exclusivity," Haines said.

"I beg your pardon?"

"I mean, it was your decision never to appear on this airplane before anyone except me." He watched the ghost closely. "You damned near did, though, didn't you?"

FDR answered him obliquely. "A very attractive lady, your Dr. Sarazin."

"Had you appeared to her, it would have solved a lot of problems," the President said.

"I was sorely tempted," the ghost admitted, "but the ground rules had to be followed."

"I'd still like to know who established those ground rules."

"And I'm still not at liberty to divulge that. Actually, I'm sorry. I'm well aware my appearance that day would have dissolved all her doubts about your, uh, mental state. However, I don't believe she really thinks you're insane. The doctor has an admirably open mind on the subject of psychic phenomena. In fact, I wouldn't be surprised if she is almost as close to believing in me as you are."

Haines grimaced. "In this screwball situation, the distance between close and actual is the width of the Grand Canyon. What are you smiling about?"

"The word you used—screwball. It reminded me of Carole Lombard, the queen of those so-called screwball comedies I loved to watch. And a real-life screwball in her own right, that Carole. She had the face of a Madonna and the mouth of a garbage pail. Y'know, she and Clark Cable visited me at the White House once. I invited them to sit in on one of my prewar fireside chats, the one in which I said the United States must be the arsenal of democracy. Now *that* was a grand phrase, one of the most memorable I ever used even though I can't take credit for it. I'll bet you can't guess its author."

Typically, he didn't wait for Haines to guess but sailed right on. "The originator was Jean Monnet, a French representative in Washington in 1940. He used the phrase in a private conversation with Justice Frankfurter, and Felix instantly recognized its aptness. He even asked Monnet never to mention *arsenal of democracy* again and told him it should be uttered only by the man who could say it best and most effectively—namely myself. The minute I saw that line, I loved it! That was my forte, of course—compressing and distilling complex issues into a single descriptive and powerful phrase. As I've mentioned before, I didn't compose all of them myself, of course, but you'll have to admit I could recognize a great line when I saw one. I've given *you* a few, haven't I? Ha-ha!"

"You have," the President acknowledged. Roosevelt's stream of thought fascinated him. That mere mention of the single word *screwball* had touched off one of those nostalgic reactions to which the ghost seemed addicted. It was exasperating yet revealing—FDR's vanity reflected in a childish need for praise, his facile jumping from the inconsequential to the vital, his sentimentality combined with an acute sense of historical perspective. Roosevelt was a brilliant if undisciplined mind at times, Haines decided, employing a circuitous thought process that somehow managed to arrive eventually at the chosen destination.

He was aware that the ghost was watching him intently, as if it were trying to read the President's mind. The surveillance made him feel uneasy; it coincided with the sudden realization that perhaps he *was* getting tired of the whole affair. Jessica may have been right—maybe it was time to break away from the pervasive, unreal influence of a being who had become more man than ghost.

With uncanny intuition, Roosevelt remarked, "Actually, my friend, I've begun to consider an early termination of our relationship. I believe I've charted a correct course for you in several essential areas, with only one major piece of business yet to be accomplished."

"And that would be?"

"What we're going to do about the Russians. Frankly, I haven't been able to come up with any solid suggestions. Eliminating aggression without armed intervention is a dilemma that boggles the mind. Even *my* mind."

As he had on several occasions, Haines almost laughed at Roosevelt's conceit. There was a naïve quality about it that invited amusement instead of annoyance. FDR didn't really boast in an offensive way; he merely stated what he himself perceived as a perfectly factual declaration of his ability and intelligence. It was more self-confidence than bragging, which was precisely why the President tolerated a personality that otherwise could have been abrasively arrogant. The ghost, Haines had learned from the start, was fun to argue with but also challenging. He had to be constantly alert to every nuance, each supposedly casual phrase, for one of Roosevelt's traits was the knack of apparently agreeing with an opposing view while subtly undermining it.

The President said, "You just used a curious choice of words. You said *eliminating* aggression. I think *containing* would be a more apt description of our policy."

FDR dismissed this with the wave of an arm. "Pure semantics. If we contain, in effect we also eliminate."

"Try *tough diplomacy* as opposed to *armed intervention*. The first is a synonym for *containment* and the second is synonymous with *elimination*. We're not quibbling over semantics here, Mr. President. We're discussing peace versus war."

"Balderdash," Roosevelt snorted. "The very definition of diplomacy precludes the use of a descriptive adjective like *tough*. You sound just like those nervous nellies in the State Department."

"And you sound as if you're urging some kind of military venture against the Soviets."

"On the contrary, I would consider that foolhardy. However, I shouldn't have to remind you that Russia is a paranoiac bully. Its long record of aggression is almost equaled by its long record of loudly crying, 'Foul,' whenever the United States has gotten its Dutch up. The Soviets backed down when Kennedy confronted them over the Cuban missile bases. They were furious but helpless when Reagan invaded Grenada. But in recent years they've gotten away with a series of aggressive acts and our only response has been to waggle a finger at it and whine, 'Naughty, naughty.'"

"Right out of Duane Collison's mouth," Haines said with a touch of bitterness.

The ghost laughed. "I wouldn't go so far as to say that, Jeremy. Your esteemed hair shirt, General Collison, *is* a bit trigger-happy, but his instincts are right in that he recognizes the mistakes of the past. We keep backing away from any major confrontation with Russia until there's nothing behind us but the cliff of surrender."

All of a sudden, the President felt his old fatigue come over him, like the vague, almost indefinable ache that precedes the flu. "We cannot commit this nation to putting out communist brush fires all over the world," he said. "Just one Vietnam was a bottomless pit. I should know—I lost my son there."

FDR said sympathetically, "I know you did, my friend. Believe me, I'm not urging more Vietnams—we're too thin in conventional weapons to be the world's policeman. Now if this Operation Umbrella of yours really works, we may be able to change our posture. A bit more clout and muscle, so to speak."

Haines bristled. "Are you siding with Collison?"

"Good Lord, no. He wants ultimatums. I simply suggest that the very presence of an effective anti-missile shield is a silent, subtle ultimatum. We don't have to threaten. We merely assume a tougher stance, knowing the shield is in existence and knowing the Soviets are only too well aware of it. I suspect they'd be a bit more tractable. We just have to stop being afraid of them."

"I'm not afraid of them," Haines said wearily. "I'm afraid of nuclear war, period."

"As well you might be. As well anyone should be, Collison included. Yet we mustn't let fear dominate every action and every word. Nobody wants another Vietnam, but perhaps we could use a few more Grenadas. That fellow Reagan—great intestinal fortitude even if he was a damned reactionary. Very persuasive speaker, too."

Haines decided abruptly he was tired of the subject and jumped at what the ghost had just said. "A debate between Roosevelt, the master politician, and Reagan, the polished actor," he suggested slyly. "Now *that* would be something to hear."

"I love it!" FDR exclaimed. "I absolutely love it! Of course, I would have eaten him alive! Fascinating fellow—basically kind and decent, yet suppressing these qualities under his abominable right-wing political and economic beliefs. The man's personality was in amazing contradiction to his policies. I would have been delighted to debate him, though. Y'know, I believe I mentioned on a previous occasion how I wish television had been around in my day. Imagine what I would have done to that pipsqueak Dewey in one of those televised debates. Alf Landon would have lost all forty-eight states, ha-ha! Willkie would have been tougher, but I think I could have mastered him."

The ghost's eyes, bright and excited, intercepted Haines's amused glance. "Well," FDR chuckled, "there I go again. I *loved* to make speeches. And I must say, Jeremy, you apparently have gained some of my forensic skills by osmosis or something. Your speech to those cadets was more of a performance than a presentation. Pity I didn't agree with the contents, but that's neither here nor there. I never expected you to agree with me on everything. Ours is a partnership, not a ventriloquist–dummy act. It is important only that we agree on mutual goals; methods are inconsequential, Jeremy, particularly so when we face our greatest challenge: the achievement of permanent peace. And when we meet that challenge, together we will present a denouement that will shake the world—that I promise you!"

The President said, very quietly, "Exactly what do you have in mind for this denouement?"

"Believe me," Roosevelt answered calmly, "if I knew the specifics, I'd give them to you right now. You could reveal them in this New Orleans speech tonight. I do have some ideas, some thoughts, but they are far from being finalized. And any hint as to their direction would not only be grossly premature but unfair to you." The ghost smiled. "Have you prepared any remarks for tonight's occasion? Or were you waiting for my contributions? If it's the latter, I'm afraid I'll have to disappoint you—I feel a bit barren mentally, largely because I've been concentrating so on this whole Russian business."

Haines, thinking of Jessica Sarazin, somehow felt relieved. "I had already prepared some remarks just in case you didn't make your usual appearance, Mr. President. Mostly they're aimed at reassuring Congress that I'm not out to exterminate the legislative branch. A kind of olive branch, if you will, along with what I hope will be additional telling arguments on behalf of the four-year term for representatives and the amendment banning riders. Both proposals are having a rough time. I'm learning what John F. Kennedy learned—popularity isn't necessarily power."

Roosevelt beamed at him, the look of a father whose son has just come home with a straight-A report card. "Excellent!" he said. "Y'know, we may have been wrong in alienating Congress to the extent we did. But then, as a wise man once said, an error does not become a mistake until you refuse to correct it. My friend, you are on the way to becoming a *great* President, one who will march through history in the company of Washington, Jefferson, and Lincoln."

"You left out your own name," Haines remarked blandly.

"An omission of modesty," FDR explained with an air of total seriousness.

* * *

Duane Collision examined the man sitting in front of him, revulsion for his profession blending with grudging admiration for his professionalism.

This second meeting, like the first, was being held in the study of Collison's McLean, Virginia, home, the night after Jessica left for Philadelphia. It was an edifice of which the general was inordinately proud (even though it had been purchased with his wife's money), and one that he loved to show off to visitors with an elaborate guided tour. This particular visitor was an exception; there was no guided tour, only a quick escort through the foyer and living room to the study. As on the night of their first meeting, Collison had dispatched his wife to a bridge game an hour before the man arrived, with instructions to phone when she was leaving the game. Duane Collison took no chances.

The man's appearance was unimpressive—medium height, rather heavyset, with shaggy, unkempt hair and sad spaniel eyes peering sleepily out of a jowled face. His clothes were neat enough but cheap-looking, as if they had been purchased off a rummage-sale rack. He reeked of an after-shave lotion so strong that Collison suspected it had been splashed on in lieu of a bath. But what the general noticed most of all were his hands—the fingers were long, tapering, almost feminine, yet with a hint of latent strength. Those hands kept Collison from dismissing him at their first session; somehow they reflected the man's personality more than his coarse facial features and flabby build.

"I appreciate your coming, Mr. Penn," the general said. "Do you have anything to report?"

Penn's voice was cotton-soft but not obsequious. "As you instructed, I obtained entrance to the subject's office last night, after making sure her receptionist had left and that Dr. Sarazin had gone home. I inspected the interior premises thoroughly and ascertained exactly what has to be done during the period she is out of town, starting today."

"And that is?"

"Her confidential files apparently are kept in two places. One is a locked file cabinet. The other is a small safe. Neither presents any difficulties. The file cabinet will be child's play. The safe will be a tougher problem, but nothing I can't handle. I can open both without leaving any trace of tampering."

"Please repeat to me the nature of what you'll be looking for."

"I am to examine, as quickly but as thoroughly as possible, the patient files dating back to the first of this year. I will be looking for any hint, clue, or suggestion that one of her patients is the person in question—being aware, as you cautioned, that his actual name may not have been used. In that event, I will examine only those files corresponding to this person's known age, physical characteristics, background and so forth. If I find nothing in those files, of course, I'll check the contents of the safe. As I explained to you when we first met, my previous experiences with what a psychiatrist foolishly assumes is tight security indicates that patient interview tapes are stored separately from the regular typed or written files. You've already advised me of your information, obtained from someone who knows the woman, that she tapes all interviews. It is my belief that the tape you want, if it exists, will be in her safe."

"And tell me once more what you are to do with the tape or tapes, assuming you're successful."

"First, I'll listen only to those tapes within the same time period as the files, and which bear any suspicious label or possible code. As you've already pointed out, I should be able to recognize the patient's voice so I shouldn't have to spend much time on tapes that obviously do not involve him."

"Remember," Collison interrupted, "I don't want you to spend any unnecessary time listening to the whole damned thing. All you have to do is identify the voice. The minute that's done, you're to cease listening. Now, give me the rest of your scenario."

"If I unearth a tape with the person's voice, I'm to put it into your hands as quickly as possible. If the evidence is contained in the written files, I'm to photograph all pages and also bring these negatives to you. The original files are to be put back before I leave. If there is *any* tape, I'm to return it to the subject's office the following night after you've had a chance to duplicate it."

"Both time and extreme caution are of the essence," Collison warned. Penn nodded placidly.

"Not to worry, General," he said. "I assure you I'll complete the job on schedule and the subject won't know the files have been touched. There will be no fingerprints—as the person who recommended me to you must have told you, I wear surgical gloves. And"—the spaniel eyes took on a slight twinkle—"my work's guaranteed."

Duane Collison rose and put out his hand; the responding shake was surprisingly strong. "If you come up with what I hope you do, I'm not going to limit your fee to five thousand. There will be an additional twenty-five hundred if you unearth anything significant. Let me see you to the door."

After Penn left, the general poured himself a drink and sat in his study. He was satisfied but not entirely happy. It wasn't the mysterious Penn that worried him—the man seemed devilishly competent—but rather the size of the bet Collison had thrown on the table. He was a good enough soldier to realize that overconfidence was the military man's greatest enemy, and he knew the longshot he was playing did not warrant the optimism he so wanted to feel. He was only too well aware that Penn would have trouble finding a file or tape that would almost certainly be labeled anonymously, assuming there even were such unidentified records.

But suppose Penn did produce the evidence? Collison already had decided his course of action. He would tell Rafferty, of course, but advise the Speaker not to do anything until those "certain developments" bore fruit. Then if Haines resisted acting on those developments, Collison was ready to expose him as insane. Vice President Geoffrey Mitchell would take over the Presidency, and the general was sure he could convince him of the only sensible decision.

It was going to work out, Duane Collison told himself with renewed confidence.

It had to.

* * *

It was 2:13 A.M. when Leo Penn entered Jessica Sarazin's office for the second time, again by the simple process of forcing the outer door lock of the building with a plastic VISA card. He was wearing paper-thin surgical gloves. It always amused him, the sense of false security that people displayed toward locks. The one on the doctor's front door wouldn't have stopped a rank amateur, let alone a skilled practitioner like himself.

He did not turn on the lights in the reception area, but groped his way into Jessica's windowless office with a shielded flashlight. Once inside, he closed the door leading to the reception room, put his jacket over the lamp on her desk, and turned it on—enough illumination to work by, he thought with satisfaction, yet dim enough so it couldn't possibly attract attention.

He had parked his own car three blocks away and he was puffing a little now from the walk—he should cut down on smoking, he told himself. Anyone else might have supposed that his slightly heavy breathing was due at least partially to the import of the task ahead of him—a break-in involving the reputation of the President. Not Leo Penn. It was just another job for which he would be well paid, and the identity of his target was inconsequential. He was, indeed, a nerveless professional.

He began by gently prying open the indented locks on the file cabinet and riffled through the patient folders for almost an hour. As he expected, there was no folder labeled Haines or President—that would have been too obvious. He looked for initials, a possible code, or some other clue to this very special patient.

By 3:00 A.M., he decided he was wasting his time and relocked the file cabinet; as usual he had left no trace that it had ever been opened. He aimed the shaded flashlight in the direction of the small safe in back of and just to the right of the psychiatrist's desk. Penn knelt down and examined the dial. It was an old safe, and the dial looked about as complicated as a padlock on a child's bicycle. He could have opened it by sensing the combination with his skilled fingers as he twirled the dial, feeling and listening to the telltale clicks. But Leo Penn was too much of veteran to try this if there was an easier way.

And often there was. Many people, he knew, set a safe combination by using easy-to-remember numbers. Birthdays were the most frequently employed sequence, and Penn shone the flashlight on the wall bookcase. He quickly found what he was looking for: *The American Directory of Psychiatry*.

He opened the book to the *S*'s and located *Sarazin, Jessica Vaughn. Born March 28, 1951*. He put back the book and kneeled again in front of the safe. He dialed 3–2–8–5–1.

The safe opened.

Penn chuckled to himself. Ah, the gullibility and naïvité of people! He focused the flashlight on the contents, mostly small metal boxes secured with tiny padlocks. Childs's play to pick, he knew. It took him no more than ten seconds to open the first box he took out of the safe. Inside was a tape cartridge marked Goldman—not likely. He reached for a second box, quickly manipulated the padlock and opened it.

Inside was a single cartridge, one side designated X-1 and the other X-2.

Bingo! thought Penn. He would wager his entire fee that he had just hit the jackpot. He carried the cartridge to the desk and inserted it into the tape recorder he had noticed on Dr. Sarazin's desk; he had a standard-size tape recorder of his own in his pocket just in case, but he figured he might as well use the doctor's.

He turned the volume knob down low and pressed the Play button, nodding as he caught the familiar voice. It was typical of Leo Penn, following Collison's orders to the letter, that he let the tape run only long enough to identify that voice positively. His curiosity extended solely to identification—that was what Collison was paying him for, and in his own way Penn had a certain sense of integrity. He merely did the job for which he was exquisitely trained and never exceeded the limits of a specific assignment. The idea of using a tape for blackmail would have repelled him; he considered blackmail the cruelest and crudest of crimes.

So he resisted the temptation to listen further, put the cartridge in his pocket, and sauntered nonchalantly out of the office and into the still-deserted street. He walked with leisurely steps to his car, drove to his small apartment on P Street, and went to bed, sleeping the sleep of the innocent. As Collison had instructed him, not until the following night did he call the general at exactly 10:00 P.M.

"I have something for you, General."

"Tape or file?" Collison asked in a guarded voice he barely keep steady.

"Tape. I played the first side just long enough to identify the voice. It was him, no mistaking it."

"Get over here right away," Collison ordered.

As soon as he hung up, he dialed Speaker Rafferty's number, conscious that his hand was trembling. He misdialed the first time, cursed his own nervousness, and dialed again, feeling relief as he heard Rafferty's gruff voice.

"Duane Collison, Mr. Speaker. Sorry to disturb you at this late hour but I wonder if you could drive over to my house. It's extremely important."

"Tonight? Goddamnit, it's after ten."

"The trip will be worth your while," Collison said with a dramatic softness. He heard the annoyance disappear from Rafferty's voice.

"What's it all about? And how about your coming over here? Hell, I'm already in my pajamas."

"I'm waiting for someone—someone who's bringing me a tape recording. It will save time if you drive out to McLean. I'll get rid of the person before you arrive—he'll be here in twenty minutes, and it will take you about thirty. I'd deeply appreciate it, Mr. Speaker."

"Oh, all right," Rafferty grumbled. "I can't get hold of my chauffeur at this time of night so I'll have to drive myself. And Duane . . ."

"Sir?"

"This had better not be some wild goose chase."

"It won't be," the general promised.

Penn showed up twenty-one minutes later and handed Collison the tiny cassette.

"Want me to stick around while you listen to it?"

"Are you positive about the voice?"

"Oh, it's him, all right. I only listened to a couple

of lines, but believe me, they're enough to make you want to listen to the rest."

"Then it's not necessary for you to stay. I'll duplicate this on my own recorder tonight and will be in touch with you tomorrow as to when you can pick up the original and return it."

"It'll have to be tomorrow night," Penn warned in his mild voice. "She's due home the following day."

"I realize that." Collison handed him an envelope. "Here's five thousand in cash, as promised. When you pick up the tape tomorrow, I'll give you another twenty-five hundred—provided it made for enjoyable listening."

"I have a hunch you won't be disappointed," Penn said blandly. "Good night, General."

Collison had to fight temptation. He wanted to hear the tape before Rafferty arrived, but he settled for playing just enough to identify the President's voice. The first few seconds were enough to confirm Penn's identification. It was Jeremy Haines, all right. Collison listened for another minute, then shut off the recorder, made one more phone call, and waited for both Thomas Patrick Rafferty and Peter Frain to arrive.

THREE

THIRTEEN

Jessica's driver on the seventy-mile trip to Camp David was Special Agent McNulty, a choice that pleased her because she had grown quite fond of Mike. He had picked her up at National Airport and proceeded to Camp David without stopping at her office or at her home.

His burly physique, with its goalpost shoulders and a chest that could have belonged to the front end of a diesel locomotive, was deceptive; McNulty, she learned, was a surprisingly erudite and articulate person who read good books voraciously and harbored a secret desire to write one of his own.

He confided this to her as their car left the ribboned expanse of busy Interstate 70S north of Frederick, Maryland, and nosed into US 15.

"I like long books," he said. "I guess if I ever

write one myself I'll try to emulate somebody like Michener. He not only tells, he teaches. A couple of agents have written nonfiction books. Edmund Starling—he had the White House detail from Wilson to Roosevelt—did his autobiography. Then there was Mike Reilly—he wrote a book on his experiences when FDR was in the White House. I've got both of them, Doctor, if you'd like to borrow them sometime."

"I'd like to," Jessica said, "particularly Reilly's. Was he FDR's favorite?"

"From all I've heard, yes. And it was mutual—Reilly must have been like me in that respect. Mr. Haines could beat up kids, kick dogs, and spit on his mother's grave—I'd still think he was a great man."

"Don't most agents rather worship their Presidents?"

"Not necessarily. I've heard some of the veterans talk about previous Presidents. Lyndon Johnson wasn't exactly popular among some of the guys. Neither were Nixon and Carter. Every President has had his favorite agent, though."

"And you're Jeremy Haines's," she said. It was a statement, not a question, and McNulty looked pleased.

"I hope so," he said. "I figure he must think something of me to assign me to the Dr. Sarazin detail on a regular basis. You might as well know my colleagues envy me."

Jessica laughed. "I've never been a detail before, but I'll take it as a compliment. I'm only sorry you have to give up your weekend to chauffeur me around. The President told me you have a lovely wife—a stewardess, he said."

"She's flying a four-day trip anyway, and she's used to my screwball schedule. Take a look at that sign coming up on the right, Doctor."

THURMONT 5 MILES, she read.

"That's where Camp David is?" she asked.

"Not too far beyond it. Know much about the Camp?"

"Only that it's a Presidential retreat and has been since Eisenhower was in office."

"Longer than that. It was built during the Depression as a Civilian Conservation Corps installation. During World War Two, Roosevelt wanted a secluded place he could go to and relax, and it was fine with the Secret Service—Hyde Park was too far away for a wartime President. FDR called it 'Shangri-La'—you know, after the sanctuary in *Lost Horizons*—but Ike changed it to Camp David, named after his grandson. We agents like it because we don't have to worry about security. Camp David's actually a Navy installation, staffed by Navy personnel and guarded by the Marines. By the way, I guess that calls for another compliment."

Jessica said, puzzled, "I don't follow you."

"The Boss used to hate Camp David. He ordered it closed shortly after he took office—said it was too expensive to maintain, but the scuttlebutt around the detail was that it was just too lonely for him. The only time he went up there was for the Bujesky meeting, when Air Force One crashed. This is the first time he's been back since then."

"I still don't understand why that's a compliment."

"You don't?"

"No, I don't."

McNulty cleared his throat. "Well, I figure he just wants to show it off to you."

Jessica decided to play discreet. "Mike, you're an incurable romantic. His back still bothers him, and he probably decided it's a relaxing atmosphere for therapy."

McNulty kept to himself a firm belief that physical therapy could have been conducted just as well at the White House. He was relieved of any need for further comment by the sight of another road sign, STATE ROUTE 77.

He turned right. "We're getting close." Jessica's excitement grew. A few hundred yards beyond the turnoff, the Mercury thumped noisily over a one-lane wooden bridge and continued up a bumpy, winding road with the curves and dips of a roller coaster. Just past an unmanned ranger station, the agent turned sharply to the left and headed up an even narrower road for another two miles where Jessica saw a sign, CAMP 4

"Almost there," McNulty murmured, and turned right again into a gravel road. Peering ahead, Jessica noticed a posted warning, FEDERAL PROPERTY—NO TRESPASSING; through the thickening foliage that lined the road she glimpsed three rows of barbed-wire fencing.

"My God, it looks mean," she muttered.

"Electrified," the agent said laconically. "Not enough to kill but sufficient juice to knock an intruder right on his butt." He slowed down and stopped next to a small booth built out of logs. Alongside the booth, stretching across the road like the barrier at a railroad crossing, was a long pole. Out of the sentry box stepped a tall Marine, a .45 nestled ominously in his waist holster, a not-so-ominous clipboard in his hand. He approached the car; McNulty flashed his Secret Service badge and ID.

"Agent McNulty and Dr. Sarazin," he told the Marine, who consulted the clipboard, nodded perfunctorily, and turned to a second Marine standing by the side of the log booth. The latter, Jessica noticed, was carrying a submachine gun over his shoulder.

"Okay," the first Marine called, and his companion pushed a button on the side of the sentry box. The pole raised and McNulty drove through, maneuvering the Mercury down the gravel road until they came to an open field adjoining it.

"That's where the President's helicopter lands," McNulty informed her. There was no chopper on the pad. "Is he here?" Jessica asked.

"Oh, he's here. See the flagpole in the center of the pad?"

She looked. A purple and gold banner was flapping languorously in the warm breeze, the same kind of flag she had seen in the Oval Office. McNulty's calm voice took on the tone of a tour guide. "The Marines raise the flag when he arrives and lower it when he leaves. We're a mile from Aspen Lodge—that's where the Boss is. You're staying in a smaller lodge just down the road from the Presidential cabin."

He picked up the microphone connected to the car's two-way radio and pressed the Transmit button. "Aspen, this is McNulty. We just passed the pad. Please advise Buckeye we'll be there in five minutes."

"Roger," said a metallic voice.

"Who's Buckeye?" Jessica wanted to know.

"Code name for the Boss. His being from Ohio, you know. The detail can come up with some lulu codes for the President. Jimmy Carter's was Deacon."

Dr. Sarazin's first view of Aspen Lodge's rustic, resortlike structure was preempted by the sight of the President's tall figure standing expectantly on the porch, the smile on his face broadening as the Mercury rolled to a stop. Jessica climbed out without waiting for McNulty to sprint around to her side.

Haines greeted her with a handshake that was outwardly circumspect; the pressure told her otherwise. "Welcome to Camp David," he said. "Mike, I'd appreciate your taking Jessica's things over to Laurel Lodge. Then go get yourself some lunch. The mess menu's chili, and I know that's one of your favorites."

The agent watched them walk into Aspen, talking animatedly; it did not escape him that they were holding hands as naturally as a pair of young lovers. McNulty emitted a sigh of pure Irish sentimentality and climbed back into the car, feeling deliciously pleased. He was thinking how much healthier and relaxed Haines appeared and he was convinced the reason had to be more than medical therapy. The Boss had even called her Jessica in the agent's presence for the first time. Things were progressing satisfactorily, McNulty decided.

Jessica thought so, too. She felt instantly at home in Aspen Lodge, away from the cold magnificence of the White House. Even Jeremy seemed different; dressed in casual gray slacks with a maroon polo shirt, he looked ten years younger than the man she had first seen in her office.

They spent much of the afternoon touring the sprawling facility, with a Navy mess steward serving cocktails and dinner in Aspen later. "I can't help but notice that you seem very pleased with yourself—or pleased about something," Jessica told him.

He smiled mischievously. "I'm pleased you're here, of course."

"That *of course* seems to indicate that's not the only reason."

"Could be," he said enigmatically.

"Jeremy, I hate secrets. A secret is like having an itch in a place you can't scratch."

"You can scratch later. When I'm ready to tell you—and I can't tell you yet—it's something that . . . that's up in the air right now. When it comes down, I promise you I'll provide all the details. Good or bad."

Jessica shook her head. "From that smirk on your face, I rather assumed it was good. Now I gather something could go wrong."

The grin vanished, as if a hot iron had been pressed down on his mouth. "Anything can go wrong at any time, for whatever reason—I should know that better than anyone else. Such as that supposedly harmless, foolproof flight to Palm Springs two years ago. Overoptimism is a twin brother to overconfidence, and taking things for granted is a worse drug than cocaine."

Somehow, she understood his sudden shift in mood, sensing that it was not the mercurial flow of emotional instability but rather the safety valve of caution built into the mind of a man who has known disappointment and defeat.

She said simply, "When you're ready to tell me, I'll be ready to listen."

The grim lines on his face relaxed into the small grin he had worn earlier. "You're quite a person, Jessica—curious without being nosy. A most unusual attribute and one that complements the rest of you—beautiful, intelligent, caring, sensitive, and very perceptive. All those qualities Barbara possessed, qualities I never thought I'd find in anyone else."

Jessica Sarazin looked into his expressive gray eyes with a directness that flustered him. Her voice was soft but gave the impression of a steel ball buried under cotton. "That sounds like I'm getting a proposal from the President of the United States."

The grin melted into a sad smile. "Not quite. I wouldn't ask you to marry the President of the United States. I'd rather the proposal come from ordinary citizen Jeremy Haines, ex-President."

"Assuming I'd seriously entertain a proposal from either man, why is the former more afraid of marriage than the latter?"

"Because as President, I'd probably make a lousy husband. Thanks to that damned ghost, I've fired a hundred clay pigeons into the air, and I'm trying to hit every one of them. I don't have time for a wife who deserves at least 50 percent of my attention and 100 percent of my affection. A wife who'd have to share me with every crisis, every distraction, every petty and major headache that goes with the job. Plus the fact that I seem to have fallen in love with a woman who has her own profession. Do you realize, Jessica, that no First Lady in American history has been a working wife?"

Jessica laughed. "You just flunked your history test. Eleanor Roosevelt, of all people, was for all intents and purposes a working First Lady. She had a daily syndicated column, for one thing, and God knows how many fact-finding missions she performed for FDR. Maybe you should talk to your ghost about marriage to women with minds and interests of their own."

"*Our* ghost," Haines corrected her with just a fragile hint of regret. "That's another block in the way of what I really want. I can't ever forget the reason that brought us together."

"Nor can I," Jessica murmured. "Jeremy, if you were any other patient. I'd recommend that you consult another psychiatrist."

"Why? Because I'm beyond your help?"

"No. Because I've committed the cardinal sin of a doctor–patient relationship. I've fallen in love with the person I'm trying to treat."

He put both hands on the cheeks of her chiseled, glowing face and gently kissed her. "I've also fallen in love with you, which would seem to take it out of the sinning category."

"It's not that easy. I've lost all objectivity, all sense of proportion. Yet, medically speaking, I can't let go. I can't turn you over to someone else. You're not just another patient. You're the President, and each additional person who knows about your experiences multiplies the risk of exposure. In other words, Jeremy, you're stuck with me for better or worse—which, come to think of it, sounds suspiciously like part of the marriage vows."

Haines said quietly, "I could think of far more distasteful fates." He took her hands and was drawing her to him again when the uncaring ring of a telephone sounded in the study adjoining the living room where they were sitting.

Haines frowned. "That's my private line. It may be the call I've been waiting for. Excuse me, Jessica. I'll be back in a minute."

She watched him stride into the study and close the door behind him. That very gesture, she thought wryly, underscored what he had said. Being married to an embattled President could be a succession of closed doors. For a self-sufficient, proud woman who had constructed a career of professional involvement, it could be a degrading environment in which her husband too often would have to shut her out of his own career. She knew Presidential wives could be protective—Rosalynn Carter and Nancy Reagan were—but she also suspected she would not be satisfied with merely being defensive. Jeremy would confide in her—of that she was certain—but to what extent she had no way of judging.

And there was one more thing.

The ghost.

It was both part of their relationship and a barrier to its natural development. As Jeremy had said, it had brought them together yet threatened to destroy them.

A long ten minutes went by before the study door opened. She could not quite interpret the expression on his face. It fell between grim and satisfied, as if something unpleasant had occurred, yet not in an irretrievable sense. The President faced her, still standing, and she wondered if some new crisis was to shatter this weekend to which she had looked forward with the anticipation of a child at Christmas. He's so tall, she thought disjointedly—the stooped shoulders had straightened out and there was an aura of authority about him that she had never seen before, worn like an invisible uniform under the incongruity of his sports clothes.

"Jessica," he began quietly, "you might as well know that someone broke into your office while you were at that medical meeting. They stole the tape of our first session."

She turned white, so colorless that even the pale shade of her lipstick seemed blood red.

She tried to keep her voice calm, but the sound propelled from a constricted throat was choked, almost guttural. "They'll destroy you," she said hoarsely.

"I doubt it," Haines said with a calmness she could not believe. He poured sherry into a tumbler and handed it to her. "Work on this while I tell you the whole story."

Peter Frain had already arrived when Collison ushered Speaker Rafferty into his study and made a ceremony out of locking the door. At the sight of the columnist slouched comfortably on a couch, Rafferty frowned unhappily.

"What the hell's *he* doing here?" he demanded.

"I was invited," Frain said demurely, and Collison added hastily, "I thought it best that you both hear the tape, Mr. Speaker. Pete, as you know, has been most helpful and warrants our confidence in his discretion."

Frain interjected dryly, "He means I deserve to be in on the kill. I seem to have supplied the gun."

Rafferty merely grunted. Collison said, "Sit down there, Mr. Speaker. I have a hunch we're going to be hearing dynamite going off."

Rafferty lowered himself into the proferred armchair. "A hunch? Haven't you played the damned thing yet?"

"Only far enough to ascertain that the voice on the tape is that of Mr. Jeremy Haines. Well, shall we start?"

The Speaker grunted again, leaning his head back against the chair with his eyes half-closed as if he were a classical music lover about to listen to a symphony. Frain lit his pipe, his jaw muscles working. Collison pressed the Play button on his tape recorder and sat down himself, nodding with satisfaction as the President's voice filled the still, small room.

"Dr. Sarazin, how much do you know?"

"Captain Baxter has briefed me in general terms and I've been going over your medical history."

"Did he tell you what I've been seeing? Or thought I saw?"

Rafferty leaned forward expectantly, his eyes now wide open. But instead of an immediate answer from the psychiatrist, there was nothing but silence for about fifteen seconds. Then Dr. Sarazin's voice crackled through the recorder's tiny speaker.

"Mr. President, what is your honest opinion of my profession?"

"It would be a . . ."

Rafferty leaned forward and pressed the Stop button. "Wait a minute," he rasped. "She didn't answer his question. What he was seeing or thought he saw. What the hell's going on here?"

Collison said soothingly, "She apparently stopped the tape, or there was a brief malfunction. Don't worry, the rest of their conversation appears to be intact—I listened to a little of it before I exercised my willpower and decided to wait for you before I heard the whole thing." He pressed Play.

". . . subjective opinion. You're the first shri— psychiatrist I've ever seen. Other than Cat Baxter, of course."

"You started to say shrink. *Which indicates that your opinion is somewhat negative."*

"I'm sorry. I should . . ."

"No apology is necessary. A good psychiatrist, if he or she is honest, will recognize the limitations of the profession. Psychiatry, Mr. President, is easily the most imperfect branch of medicine. Too often we have to deal with intangible theories and pure guesswork. A surgeon can spot cancer. An ophthalmologist knows when he has a patient with glaucoma. A general practictioner can diagnose a case of measles. But psychiatry deals with the human mind, the most complex and least understood of all living organisms. So let's establish something right from the start. I'm not sure I can help you. I'm not even sure there's anything wrong with you. But I'm going to try to help. And for that, I will need total honesty and unquestioning cooperation on your part. Is that clear?"

"Perfectly."

The tape ran on wordlessly a few seconds before Dr. Sarazin's voice resumed.

"Have you ever believed in ghosts?"

Collison punched Stop and turned to his guests. "That's where I stopped listening. I wanted us to hear the rest together. Haines's answer to that last question should prove illuminating."

The Speaker's homely face wore an expression of puzzlement that seemed to be set in concrete—a frown that locked creases of uncertainty into mouth, eyes, and forehead. "I wonder why she asked the question," he muttered. "Haines said he was seeing something or thought he was seeing something. Then she went into all that crap about her profession before she asked him if he believed in ghosts. Do you suppose the crazy son of a bitch is consulting some quack medium at seances?"

The general said easily, "I suggest we continue listening." He hit Play again. The tape rolled silently on for what seemed to be interminable minutes and Rafferty, fidgeting impatiently, grumbled, "Why in Christ's name doesn't the bastard answer that question?"

For the first time, a splinter of doubt edged into Collison's mind. He murmured, "I hope it's not another malfunction. I can't believe a responsible psychiatrist would interview such an important patient with defective equipment."

"Maybe somebody's tampered with the tape," Frain suggested, a note of cynicism blended with harshness creeping into his voice.

"Impossible. I'm absolutely certain this is the original . . ." He stopped, for a voice emanated from the recorder. The three men tensed.

Only it was not the voice of the president, nor of Dr. Sarazin. A third person was speaking, a man.

"Mary had a little lamb,
Its name was General Duane.
He fell hard on his goddamned ass
Trying to prove his boss insane. Ha! Ha!"

The laughter continued and Collison, his hand shaking, shut off the recorder. The three men exchanged horrified looks. Rafferty jumped to his feet and roared, "What the fuck's going on?"

Collison, his features contorted and flushed, shook his head slowly, like a stunned fighter trying to shake off the effects of a pulverizing punch. "We've been had," he muttered. "I recognize that voice."

Rafferty's facial thermometer reached the intensity of a terminal fever. "Who the hell was it?" he breathed.

"That," sighed Duane Collison, "was Admiral Rhino Robertson."

"A slight correction," Peter Frain said calmly. "*You've* been had."

Jeremy Haines refilled Jessica's tumbler for the second time before resuming his account.

"It was the admiral who blew the whistle," he explained. "I don't know the full story yet, but it seems Robertson became worried about a remark he had made to General Collison at lunch, about my seeing Captain

Baxter. Fortunately, Rhino's an old friend of Baxter and confided his fears to him. The upshot was that they had your office under Naval Intelligence surveillance twenty-four hours a day. But first they lifted the tape before any break-in occurred and Baxter himself listened to some of it. Then Rhino suggested the ultimate revenge. They simply reproduced the first few, unincriminating minutes on another tape, and at the very point where I was about to describe my first encounter with the ghost, Roberston inserted his own little message. He wouldn't tell me what he said, but it must have been something because he was laughing so hard he could hardly talk. Jessica, what the devil are you frowning about?"

She said sharply, "I don't find anything funny in this. When we started out, only three people knew our secret—Baxter, me, and yourself. Now some admiral knows and there's no telling how many others."

"No others—and if I know Rhino, he won't talk. He's an irascible old bastard but pure Navy, with a sense of loyalty the width of the Grand Canyon. Besides, in a way I've paid him off. I've promised to take another look at an idea he has for a high-speed aluminum aircraft carrier."

"There must be others, Jeremy. There has to be. Maybe they didn't get that tape, but they knew enough to try for it. Duane Collison—you said Baxter and Robertson believe he was behind the theft. What are you going to do about him?"

Haines stroked his jaw as if the motion was helping him decide. "For the moment, nothing."

"Nothing? The man's obviously a menace. Your own chief security adviser!"

"The Navy agents took infrared photographs of the man who did the actual break-in. He's been identified as an expert in escapades of this kind. If we arrested him, he'd probably squeal on the one who hired him. But I don't want him arrested—not yet."

"For God's sake, why not?"

His answer came in a tone of sadness. "Because the inevitable publicity would be almost as harmful as if the real tape had been stolen. Put yourself in Collison's shoes, Jessica. Suppose we nailed the break-in artist, and he implicated the general. Collison's only recourse would be to reveal I was seeing not just one psychiatrist but two—Baxter and yourself. He'd portray himself as a patriot who was merely trying to find out if the President was mentally ill. He'd defend his action as being within his own province as the country's top security official. He would justify an illegal break-in as a matter pertaining to the security of the United States, in principle no different from our spying on suspected subversives. I know the man, my dear. He's capable of erecting a defense that would be accepted by a great many people."

"We could give some harmless explanation for those psychiatric visits—insomnia, recurring nightmares, fits of depression. I'd be willing to testify you were consulting me for some minor trouble."

He took her slim hands in his. "In other words, you'd lie under oath."

"Yes, I would!" she said defiantly.

"But Cat Baxter wouldn't. Besides, whatever Perry Mason Collison would hire could tear you apart. Remember, you're also an expert in the field of parapsychology. That little professional sideline of yours would be brought up." He hesitated, a momentary delay she instantly recognized as a prelude to confession. "You might as well know that if Collison heard that bogus tape, he heard just enough to whet his appetite. Baxter left in a reference to my telling you I had seen something. And a question you asked me—whether I believed in ghosts. Rhino lowered the boom, so to speak, just at the point I was about to answer. Some ribald nursery rhyme, I gather."

She turned pale again, and now her tone was accusatory. "You love to play games, don't you? All you really had to do was remove the original tape from my office, and the man who broke in wouldn't have found anything. And you could have done just that. You told me those Navy agents had no difficulty opening my safe and the locked box as well. That's how you duplicated the first few minutes and then substituted the fake tape for the original. Why, Jeremy? Why? Was it another Air Force One scenario you scripted? An urge to make up for the plot that backfired and gave you a guilt complex the size of your damned airplane?"

He released her hands and stood up. Never before had she seen him so stern and commanding, yet with a hurt look on his face that made her regret what she had said.

The President said, "I told Rhino and Cat Baxter I *wanted* the theft to occur, for a very good reason. Something will happen in the next few days that will put me in direct confrontation with Duane Collison. Confrontation may be too mild a term—collision would be more apt. When that happens, I need ammunition for a trade-off, some kind of leverage to use against him. I can't think of anything better than to threaten him with exposure as a thief if he decides to fight me on the most important issue ever to face this nation. I'm sorry, but I can't tell you any more than that. You'll just have to trust me."

She could not prevent the tears that glistened in her eyes. "Then I won't insist you tell me. Even though I still don't really understand what you're doing or why. This so-called ammunition or leverage against General Collison—it doesn't seem very effective when you believe he could defend himself against any break-in charges."

Haines smiled wryly. "True, but if I'd bring up exposure as a last resort, by the same token, his own attempt at justification would be a last resort. We've got a standoff there, and that's the best I can hope for. A chance to argue the issue solely on the merits as both Collison and I see them."

"In the end, the decision has to be yours. You're the President."

He nodded, so slowly that it almost seemed as much doubt as agreement. "He'll try to swing the cabinet against me. Maybe key members of Congress. Even the public. Exposure may be the only curb at my disposal, and it could backfire." He suddenly grinned and in the process shed ten years. "You might even wind up committing perjury. This is some sweet mess I've gotten you into."

"Captain Baxter got me into it," she corrected. "And if you want to know the truth, I'm glad." She rose and moved swiftly into his arms, kissing him first with tenderness and then unexpectedly opening her mouth and letting her tongue slide moistly against his.

"I love you," she whispered huskily. "I didn't want to, but it happened and I don't give a damn—about anything or anyone except you."

"I love you, too, Jessica," he said in a half-choked voice.

She broke away from his embrace long enough to stare into his taut, tense face. She had felt his body tremble at the unexpected sensuality of that kiss, and she knew she had ignited long-dormant emotions in a President who was now remembering that he also was a man.

"How about walking me down to this Laurel Lodge?" she asked. There was no coyness, no false demureness, in her tone but rather the typical directness that already had endeared her to him.

He held her at arm's length, with a grip that startled her.

"McNulty will escort you to Laurel," he said almost gruffly. But just as her face fell with the rejection, he added, "I'll come by a little later. I've got some calls to make."

An angry, disappointed, and disconcerted Speaker of the House snarled, "Okay, Collison, what the hell do you do now? And I mean *you*! I said right from the start that if this caper boomeranged, I don't know a goddamned thing. You're deep in a hole you dug yourself, and I'm not about to throw you a rope."

Collison's response was etched in such calm tones that Rafferty could not help but feel grudging respect for the man. "For the moment, I intend to do absolutely nothing. I see no reason to panic. We've failed to acquire specific evidence that Haines is mentally unbalanced, but we still have undisputed proof he's been receiving psychiatric help. The President undoubtedly knows about the break-in, and I suspect he knows who was behind it—that buffoon Robertson must have put two and two together after our lunch. But by knowing that much, Haines also is aware that *I* know something, too. He'll be afraid to act against me because of that fact. If he tries to expose me, I'll expose him. Believe me, gentlemen, this is only a temporary setback. I assure you, your own skirts will remain clean. Pete, you wouldn't be implicated because Mr. Penn doesn't know where I got his name. He asked me and I refused to divulge it. Mr. Speaker, I've already given you my word of honor as a retired officer in the United States Air Force that I would never incriminate you."

"I appreciate that pledge," Rafferty said with just a faint glimmer of sarcasm, "but how about the clown you hired to steal the tape? They've probably got twenty-eight-thousand feet of home movies showing him breaking and entering. He'd spill the beans at the drop of a bargaining plea."

"The only beans he'd spill would fall on my own head, and as I've explained to you, I'm not worried. He knows nothing about you."

Rafferty turned to Frain. "I'd like to hear your reaction to this—this goddamned fiasco."

"I have to agree with Duane. It's only a setback—major but not fatal. We still know Haines has been seeing psychiatrists. This is damaging to him in itself, even if we don't know the reason. When the general here is ready, I'll blow that loud whistle in my column and let the President come up with an explanation—which could very well be most unconvincing. That question about believing in ghosts intrigues the hell out of me."

The Speaker of the House climbed to his feet and took one final look at the silent tape recorder.

"Son of a bitch!" he mourned. "I really thought we had him by the balls."

Collison murmured, "We may still have him. Operation Umbrella is scheduled for its full-scale test within the next seventy-two hours."

Jeremy Haines, as he expected, encountered the ubiquitous figure of Special Agent McNulty as he started out the front door of Aspen Lodge.

"Going for a walk, Mr. President?"

"I am, Mike. Alone, if you don't mind."

"Sir, I can't let you go alone. You know that."

"You can this time. I'm going over to Laurel."

The President would never forget the conflicting emotions that sailed across McNulty's face—duty wrestling with sentiment, responsibility struggling against the sympathetic understanding of one man toward another.

Duty and responsibility lost.

"Good night, Mr. President," said Special Agent McNulty.

"Good night, my friend."

Haines walked briskly down the narrow road that trailed from Aspen to Laurel, unheeding the slight chill in the mountain air. He had not bothered to take a flashlight and didn't need one. A full moon illuminated his path like the glow from a diffused searchlight. He found himself whistling some obscure march, happy with the delicious anticipation not of conquest but of sharing.

When he reached Laurel, he knocked discreetly and heard Jessica's soft voice, "Come in." He opened the door and entered, conscious that somehow he was crossing a momentous threshold of his life.

She was standing by a small sofa, her tall, supple figure encased in a negligee of pale blue. He caught his breath. She wore nothing underneath the flowing, almost transparent gown and he could see the outline of her firm breasts.

He managed a simple but fervent, "You're beautiful, Jessica."

She approached him slowly, took his hand, and led him wordlessly into the bedroom. He caught the fragrance of her perfume, a scent that invaded his senses with the impact of a strong drug. His legs felt weak, as if the heat of desire had softened the muscles.

"Get undressed," she murmured.

He stripped, thinking how long it had been since any woman had seen his naked body. The bedcovers had been tossed back and Jessica, her negligee thrown on the floor, lay supine, her body almost as white as the sheet, contrasting starkly with the long dark hair strewn wantonly over the pillow.

She held out her arms and he lay down beside her, fingers groping first tentatively, then firmly, between her thighs, feeling the oily, warm moistness. He caressed her breasts, and his tongue flicked the jutting, hard nipples. She drew his mouth to hers, her tongue lashing with frantic motion.

He had one last fleeting thought of his dead wife before he succumbed, a momentary stab of guilt wiped out by the sound of panting that turned into gasps and cries as he fondled her, then entered.

Dawn had already lightened the dark bedroom when he awoke to find her staring at him.

"Do I say good morning before I say I love you?" he asked.

"The latter order is preferred. I love *you*—and good morning, Mr. President. Except that's not how I should address you. I've been made love to by a man, not a President."

He raised himself on one elbow and kissed her. "For the sake of discretion, your reputation, and my duties of office, I supposed I'd better get back to Aspen. I'll bet that damned McNulty has been waiting up for me."

They embraced and both felt the stirrings of renewed passion. It was a half-hour later when Haines climbed out of bed and began dressing. She watched him with the half-amused, satisfied smile of a satiated woman.

"We've got a lot to talk about," she observed.

"We do. And we will, as soon as I get back."

Jessica sat up, heedless of her nudity. "Get back? From where?"

"Houston. I have an important meeting at the White House this morning, and then I'm leaving for Texas. And don't ask if you can go because you can't. This flight is top secret."

Jessica's maturity kept her from pouting. "When are you coming back? I feel like a neglected wife."

"Neglected wives go with the territory—I already

warned you against marrying a President. I would have told you about the trip last night but you were in too much of a hurry to seduce me. I'm not sure when I'll be back. Maybe a couple of days."

She donned the negligee while he pulled his sports shirt over his head and slipped into his loafers.

She said, "I gather this trip's important."

"Very important. And so is this morning's meeting. I'll have to take the chopper back, Jessica. McNulty will drive you to Washington—if you want to stay here until Sunday, you're certainly welcome. You'd get a good rest."

She pondered this. "After last night, I could use one. But I think I'll ask Mike to drive me back today. I don't like the idea of being here without you."

He hugged her but she broke away, propelled with a sudden thought. "Jeremy, you'll see him again."

"Him?"

"The ghost. Roosevelt."

Grimness edged into his voice. "I hope so. It'll give me a chance to say good-bye."

FOURTEEN

President Jeremy Haines's eyes swept around the Situation Room, taking a visual roll call of those present.

The comfortably pugnacious face belonged to Secretary of State James Sharkey.

Chairman of the Joint Chiefs of Staff Admiral Gerald Cosley, a beribboned veteran of three wars, had leathery features that could have been dipped in brine and left to harden over the years. One hand was terribly scarred, the residue of burns suffered in a World War II carrier fire—a tough old seahawk, Haines knew, and Rhino Robertson's closest friend.

Air Force Chief of Staff George Silvius, tall, whipcord-lean, with a pleasant, mild countenance that belied his hard-won nickname of "Tiger." Collison's successor, the President remembered with satisfaction, for Collison had lobbied energetically for someone else, largely because he knew Silvius considered him more of a politician than a military tactician.

General Terrell "Gus" Ganoe, Army Chief of Staff and another old crony of Robertson, was a taciturn West Pointer whose twinkling eyes offset his stern visage. He had risen from tank commander to the best armored corps leader the Army had known since Patton. He had the vocabulary of a dock worker, the cold, killer instinct of a Mafia hit man, and a charisma with enlisted men of the kind that earned affection without diminishing respectful discipline.

Dave Pearson, director of the National Aeronautics and Space Administration, had a butterball build that always seemed at odds with the fact that he had once been an astronaut and an expert in space shuttle operations. His gelatin physique had also fooled a street mugger, who had no way of knowing the intended victim held a black belt in karate; the mugger wound up with a broken arm and three cracked ribs. Haines considered Pearson one of his better appointments—under the blubber was intelligence and the integrity of galvanized steel.

Vice President Geoffrey Mitchell, probably one of the few Vice Presidents in American history who didn't like being the proverbial heartbeat away from the Presidency. He admired Jeremy Haines unabashedly, considered his own high status freakish luck, and spent every night praying that Haines would stay healthy. But the President knew him for what he also was—a simple, hard-working rancher drawn into politics by sincere convictions and a sense of duty that told him politics was dirty mostly because not enough clean men were willing to get involved. He had served one term as Arizona's Governor before going to Congress, where Haines spotted him as a solid conservative unafraid of a few liberal ideas. Haines winked at the Vice President and could not help but smile; being the second-highest elected official in the United States had never kept Geoff Mitchell from wearing his inevitable jeans, a trimly fitted western shirt, and a bolo tie. He looked as much at home in this outfit as an opera lover would in traditional tails, nor did he care in the slightest that most of Washington society considered his taste in clothes inappropriate for anything but an outdoor barbecue.

Secretary of Defense John Hammond's white hair served as a dignified crown above a hand-tailored Brooks Brothers suit and regimental tie. Compared to Mitchell, with his informal garb, Hammond was a Cadillac parked next to a pickup truck.

The President shifted his glance to the ninth and final occupant of the Situation Room, Duane Collison, who returned the inspection with a sardonic look. They already had clashed; when Haines summoned these specific eight men to the meeting, Collison suggested that the entire cabinet be present.

"I want only those who've been directly associated with Operation Umbrella," Haines said in a firm but mild tone.

"Mr. President, I think the subject under discussion is important enough for a full cabinet meeting—plus the Joint Chiefs and Dave Pearson, of course."

"I don't want the meeting to turn into a Chinese fire drill, Duane. Even nine people are unwieldy. Throw in the cabinet and you've got a Town Hall debate. For that matter, the subject on the agenda isn't exactly debatable, and it's more of a briefing than a discussion."

"That remains to be seen," Collison had said tartly.

Well, Haines was thinking as he completed his survey of the Situation Room, Collison had thrown down the gauntlet and he was about to pick it up. He gave his chosen battleground one final look. The Situation Room was relatively small, about fifteen by twenty feet, located in the middle of a complex of other rooms filled with computers, teletypes and enough telephones to give the area the appearance of a network news center. Fortunately, the room itself was soundproofed, a quiet oasis in the midst of noisy if organized confusion. At one time it had been the only conference room in the White House equipped with contemporary furniture, but one of Haines's predecessors—he wasn't sure which—had decided to install French provincial chairs that circled an antique oak table.

Haines was rapping on that table now, and eight pairs of eyes fixed on him expectantly—except for Collison's, who carried the look of a wary prizefighter, uncertain of what strategy his opponent was about to use and waiting for the first opening to counterpunch.

The President began, "Gentlemen, at five A.M., Eastern Daylight Time, NASA and the Air Force jointly launched the first of the three hundred and ninety anti-missile satellites that will constitute the major phase of Operation Umbrella, our ninety-eight-billion-dollar shield against nuclear attack. Within the next twelve hours, the remainder of these satellities will be in orbit.

"As I indicated when I asked you to attend this meeting, we will leave shortly for Houston, where temporary control headquarters have been established for a major test of Operation Umbrella's capability. A dozen nuclear submarines stationed off the West Coast will fire some two hundred dummy missiles aimed at three remote desert areas. Simultaneously, the Alaskan Defense Command will launch a number of similar unarmed missiles targeted for five other deserted locations—the latter, of course, will simulate an attack from Russia itself. If just one of these ersatz enemy missiles slips through Umbrella, we're faced with going back to the drawing board. However, I'm confident that all of us will witness firsthand a dramatic if temporary shift in the power of balance between the United States and the Soviet Union.

"Anticipating the success of the test, I believe it is time to consider the consequences of this enormous accomplishment, one whose seeds were sown in the spring of 1983, when Ronald Reagan first proposed an ABM system. At the time, two serious objections were raised. The first was technological—namely, that development of a impervious shield was not only technically difficult but might well be impossible, which would mean wasting billions of dollars on a dangerous illusion of security. I believe that Operation Umbrella will refute those fears, for which we owe an enormous debt to the scientists and military technicians involved.

"But the second objection was one that we must still address. Namely, that once the Soviets know we have an effective ABM system—and I have no doubt they've been anticipating this for a long time—we will have touched off a disastrous arms race in space. I'm well aware that such a race already is in progress; we know the Soviets are trying desperately to create an Umbrella of their own, along with the means of destroying the one we've erected. Their efforts to regain equality or even superiority will now be redoubled.

"This is the primary reason I asked you to meet with me this morning, prior to boarding Air Force One. I need your input on the implications of a successful Operation Umbrella. Each of you in this room represents a major facet of foreign policy—diplomatic, military, scientific, and the intelligence activities associated with each. In essence, Umbrella is a defensive measure but one with potential offensive consequences depending on the extent and direction of Soviet response. I'd like to give our distinguished Secretary of State the floor."

Sharkey cleared his throat nervously. "Mr. President, when you decided about three years ago to give completion of Operation Umbrella the highest priority, I told you at the time we might be opening a Pandora's box. That any major tipping of the balance of power would worsen our relations with Russia. That they would undoubtedly try to match us, in which case we'd be back to square one. I also conceded, however, I could see no sensible, safe alternative. If the Soviets had achieved an ABM system ahead of us, I haven't the slightest doubt World War Three would have started and probably would have ended with our destruction. My own feeling is that we should use what may very well be only a momentary period of military advantage to attempt once more to ease tension. Make some fresh overtures for settlement of differences—anything to allay their inevitable fears of new American nuclear superiority."

Haines asked, "Are you suggesting a summit meeting, Jim?"

"I'd seriously consider it, Mr. President. Even if they insisted it be held in Moscow. You wouldn't be going there hat in hand—not with Operation Umbrella hanging over their goddamned heads."

"An interesting suggestion," Haines commented. "General Ganoe?"

"Diplomatic meetings aren't within my province, Mr. President, and the one Secretary Sharkey has proposed seems to fall into the category of giving an enema to a dead man—it may not do him any good but it won't do him any harm."

There was general laughter, but Ganoe shook his head as if he resented the reaction. "I wasn't trying to be funny, sir. If a summit meeting would help in the slightest way, I'd say go for it. What worries me is that the Russkies' reaction would be the opposite of a Cold War thaw."

"Meaning some new aggressive move?"

"Precisely, sir. A flexing of muscles to show us they can't be intimidated by anything like Umbrella."

Admiral Cosley took the floor. "I can't say I agree with you, Gus. If they tried anything major, they know we could clobber them from behind Umbrella with no chance of retaliation. One move against Western Europe, for example, and they'd be opening the gates to Hell itself."

The Secretary of State grimaced. "I have to remind you, Admiral, the United States for many years has been committed to a pledge that we will never be the first to launch a nuclear war."

Duane Collison charged. "That pledge, Mr. Secretary, is as obsolete as the piston engine airplane. If Russia should attack Western Europe, we're committed to act in accordance with our NATO treaty. War against Western Europe is, in effect, war against the United States."

The Air Force's Silvius threw Collison a suspicious glance.

"Honoring the NATO treaty doesn't mean we have to do it with nuclear weapons."

Ganoe snorted, "How the hell else would we stop the bastards? In conventional weapons—tanks, artillery, and manpower—they outnumber NATO forces ten to one."

There was a flurry of noise as several men tried to

speak. Haines rapped the table. "Gentlemen, I'd prefer a discussion to a free-for-all," he said calmly. "It seems to me that we have to be influenced by one key factor yet unmentioned—how close is the Soviet Union to developing an ABM system comparable to Umbrella? Duane, as head of the Security Council you're sort of representing the CIA defacto. What's the best and latest estimate of our intelligence people?"

Collison's answer came so fast he seemed to have anticipated the President's question, like an anxious actor jumping on his cue. "They're at least a year behind us, perhaps two, mostly because they've never been able to match our electronics technology. They can put anything into space we can, as we well know, but their hardware isn't the ultimate in sophistication. They already have an ABM system of sorts, but its accuracy and coverage are doubtful. Our estimate is that we probably could get at least 50 percent of our missiles through their ABM screen and maybe more. Which, I might add, is highly significant."

"Significant in what way?" Geoff Mitchell drawled.

"They're moving heaven and earth trying to catch up. What they can't steal they're trying to buy. They've offered Japan everything but the keys to the Kremlin for technical help but, thank God, our friends in Tokyo have thus far resisted temptation. The point is, gentlemen, our one-year margin of superiority has to narrow. We must accept the fact that we can do a hell of a lot in the one year we have left."

The room took on a silence so intense that each

man could swear he could hear his own heart beat. The President was the first to respond.

"Exactly what do you think we should do—or could do?"

Collison tensed, his face pale. "With Umbrella operational, we should knock them out once and for all."

The final gauntlet had been thrown.

Haines asked calmly, "What hapened to your proposal that we should send them an ultimatum first?"

"I never made such a proposal, not publicly," Collison retorted.

"You did in private, to me. And I told you then I wouldn't stand for it. So you got your pal Peter Frain to suggest it, just to see if anyone would stand up and salute."

"I don't deny it. And if I'm any judge of public response, a hell of a lot of people favored it."

The President said with a deadly softness, "And a hell of a lot of people didn't, including myself. I told you I'd never allow Umbrella to be used as blackmail. Nor would I go that criminal step further—to attack without any advance warning. I repeat, Duane, what makes you think I'd buy an even more drastic step?"

"Because I honestly believe an ultimatum would be a waste of time. They'd think we were bluffing and they'd call our bluff. Furthermore, they'd probably respond to an ultimatum with one of their own—they'd threaten to attack Western Europe, or Japan, or any friendly nation that didn't have an anti-missile system. A surprise attack on the Soviet Union is our only sensible course, as difficult and even abominable as it may seem."

"Abominable?" the fiery-tempered Sharkey cried. "It's crazy! You're out of your goddamned mind."

"Am I?" said Collison easily. "Is it really insane to destroy the one enemy who's been blocking world peace for the past four decades? Operation Umbrella is misnamed. We should call it Operation Last Chance. Because that's what it really is."

Admiral Cosley, his face red, said unhappily, "I see your point but in the eyes of the civilized world you'd be damning us to Hell and perdition, dooming millions of innocent civilians, and probably poisoning the atmosphere for the next four decades. The residue of nuclear war is as bad as the initial destruction."

Collison leaned forward, his elbows on table and his face intense. "We only have to wipe out selected military targets with a pinpoint attack. You should know that as well as any of us—you, too, Silvius, and General Ganoe. We don't have to destroy all of Russia. We'd simply eliminate their ability to resist anything stronger than a few popguns."

NASA's Pearson opened his mouth for the first time, his jowls quivering. "And you should know there's no such animal as a limited nuclear attack. A handful of bombs is enough to damage the entire earth for generations to come. The ones in our arsenal are twenty times more destructive than the ones we dropped on Hiroshima and Nagasaki."

Collison said, "We don't have to use the biggest ones. We only have to employ what's necessary to eradicate the Soviets' military machine—their naval bases, airfields, missile sites, and major Army installations."

"And Moscow?" Vice President Mitchell asked with an equanimity he did not feel.

"And Moscow," Collison replied. "The very heart and brain of communism. It would be like killing an octopus. Smash the head and the tentacles are powerless."

"Killing a few million women and children in the process," Sharkey said, with undisguised contempt.

Collison clenched his fists so hard that the knuckles were white. "We killed thousands of them at Hiroshima and Nagasaki because we had a justifiable reason for sentencing them to a horrible death. We thought it was the only way to end the war quickly. We rationalized, and correctly, that killing Japanese civilians had to be weighed against the estimated million casualties that would have resulted from an invasion of the Japanese homeland. Is there any difference in what I propose? Even if we kill a million Russian civilians, we bring peace to many more millions—including those enslaved by communism. In my opinion, that's a very reasonable price to pay. A tragic one, but justified by the results. I repeat, gentlemen, this is literally our last chance. Sooner or later, Russia will have its own Operation Umbrella, and as Secretary Sharkey himself stated, we'll be back to square one. Back to the same unbearable, unrelievable tension, the same Red aggression that always stops just short of all-out war and leaves us frustrated, helpless, and hopelessly ineffective. You all know that inevitably we could drift into a nuclear war. How many millions will die in that war? A hell of a lot more than would die in what I regard as nothing but a holy crusade! For God's sake, don't you see the opportunity Umbrella has given us? Our final means of eradicating a plague that has murdered, suppressed, robbed, and tortured without pity."

Again there was an uneasy silence. Haines's eyes cruised around the table, searching for visual clues to inner feelings. He saw horror on their faces, yet it was horror diluted and weakened by reluctant interest. Even Sharkey seemed affected, and the President knew why. There had been a deadly kind of logic in Duane Collison's arguments; Haines, too, had been shaken and swayed in spite of himself. Yet it was that cold, unwelcome realization that snapped him out of what was almost a hypnotic spell.

He said, "You're forgetting one thing, Duane. The Soviets wouldn't roll over and play dead even if we devastated every strategic and tactical target in Russia proper. They'd be insane with rage, and they'd strike back in any direction they could—such as Japan and Western Europe, neither of which are protected by Umbrella. You said yourself they'd threaten us if we threatened them."

Collison had sensed the inroads he had made on more than one conscience, and his answer was in a tone of confidence that came close to triumph. "A highly spurious assumption," he declared. "Kindly recall my analogy of the octopus. Destroy their primary military nerve centers including Moscow and you have nothing left but lifeless tentacles. There would be no leadership, no direction, no strategy on which to act. Nothing but aimless, short-lived floundering that we and our allies could crush in less than a month."

Secretary Sharkey recovered his senses. "What allies?" he demanded. "Do you think any civilized nation is going to applaud our starting a nuclear war? Admiral Cosley is right. We'd earn not gratitude but irreparable hatred, especially from those caught in the backlash of a mortally wounded nation."

Cosley's seamed face wore an expression of gratitude. "An excellent point, Mr. Secretary. And let's not forget their sizable submarine fleet. Most of it could survive a first strike, and they'd be prowling the seven seas looking for bloody revenge."

Collison said hurriedly and with a touch of anger, "Not against us they couldn't. Umbrella would stop anything nuclear they threw at us, and I'm quite sure, Admiral, your fleet is fully capable of countering a few conventional torpedo attacks."

General Ganoe snapped, "Goddamn it, Collison, they've got enough tactical nuclear weapons outside of Russia to blast all of Western Europe. Pandora's box describes the situation."

"They also have a network of air bases throughout their satellite countries—Poland, Czechoslovakia, Bulgaria, and so forth," Silvius added. "Our estimate is that the aircraft stationed at these bases number approximately three hundred strategic bombers, two thousand tactical bombers, and about fifteen hundred fighters. As the President has pointed out, this sizable force could be turned against Western Europe out of sheer revenge and probably would be hurled against the continental United States, even if they were largely suicide missions. Russian leaders may be a pack of gangsters, but the Russian fighting man is courageous, persistent, and unafraid of dying. I prefer the Pandora's box analogy to yours of the octopus."

Jeremy Haines felt his tension evaporating—the mood had turned against Collison.

The security chief knew it, too. "Who are you being loyal to?" he cried. "I'm only asking you to think of our own beloved country, reviled, despised, and humiliated for years by these godless monsters who break treaties at their leisure, enslave countless millions at their will. All I've heard from any of you is concern not for the United States but our so-called allies. Allies!"

His voice descended into a tonal valley of utter contempt. "Some allies—a bunch of greedy, selfish, self-centered hypocrites. They take but give nothing in return. We've saved their asses in two world wars and they continue to mock us, oppose us, even sneer at us. They desert us when the going gets rough, but when they're threatened they come whining for help. They extort, compete unfairly, and behind our backs regard us as suckers. We've financed their wars, their economies and their commerce, and our reward has been an unpayable, uncollectable debt with a collateral of ingratitude. We've given them the blood of our fighting men and the sinews of our industries. They've given us precisely nothing but burdens strapped to the backs of every American man, woman, and child since 1917.

"Well, it's time we considered our own welfare, not Europe's or anyone else's. I totally disagree that an attack on the Soviet Union would result in a counterattack on Western Europe. But even if it did, the stakes justify that risk. And in years to come, generations yet unborn—including those in *all* nations—will thank us for giving them freedom."

For a long, uneasy moment, the only sound in the room was a muffled cough from NASA director Pearson. Now, once again, Haines sensed the unstable shifting of emotional tides in that room back toward Collison. The President started to speak, but Admiral Cosley's gravelly voice broke the silence first.

"When you came to my office last week, Duane," he said, "you talked only about using Umbrella as a bargaining weapon. You didn't mention being in favor of a surprise attack."

Ganoe's hamhock-size fist was clenched as tightly as the lips that held his unlit cigar. "That was the same approach you used with me. You said nothing about precipitating a war."

"Likewise." This was from Vice President Mitchell. Jeremy Haines, white with anger, turned to Collison.

"So you've been running around town lying about your real intentions," he said coldly.

Collison said calmly, "I would have been tossed out of every office I visited if I had said what was really on my mind. My purpose, Mr. President, was to get a few influential military and civilian leaders at least to start *thinking* about what's at stake. Including yourself, sir."

"Nevertheless, campaigning behind my back amounts to disloyalty. You've exceeded your authority."

Collison retorted, "Sir, my job as chief of the National Security Council implies such authority. May I remind you, Mr. President, national security *is* the issue before us."

"You have a weird definition of national security," the President snapped. "It represents a line of reasoning that borders on sheer insanity."

A strange smile crossed Collison's handsome face, a flicker of triumph, a hint of smugness.

"If insanity is the issue here," he said with deadly evenness, "I suggest you explain to the Secretary of State, the Vice President, Mr. Pearson, and your top military advisers why you've found it necessary to have consulted at least two psychiatrists over the past few months."

Someone around the table gasped—the President, his furious eyes fixed on Collison, could not identify the source—and Sharkey blurted, "That's the most slanderous chunk of garbage I've ever heard!

Collison's smile tightened and hardened into a smirk. "Mr. Sharkey, it's neither slanderous nor garbage. I have been informed by sources I consider unfailingly reliable that the President apparently is suffering from some kind of mental aberration, serious enough for him to have sought medical help. I can even provide the names of those he consulted. Captain Catlin Baxter, chief of psychiatry at the Navy Medical Center, and a Dr. Jessica Sarazin, a prominent specialist in mental disease."

Sharkey snapped, "I don't believe it!" But as he turned toward Haines in a unspoken plea for denial, to his surprised horror the President was nodding placidly in obvious confirmation. Sharkey said in a stricken voice, "For God's sake, Jeremy, is he telling the truth?"

Haines said softly, "He is." The stern eyes of Admiral Cosley, set deep in his craggy face like two gun holes planted on the side of a lava-formed cliff, seemed to flash sparks of pained accusation. His strong, thin lips parted as if he were about to voice his thoughts but then pursed and all that emerged was an almost imperceptible whistle.

From the dry mouth of Gus Ganoe came one earthy expletive. "Shit," he muttered.

The President looked at Ganoe, who turned so red that Haines chuckled. He said affably, "An apt description, Gus, if we apply it to General Collison's inference that my seeing a pair of shrinks proves I'm going off my rocker. It would be interesting to reveal the source of his information, but I don't want to embarrass him in front of his peers."

He shifted his gaze toward Collison and his amused voice took on a tone of hardness. "Inasmuch as you've seen fit to bring up the matter, I believe I owe all of you an explanation. Yes, I've seen the two doctors the general has mentioned, for a very simple reason. Several months ago, I saw what appeared to be a ghost walking through one of the White House corridors. I thought I was imagining things, but a few nights later it happened again. I was concerned enough to confide my experiences to Cat Baxter who, in turn, recommended that I consult Dr. Sarazin. The latter happens to be not only a psychiatrist but a parapsychologist—in layman's terms, an expert on psychic phenomena or, if you prefer, ghosts."

Defense Secretary Hammond retrieved his voice. "A ghost of what?" he asked huskily.

"It was rather nebulous, but it appeared to be Abraham Lincoln."

The lie had come so easily that Haines felt like laughing, but the faces of his listeners—except for Silvius and Hammond, he noticed—wore expressions of disbelief. Hammond said in a hushed, almost reverent tone, "The White House is supposed to be haunted by Lincoln—I've heard that story many times. Up until now, I thought it was an old wives' tale."

A frowning Admiral Cosley asked, "Mr. President, forgive my curiosity, but what did this—this parapsychologist tell you? Did she have any explanation?"

Haines continued with fluid skill. "She reached no definite conclusion. She cited previous reports of Lincoln's ghost being seen around the White House, and as a parapsychologist she didn't discount the possibility that this place could be haunted. But she also told me anyone who's mentally and physically tired can imagine some weird things—a temporary form of hallucination at worst or a visual misinterpretation of what's being seen. Naturally, I lean toward the latter explanation. At any rate, I haven't encountered Mr. Lincoln's alleged ghost for quite some time, so I consider the matter closed—or did until General Collison chose to share his fears with you. Have I satisfied your curiosity, General?"

His tone was friendly, yet the underlying sarcasm was unmistakable, and Collison said sullenly, "Not quite. According to press reports, this Dr. Sarazin has been a rather frequent visitor to the White House—more frequently than your glib explanation would indicate. I believe you even spent a weekend with her on your brother's boat. Yet the official . . ."

Sharkey interrupted. "Collison, the President's social life is none of your goddamned business!"

"Please let me finish. I'm not talking about his social life. I'm referring to a frequency of contact with a psychiatrist that indicates a more serious problem than the President would have us believe. Press Secretary Dillman has publicly categorized Dr. Sarazin as a physician treating Mr. Haines for some back ailment. We now know that was an absolute falsehood—he's been seeing ghosts!" Collison's tone was self-righteously accusatory, and he gave the President a look of defiance.

Haines said, "Do you think I'm damned fool enough to announce to the world that Jessica Sarazin is my psychiatrist? The very word connotes the possibility of mental disease and my reason for passing her visits off as physical therapy is obvious, as your own wrong interpretation has demonstrated."

"Would you care to announce to the world you've seen the ghost of Abraham Lincoln?" Collison asked.

"I don't care to, but if it's necessary, I will."

The President's eyes swept the faces of the men around the conference table, trying to gauge their thoughts. He did not like what he saw. Of the three civilians, only Sharkey seemed sympathetic—Pearson and even Mitchell were watching him with expressions of disbelief. Cosley and Ganoe seemed stunned to the point of horror. In Silvius, however, Haines found a welcome ally.

"Let's drop it, Collison!" the Air Force chief barked. "I'd like to have a dollar for every sane man who's seen things that made him doubt his own sanity. And that includes me."

Admiral Cosley tossed him a quizzical glance but Silvius ignored it and continued.

"When I was a captain flying F-15s, I reported a UFO sighting that scared the hell out of me. It turned out to be an illusion caused by a temperature inversion. At least that was the official explanation, but to this day I'm not sure of what I *really* saw. I don't give a damn if the President thinks the ghost of Marilyn Monroe is stalking through these hallowed halls. The issue before us is your asinine notion that we should clobber the Soviets the minute Umbrella is activated. I not only vote no, but I must remind you that if the President followed the course you propose, it would horrify not just other nations but our own people."

"Are you quite sure of that?" Collison demanded.

"Very sure. Only a blind, jingoistic nut would favor it."

"There are more of your blind, jingoistic nuts out there than you're willing to admit. Every American would welcome the eradication of the Red menace, at a minimal cost to ourselves. A final, irrevocable removal of the sword of Damocles that has been hanging over our heads since Stalin."

The President said angrily, "No one would favor it if they understood all the ramifications. Gentlemen, I think I'll bring this meeting to a close. We'll be boarding a helicopter to Andrews in ten minutes."

Collison said hurriedly, "If I may, I'd like to ask one more question of my three military colleagues. Would you give me that privilege, sir?"

Haines sensed he was handing Collison a key to a locked, forbidden door, and he hesitated.

Collison pressed, "Just one question, Mr. President."

Haines nodded reluctantly.

"Admiral Cosley, General Silvius, and General

Ganoe, given the successful implementation of Operation Umbrella, do you believe a carefully selected nuclear attack on the Russian mainland would destroy the Soviets' capability of waging any kind of major offensive retaliation against the United States?"

Sharkey frowled impatiently, "For Christ's sake, we've already gone over that."

Collison said, "The President has allowed me to ask that one question. I deserve the courtesy of an honest answer."

Cosley exchanged glances with his two uniformed compatriots.

"Go ahead, Admiral," Silvius said, "I think you can speak for us. We've discussed this on more than one occasion." Ganoe nodded agreement.

"Very well. The answer to your question is yes. Ignoring all other considerations, we could destroy the heart of Soviet military power. They probably would fight on elsewhere, but in the end they'd be totally defeated."

Collison said with an air of justified triumph, "Out of your own mouth, Admiral. You've just admitted what I've been trying to tell all of you. And I implore you not to buy the Secretary of State's view that a summit meeting would ease tension. The only thing that would achieve is time—not time for us but for the Soviets! They'll stall and delay and promise anything, and you know what a Russian promise is worth. I tell you, when they achieve Umbrella, all their so-called talk will turn into renewed threats and demands. At which point the standoff the President is so willing to accept will become reality and we'll have to spend another hundred billion dollars on conventional weapons or let them rule the rest of the world. For God's sake, is that what you want?"

He glared defiantly at Haines, who saw once more in all their faces the terrible uncertainty that Collison had planted. His own throat was so choked he could not speak. It was Admiral Cosley who found his voice first.

"I suggest that the subject is moot until we see whether Umbrella works. Then we can discuss this on the way back from Houston."

Sharkey murmured, "I hope the goddamned thing goes down the tube."

The President said softly, "Gentlemen, I would appreciate your proceeding to the helicopter pad on the East Lawn. General Collison, please stay behind."

They filed out, more than one casting a final glance over their shoulders at the security chief and the President, still standing by the table. Ganoe, the last to leave, closed the door with the reluctant air of a man fervently wishing he could stay and hear what was to follow.

The President rose. "Duane, more than any man alive you deserve to see Operation Umbrella activated. It is a monument to your perseverance and energy. Under the circumstances, however, I believe it best that you not accompany this group to Houston." He hesitated, regret grafted onto the fatigue lines in his face. "I want your resignation, effective immediately, on my desk within the next ten minutes. If you don't care to compose it in your own handwriting, I'll furnish you with a typewriter. I'm sorry."

"The hell you are," Collison said, more in sadness

than in anger. "The tragedy is that, down deep, every man in this room knows I'm right. Maybe including yourself." He paused, a cynical smile creasing his lips. "If I could have proved you crazy, I could have swung them over once they saw what Umbrella could do, and the world would have been better for it. But you shot me down by admitting you saw some ghost, and least some of those damned fools bought it. Just for the record, Mr. President, I don't believe a word of it. I still think there's something wrong with you. Nobody could have seen that psychiatrist as often as you have without being a little bit crazy. But I don't suppose you'd admit it."

"No," Jeremy Haines said, "because I'm going to shoot you down again. Dr. Sarazin and I are in love—and that's one more item I don't want you carrying to Peter Frain. You did intend to tell him about those psychiatric visits, didn't you?"

Collison nodded. "I already told him, but he can't print anything unless I give him a go-ahead. He won't get one, of course. There's no point in it. You could explain the whole thing as a romance. And if I did, you'd ruin me, wouldn't you?"

"I'd have to," the President said, and he could not prevent a tone of sadness creeping into his voice. "Your boy Penn talked. I'm letting you off the hook because down deep in *your* heart, you honestly believe this is our last chance for real peace. And maybe you're right. I just can't push a button that would doom millions of people whose only crime is enforced loyalty to the wrong philosophy."

Collison rose, standing straight and tall. "You're

the biggest fool of them all. The great leaders of history know when to accept opportunity. You've turned your back on it because you're afraid. So let me tell you something—Umbrella won't be a success. It's already a dismal failure. It's just a temporary buffer that will disappear the minute the Soviets develop their own ABM system. Then they'll resume trampling over the rest of the world and you'll have more blood on your hands than you would if you took my advice. Good-bye, *Mr. President.*"

The slur in those two words hung in the air like a frozen jet contrail as Collison strode out, slamming the door of the Situation Room behind him. Haines winced as if the sound carried the impact of a punch. He had beaten Duane Collison, yet why did he feel so drained and depressed?

He knew why. The residue of Collison's arguments still existed in the minds and hearts of the others.

And in a few hours, they might be reinforced.

FIFTEEN

"*. . . five minutes to missile launch time.*"

The President of the United States and his seven stone-faced companions were in a glass-enclosed booth high above the main NASA launch control room at

NASA's Clear Lake, Texas, complex thirty-one miles from Houston.

Below them stretched the bewildering batteries of computers and communications consoles that were the lifelines to Operation Umbrella's network—nearly four hundred satellites armed with laser and energy beam weaponry, plus ten squadrons of the new F-25 supersonic fighters, each armed with a recently developed ASAT missile capable of devastating an enemy missile traveling at thirty thousand miles an hour.

Suspended from the wall, above their heads but well within their vision, were numerous closed circuit television screens, with most of their cameras focused on the individual areas of planned interception. On three of the screens Haines could see the hordes of F-25s climbing to their assigned interception altitudes like angry bees. On several others were the laser–energy beam satellites orbiting their prescribed courses; large spiked globes resembling oversized mines.

Operation Umbrella's chief project officer, Jerome Walton, sat next to the President. He was a lanky, red-haired man in his late forties, with twinkling blue eyes and a freckled countenance belying the awesome destruction at his fingertips—"Huck Finn in the middle of Armageddon," Sharkey had murmured to Haines after meeting Walton.

"Before everything hits the fan, Mr. President," Walton was saying, "do you have any questions that weren't covered in the briefing?"

Haines pointed to one screen displaying several killer satellites. "How are you getting that picture?"

"From camera-equipped satellites orbiting above Umbrella. The photographic satellites were launched ahead of them. And we have three F-25 camera planes accompanying the intercepting aircraft. Take a gander at Screen Six."

The President looked at a group of satellites slightly larger than the armed ones. "Those are part of Umbrella's own defensive shield," Walton said. "We know the Soviets would try to destroy the weaponry satellites, and our shield satellites fire a system of magnetized electrons that confuse the guidance system of an attack missile and divert its trajectory."

"Three minutes to missile launch".

Haines noticed that the young project director's face was pale, visible tension poking through the pleasant freckles. "Win or lose, Jerome," the President said, "you've done a hell of a job."

Walton's smile was more of a grimace. "Thank you, sir, but this is one game we can't afford to lose. There are no prizes for second place."

"Are you confident or merely hopeful?"

"Both. The big breakthrough was in the development of compact power units for generating the laser and energy beams. A few years ago, we needed a unit the size of three freight cars to fire a beam of only three hundred watts. Those laser satellites on Screen Two carry a generating unit the size of a microwave oven. Why, I remember . . ."

"One minute to missile launch."

General Ganoe, still chomping hard on an unlit cigar, glanced up at the loudspeaker carrying the metallic announcements. "Voice of doom," he said, and General Silvius merely nodded.

"*. . . fifty-seven . . . fifty-six . . . fifty-five . . . fifty-four . . .*"

Walton picked up a hand mike. "All stations and units stand by on the ready. The launch signal will come from Station One."

"*. . . twenty-two . . . twenty-one . . . twenty . . . nineteen . . .*"

Haines looked at Walton's hands clutching the microphone. They were covered with perspiration, but his voice remained boulder-steady.

"Repeat, the launch signal will come from Station One. The intercept signal will come from me. Stand by on the ready."

"*. . . six . . . five . . . four . . . three . . . two . . . one . . .*"

"This is Station One. Launch signal activated."

The eyes of every man in the booth swiveled toward the TV screens, Admiral Cosley's gravitating to the pair showing missiles rising out of the Pacific like a hundred fingers clawing at the sky. "Submarine launch," Cosley said to nobody in particular, his voice hoarse.

The camera satellite orbiting over Alaska had caught the missiles fired by the Alaskan Defense Command—scores upon scores of ugly, pencil-shaped giants blasting upward and curving into their prearranged paths. Only dimly did Haines hear Walton's laconic comment, "They're doing about twenty thousand miles an hour."

He spoke into the mike. "Interception consoles,

stand by *on the ready.*" This time, however, his voice cracked slightly on the last three words.

The President looked away from the screens to stare at the scene below the booth. Hundreds of men with fingers poised at consoles. He turned back to the screens.

The metallic voice again. "*One minute to F-25 intercept.*"

"There they go," General Silvius breathed. He was watching a V-formation of the fighters streaking westward.

"*. . . five seconds to F-25 intercept . . . three . . . two . . . one . . .*"

"Signal okay to fire," Walton said into the mike and added over his shoulder, "watch Screen Five and then Twelve."

On Screen Five, they saw the red-tipped, twenty-foot-long ASAT missiles leap from under the fighter's wings. Seconds later, Screen Twelve showed the sub-launched missiles curving through the skies one minute and suddenly disintegrating seconds later as if they had collided with an unseen brick wall fifty thousand feet high. Sharkey started to ask Pearson if any got through, but he never finished the question.

"Umbrella stations, stand by to intercept," Walton intoned. "Booth personnel, watch Screen Three. Those are the incoming missiles. They're over the Pacific about a thousand miles northwest of Los Angeles, speed twenty-one thousand miles an hour. Okay, here we go. Umbrella stations, *Intercept!*"

Laser streaks and invisible energy beams slashed from the killer satellites, moving at one hundred eighty-six thousand miles an hour—the speed of light—guided unerringly by the high-speed computers hooked to incredibly sensitive heat detectors; "The equivalent," Walton had said at the briefing, "of a sharpshooter standing only five feet from the bull's-eye. Fired from a thousand miles away, they will impact a twenty-thousand mile an hour target before it can cover fifty feet . . ."

Haines was watching Screen Three carefully, but neither he nor anyone else actually saw any impact. All that was visible was a series of blinding flashes and explosions that filled the screen, with no sense of detail. Eyes shifted to Screen Four, also a laser–energy impact point—but in the split second it took to switch views, Screen Four was showing nothing but empty space.

"My God," Silvius breathed.

"Amen," Sharkey said, crossing himself.

Walton ordered, "Main tracking station, report!"

Back came the metallic voice, unable to hide a tone of glee.

"*All missiles have been destroyed. Repeat, all missiles have been destroyed.*"

Only dimly did Jeremy Haines hear the cheering from the huge room below. Only dimly could he glimpse through uninvited tears the hundreds of men embracing one another and dancing in the aisles that bisected countless rows of electronic equipment. He turned to the Secretary of State and said in a choked voice, "Well, Jim, the damned thing works. Now we'll have to see if it really was worth ninety-eight billion dollars in the long run."

The euphoria he felt after witnessing Umbrella's success was temporary, lasting just long enough to walk through the crowd of technicians, engineers, and scientists on the main floor, a beaming and proud Jerome Walton by his side.

He felt pride himself as he shook more hands than he could count and looked into faces, most of them young, realizing with some irony from their awed expressions that the privilege of meeting the President of the United States was in its own way as exciting as what they had just accomplished. Their respectful murmurs of "Thank you, Mr. President," "Very proud to meet you, Mr. President," and one impish remark from a communications specialist—a pretty blond girl who couldn't have been more than twenty-five—who chirped, "Hope you enjoyed the fireworks, Mr. President."

His hand was a little sore when he finished the tour. After all the campaigning he had gone through—two for Governor and another two running for President—he had mastered the politician's self-preservation technique of touching flesh briefly in a crowd of well-wishers. But quite deliberately he had not bothered to use the technique with Umbrella's personnel. His handshakes had been firm, some of them lasting more than a few seconds as he conversed and exchanged quips. A sore hand was a small price to pay for the gratitude he felt and that he tried to put into words when Walton asked him to address Umbrella's team over the public address system.

"I will try to emulate Abraham Lincoln's wise advice," he began, "that a speech should be like a woman's dress—long enough to cover the subject and short enough to be interesting. So let me say simply that you all have made me enormously proud and indescribably grateful for this magnificent accomplishment. You have erected a fortress protecting freedom, a barrier to aggression, a bulwark against the horrors of nuclear war." He paused, knowing the importance of his next words, not just to Umbrella's workers but to the seven men who had accompanied him here. Seven men already swayed by Collison's damnable, insidious, almost irrefutable logic.

He resumed. "You have finished your task with courage and determination. You have left me with an even greater task. To make sure Operation Umbrella is employed in the sacred cause of peace, and not in the Satanic cause of war. It is a shield protecting not merely two hundred sixty million American lives but the dignity and the dreams of each of those lives. With Admiral Cosley's permission, may I just bestow on Jerome Walton and his entire team the Navy's traditional commendation—well done!"

But amid the waves of cheers and applause, he overheard General Ganoe whisper to Cosley, "Fortress, shield, barrier, bulwark—he might as well be describing a goddamned Maginot Line!"

And he steeled himself for what had to be fought out on the trip back to Washington.

They hadn't discussed Collison's arguments on the way to Houston. They had gone along with Cosley's advice that the whole subject remain moot pending Umbrella's outcome; by silent mutual agreement, no one mentioned Collison except for the President himself. He privately told Secretary Sharkey, "I fired him, Jim, but don't ask me any questions—I don't want to talk about it and I don't want the others to know, not yet."

Sharkey had merely nodded, murmuring, "I suppose it had to be done."

That *suppose* had bothered Haines. It sounded as if even Sharkey had been infected, a possibility that haunted the President. If James Sharkey was wavering, what about the others? Geoff Mitchell, especially, a heartbeat away from the Presidency . . .

Flying to Houston, Haines had deliberately avoided contact with the ghost by the simple expedient of inviting everyone to the upper lounge for the entire journey. He told himself it was more convenient and comfortable for such a small group, but he knew that wasn't the whole reason—he did not want to see FDR, not then, anyway. Wait until after Umbrella—that was when he might need support. He was desperately afraid that he might wind up standing alone against all seven—even Sharkey—for Collison's persuasive influence was only too obvious.

Cosley's suggestion that the matter be dropped until after Umbrella, for example; the admiral should have backed the President instead of procrastinating with a plea for further discussion. The way the others had acceded—with alacrity, as if they were postponing a disagreeable but necessary decision, a decision that should have been made right then, regardless of Umbrella. The looks they had given Haines when Pearson asked innocently, just as they boarded the helicopter that would take them to Andrews Air Force Base, "Aren't we going to wait for Duane?"

"He's, uh, decided not to come," Haines had explained—too weakly, he conceded, for those looks bordered on suspicion and maybe even disapproval.

On the helicopter taking them from Clear Lake to Houston, where Air Force One was waiting, Haines toyed briefly with the idea of retreating to the upper lounge for the entire flight home. He discarded this as cowardly, and he couldn't have gone through with it anyway—it was Sharkey himself who asked if they could all come up to the lounge en route back to Washington.

"We've got to talk, Jeremy," he pleaded, and the very use of the President's first name demonstrated his agitation. Close friends though they were, rare was the occasion when the Secretary of State didn't address him as Mr. President.

So Haines acquiesced, fretfully undecided whether he was pleased or disappointed that their presence would preclude another meeting with Roosevelt. He understood this ambivalence only too well—he had grown tired of the unreality, even as he admitted missing the strange companionship. Plus, he thought with a nagging throb of guilt, the stimulating and provocative ideas springing from the agile mind and enunciated by the hypnotic golden tongue.

Maybe Jessica was right. He had become too dependent on the ghost and the real source of his discontent was his still-existing need for FDR's counsel. Especially now, shaken and awed as they all were at what they had just seen.

The Air Force steward had left, accompanied by McNulty, after serving them drinks. Admiral Cosley got to the point immediately, although his voice was unsteady as if the words were being propelled over rocks in his throat. "God forgive me, Mr. President, but what I saw today—what we *all* saw—convinces me Collison may be right. We could clobber the sons of bitches. Get it over with once and for all."

Haines let his eyes cruise around the lounge, searching their faces. On Ganoe's he saw regret—but agreement. The tight-lipped Silvius merely nodded, unable to speak.

The Vice President said chokingly, "I think we should discuss this further." Haines felt a surge of relief, but Mitchell added miserably, "We've got to sleep on this because if we took a vote right now I'd have to go with Collison."

The President's heart sank. He would have trusted Geoff Mitchell to stand by him more than anyone in his administration with the exception of Sharkey. He looked at the Secretary of State; Sharkey's face was white.

"Well, Jim," Haines asked, "whose bandwagon are *you* going to ride?"

"Yours," Sharkey muttered, "but I never thought I'd see the day when I'd be wondering if it's the right bandwagon." He saw the President's startled, hurt expression but he said bravely, "I'm sorry, but I didn't count on what happened today. I didn't really expect Umbrella to work that well, and when it did—Mr. President, as God is my witness—I began to see what Duane Collison was telling us. Believe me, I'm not saying he's justified, but the thought of giving Russia a year in which to match that system scares the hell out of me."

Defense Secretary Hammond stared glumly into the stiff Manhattan the steward had mixed. His tie was loose and askew, and for such a fastidious person it gave the impression his inner tensions had somehow disarranged his clothing.

"How about you, John?" Haines asked.

Hammond looked up and shook his head. "I just don't know. I can't believe what we just witnessed. And I don't mind admitting that when those explosions filled the screens—when I heard that *all missiles destroyed*—well, I kept thinking of what Duane told us. Operation Last Chance, he called it. And now I can't decide what's right or wrong anymore."

Dave Pearson said unhappily, "That's my reaction, too. I don't even want to give you my opinion as of right now because I'd have to say, 'Let's get it over with.' Maybe if I sleep on it . . ." His voice trailed off, diminishing in direct correlation with his sagging conscience.

Sharkey said quietly, "The eventual choice has to be yours, Mr. President. There could be no declaration of war by Congress. You would have to order an attack under the War Powers Act."

"Which applies only when the President determines there is a national emergency so grave that he hasn't time to ask Congress for authority to wage war," Haines said tartly. "In effect, you're asking me to shoot first and explain later. And what kind of an explanation am I supposed to give? What justification would I have for killing millions of innocent civilians? That Russia was going to attack first and we had to beat 'em to the draw? I yield to no man in my contempt, hatred, and even fear of the Soviets, but I can't rationalize those feelings into a claim of justifiable mass homicide."

Cosley said doggedly, "They'd attack us sooner or later if they thought they could win. We all know that."

Ganoe rasped, "And on their own timetable, when they figure the odds are in their favor. At best, they'd settle for the status quo they enjoyed before Umbrella—nobody dares use nuclear weapons, them or us, so they'd keep doing what they damn well please. Look, Mr. President, this uniform I'm wearing doesn't automatically mean I'm a war lover. Anybody who likes killing for the sake of killing is a psychopath. But I'm a soldier who believes you can kill for just cause. A professional, if you will, who knows the ugly truth about modern war—it can no longer be fought just by professionals. Civilians have to die, too. And nobody, sir—not even yourself—can tell me that wiping out a self-admitted enemy, one publicly and fervently dedicated to our eventual destruction, doesn't constitute just cause."

"Those also are my sentiments, Mr. President," Admiral Cosley said firmly.

"I regret to say they're mine, too," General Silvius declared. "Not until I saw with my own eyes the advantage Operation Umbrella gives us did I grasp the import of Collison's arguments. Sir, from the start of World War Two right up to the present, air power has been responsible for more civilian casualities than any other form of weaponry. A B-17 crew dropping bombs into the heart of a city were no less mass murderers than the men who push the firing buttons on our ICBMs. And with all due respect, sir, I don't consider myself a callous monster for feeling that way."

Vice President Mitchell sighed heavily. "As the Secretary of State pointed out, Mr. President, the decision has to be yours, not ours. I can only thank God it isn't my decision. I may be wrong, tragically wrong, but I must confess I've been impressed with what these military men have said. When Duane Collison argued for such an attack, I thought he was crazy—and if I remember correctly, so did the admiral, here, and likewise Ganoe and Silvius. But that was before Umbrella."

Jeremy Haines rose. "As Jim Sharkey said, the decision *is* mine. Gentlemen, if you don't mind I'd like to be alone for the rest of this flight. Quite obviously, I have some momentous thinking to do. I appreciate your candor, and I respect your opinions. Whether I eventually come to agree with them is something perhaps a little solitude and a lot of prayer will help me determine."

They filed down the spiral staircase. Sharkey, the last in line, turned back and said to the President, "Jeremy, I still wish the goddamned thing hadn't worked."

He sat alone, brooding, as the huge 747 sped northward. His mind was cluttered and confused; he found it impossible to resent what the others had said, for he had to admit there was a part of him siding with Collison.

He shook his head with the impatient frustration of

a man losing a battle and decided he might as well get out of the lounge. He toyed with the idea of going up to the comfortable technical sanity of the cockpit, then decided against it. Better to join the others downstairs—some convivial unity, however false, was more conducive to resisting the allurement of a holy war.

It was at that moment, as he rose from his chair, that he felt the chill.

"Good evening, Jeremy," said Franklin Delano Roosevelt.

Haines sat down heavily, again not sure whether he was glad or sorry. "I'm a little surprised to see you," he managed. "I'm accustomed to your showing up the minute I'm alone up here. When you didn't appear right on schedule, I figured our association might be over."

"Almost, but not quite. Frankly, I needed a little time to collect my thoughts. Like you and your colleagues, I was anxious to see how Umbrella went. A very impressive show, my friend. Momentous is the word for it—absolutely momentous! Its significance is earthshaking."

Haines said dryly, "A ninety-eight-billion-dollar monument to Russian paranoia and to our own fears. I can't help but wonder how much good we could do if we spent ninety-eight billion dollars on medical research, eliminating poverty, and feeding the world's hungry."

"My sentiments exactly," the ghost agreed with a sad smile. "Unfortunately, we've been making that unhappy equation for generations—our perpetual desire to turn swords into plowshares. The trouble is we can't have plowshares if we don't have swords to protect us from the world's despots. Umbrella is a sword. The mightiest known to civilization."

"A shield," Haines corrected. "And a temporary one at that."

FDR's eyes narrowed. "I know. I'm aware of that little meeting at the White House. You emasculated him, didn't you?"

"The surgery was necessary."

The ghost's eyebrows arched. "Was it? Pardon my candor, Jeremy, but he only spoke the truth as he saw it. And very effectively, too. You told me he could be most persuasive and I have to agree with that assessment. Collison's a remarkable person. God, but he reminds me of Doug MacArthur. The same eloquence. The same cool-headed, irrefutable logic."

Haines said sharply, "Cold-blooded logic, not cool-headed."

The eyebrows arched again. "Ah, but tempting logic! Sorely tempting. Don't deny it, Jeremy. I *know*. I could sense the atmosphere in that room. A kind of reluctant antagonism. A collection of consciences wrestling with convictions they were afraid to admit. Now they've admitted those convictions, and you're almost ready to yourself. Am I right?"

"You're right up to a point. But my own conscience will prevail, not over conviction but an insane temptation." He looked at Roosevelt curiously and a little dubiously. "I'm almost afraid to ask this, but are you siding with my colleagues?"

FDR laughed. "Let's say I'm playing a bit of the devil's advocate. I would admit that General Collison made a pretty good case. I absolutely loved his phrase

Operation Last Chance—that one was worthy of me! In essence, my friend, Umbrella is our last chance to avoid either of two unpleasant alternatives. A continuation of the status quo, in which the Soviets can just about call their shots because no one wants a nuclear war. Or, as Collison so beautifully argued, we're pushed to the brink of Armageddon or to surrender."

Haines stared at him. "There is a third alternative. Keeping this uneasy peace with the hope that eventually the Russian people themselves get fed up with their masters."

The great head leaned back. FDR laughed derisively. "Come now, that's a noble hope but a totally unrealistic one. No state as heavily armed and security-conscious as the Soviet Union would let revolt get off the ground. They're exceptionally skilled at stifling dissent. Furthermore, the Russian people have been brainwashed for generations into acceptance of communism as a way of life. And conversely, to regard us as a bunch of threatening, immoral gangsters. Those teachings begin at childhood, and it's a rare Russian citizen who thinks otherwise."

The President said bitterly, "You're the last one I expected to deny the existence of human dignity. The innate desire to be free."

The muscles on the massive jaw tightened. "I don't deny it," he said quietly. "I simply point out that to a child weaned by the State, communism is his *own* form of freedom. He knows nothing else nor is he allowed to experience anything else. That is communism's greatest evil and also its strength."

"If I accepted such reasoning, I'd be close to accepting Collison's."

Roosevelt said with slow deliberateness, "Perhaps you should."

An alarm bell sounded in the President's brain. The ghost's eyes were burning with intensity, and Haines could see the muscles in that jutting jaw oscillate and tighten.

He said in a harsh whisper, "You want what he wants, don't you?"

"Yes."

"A course only Satan himself would propose."

FDR managed a laugh without smiling. "If you believe I'm the Devil incarnate, forget it. Satan resides only within ourselves. No, my friend, I'm not the essence of evil. If anything, his Satanic Majesty would choose the road *you* would travel. The same highway of unrelieved tension, unchecked aggression, and unbearable suffering by the innocent."

"The innocent," Haines said bitterly, "include Russian civilians."

The ghost sighed, "Jeremy, listen to me. Listen carefully. If you have a God-given chance to wipe out a sworn enemy, not merely of us but of all free men, you must be prepared to kill these so-called innocents. Except they're not really so innocent, are they? Virtually every Russian child is a potential future menace, his hatred for us inbred and as inherent as if that hatred had been planted in his genes."

"They're no different from us," the President said hoarsely. "You can't murder millions because they've been raised under oppression and have been taught to hate."

"Under these circumstances, namely Operation Umbrella, it's a tragic necessity." The magic voice rose, the lilt and cadence hypnotic in its power. "Think, Jeremy! Think! Only a few moments ago you said how much better it would be if we could take the millions we spend on weapons and divert them to mankind's common good. Spend them on a war against starvation and disease. There's only one way to do it, and you know the answer as well as I do. So do the people on this airplane. Destroy the heart of communism and you'll achieve the dream of world peace. Accept the fact that some people must perish."

"Including innocent men, women, and children."

"Including them, if you will. I sent thousands to die. Like your General Silvius and Ganoe, I regret their deaths but not the cause for which they died. Death is the same, whether it comes from a bullet, a bomb, a shell, a torpedo, or a nuclear explosion. You cannot consider death as a reason not to follow a cause. And the cause has not changed—what you face is not one whit different from what I faced. A communist is a blood brother of a Nazi, holding the same disregard for the human dignity you hold so dear."

Haines breathed, "I'd be damned throughout eternity."

"Damned by some at first, but that's a small price to pay for a future of peace. Eventually you'll go down as a courageous leader to rank with history's greatest."

"I'll go down as a mass murderer," the President grated.

"A savior, not a murderer. God himself has given you this choice."

"I can't do it." Haines's heart was pounding, a hammer of horror as resistance weakened.

"Yes, you can. This very night. From this plane itself you could order the attack. These men with you—they're already on your side. Even Sharkey. They want this as much as you do, and you trust them, don't you?"

The President stared at Roosevelt. "They trust *me*," he said quietly. "They don't want to make the decision."

"And rightly so. *You're* the President of the United States. So get out of that damned chair of indecision, *Mr. President*. Walk through that door. Behind it is freedom for the world, with just the push of a few buttons."

"The push of a few buttons," Haines repeated dully. "With death for millions at my fingertips."

"Don't think of those who must die. Think only of those who will now be able to live."

Haines said, slowly and distinctly, in a voice as intense as the ghost's, "I have to think of both."

FDR frowned. "You're avoiding the issue."

"Postponing, not avoiding. One thing's for certain—I'm not going into that comm area to push those buttons. Not tonight. There has to be an alternative. There *must* be."

"Waiting hopefully for the Russian people to revolt?" Roosevelt asked, his tone mildly mocking.

"No. As you yourself pointed out, it is not likely to happen and if it does, it might take another generation. Perhaps longer, and maybe never. There would have to be some incentive . . ."

His voice trailed off; the ghost watched him carefully. The President's eyes had narrowed and his forehead wore crevices that seemed to have been forged by some internal pressure, like fissures in a volcanic ground.

"I venture to guess an alternative has occurred to you," FDR murmured.

"It has. Not a very pleasant one, but an alternative nevertheless."

"I would very much appreciate your confiding in me, Jeremy."

"No doubt," Haines said dryly. "Maybe I will eventually but my thinking hasn't quite jelled."

The ghost chuckled. "Your use of the word *maybe* indicates the possibility that our association is about to end."

The look Haines gave him was one of firmness tinged with regret. "The advice you've given me tonight has convinced me the relationship *must end.*"

"A pity," Roosevelt said affably. "Yet inevitable, I suppose. I seem to have outlived my usefulness. Ha-ha!" He smiled again, and Haines could not tell whether it was friendly or sardonic. "Be that as it may, I don't think you can get rid of me so easily. I feel it's essential I stick around long enough to ascertain what that devious mind of yours is concocting."

"*Devious* could be an excellent choice of words," the President conceded with a tight grin. "It seems some of that quality in you has rubbed off on me."

"Touché!" the ghost laughed. "Jeremy, you are either the greatest fool in the world—which happens to be my honest conviction—or you're a bigger gambler than I was. Good night, my friend."

FDR disappeared.

For a long time, the President sat in silent meditation, looking at the empty chair in front of him. He could almost see the ghost, hear the spellbinding voice, sense the commanding presence.

He picked up the intercom.

"McNulty here."

"Mike, tell General Silvius I want to see him. Alone."

"Yes, sir."

The Air Force chief arrived in the upper lounge less than a minute after Haines's summons. He was panting a little, and the President deduced that the general must have sprinted up the stairs. Anticipation of a strike command? No, Haines decided, the look on the officer's face was one of concern bordering on dread, as if Silvius was now having second thoughts about a decision he himself had urged.

"You wanted to see me, sir?"

"Sit down, George. I'd offer you a drink, but we'll be landing shortly and we don't have time for pleasantries."

Silvius obeyed, sitting upright and rather stiffly on the edge of the chair the ghost had just vacated. Years of disciplined emotions had painted an expressionless mask on his face, but Haines noticed that the general's hands were trembling.

"George, when we land I want you to accompany me to the Pentagon. I'm going to make a phone call of sorts."

"A phone call, sir?"

"I'm going to use the hot line to the Kremlin."

The mask disintegrated. Silvius, his eyes wide, swallowed hard, and blurted, "An ultimatum, Mr. President?"

"Not exactly. More in the nature of a firm request. I want to meet that son of a bitch Magoyan face-to-face, and with as few people present as possible. What's the name of your Soviet counterpart—the general you once told me was a pretty decent guy for a Russian?"

Silvius gulped again. "Balenov, sir. I've met him only once, at the Paris Air Show. Tough, competent, and surprisingly honest. We got along well."

"Good. I'm going to advise the Premier that only the four of us will be meeting. You and I, Mr. Magoyan and this General Balenov. I know Magoyan speaks English fluently. Does Balenov?"

"Thickly accented, but very understandable. May I ask, sir, if you're inviting them to Washington?"

"No, I'm inviting myself to Moscow. Plus yourself, one Secret Service agent—McNulty, I think—and the crew of Air Force One. In absolute secrecy, George. I don't want anyone to know about this trip, not even the Secretary of State. We'll have to brief Cardella and his people, of course. They'll have to stay with the plane while we're at the Kremlin and so will McNulty, who'll probably raise hell. And you're going to have to make the necessary arrangements for clearance into Soviet air space. I suggest you ask Balenov to expedite these matters, via the hot line. Funny thing, that hot line."

"Funny, sir?"

"Not in a humorous sense. It's just that most people think the hot line is a special telephone link between the White House and the Kremlin. They don't realize it's a teletype hookup in the Pentagon, installed after the 1962 Cuban missile crisis."

"You're the only president who's ever used it," Silvius remembered, awe in his voice.

"True, during my first term." The President's features tightened into an expression of grimness. "I used the hot line to set up the meeting with Premier Bujesky at Camp David. That beautifully orchestrated scenario for secrecy I wrote." His voice turned bitter. "Some scenario. It cost sixteen lives and all for a useless treaty that didn't last long enough for the ink to dry."

"No one blamed you, Mr. President," Silvius murmured dutifully. He had heard that Haines still wore the crash of the earlier Air Force One around his neck like the Ancient Mariner's albatross, but not until this moment had he realized the extent of the President's guilt. He had a sudden, disturbing sense of déjà vu—now Haines was proposing another secret flight of unknown consequences.

Almost as if he could read the general's mind, Haines sighed heavily and said, as much to himself as Silvius, "Well, let's hope this little jaunt turns out to be more productive."

A lifetime of unquestioning obedience to superiors failed to quell the Air Force chief's curiosity. "Sir, why am I the only one going with you? Admiral Cosley is my senior and chairman of the joint chiefs as well. It would . . ."

The President interrupted. "You run the Air Force, George. Operation Umbrella's under your direct command. I'm sorry I can't tell you any more than that at the present. Frankly, I have to solidify my own thinking before I brief you, and I'll do that on the way to Moscow. Meanwhile, I want you to promise me something. Regard it as a direct order if you find it collides with your conscience."

Silvius stared at the President and instinctively, almost imperceptibly, squared his shoulders. "You're the commander-in-chief, sir. No more need be said."

"I appreciate that," Haines said feelingly. "More than you'll ever realize." He hesitated, his own mind grappling with the enormity of what he was about to say. "General Silvius, no matter what I tell Premier Magoyan, you are to back me up completely. You will not contradict me or correct me, even if you know I'm uttering complete falsehoods. Is that clear?"

"Yes, sir," snapped the Air Force chief of staff.

SIXTEEN

Jeremy Haines would have been far more nervous facing the Soviet premier had he not sensed immediately that Andrei Magoyan was nervous, too.

From the very first, firm handshake, the beefy Russian obviously was trying to walk a tightrope between hospitable protocol and maintaining his reputation for tough belligerence. He did not quite succeed in either—the hospitality was a bit forced and the belligerence was softened by undisguisable curiosity.

The hot line request for a meeting had come to the

Kremlin's complete surprise. Almost as surprising were the conditions Haines had laid down. The visit was to be kept absolutely secret, and the meeting itself would involve only the four men the President had designated as participants. Both requisites had intrigued Magoyan.

"They would indicate some American proposal of a unique nature, don't you think?" he had inquired of General Balenov.

Balenov guessed, "Possibly something to do with their recent anti-missile system test. As I informed you, Excellency, all indications are that it was very successful."

"An ultimatum, perhaps? I seem to recall telling you that's what I would have done if our positions were reversed."

"I'm afraid, sir, we'll just have to wait for their arrival. I would hate to speculate on the motives behind this visit, except to express great curiosity as to the presence of my distinguished counterpart, General Silvius."

"You know him?"

"I met him once in Paris. An outstanding officer, in my opinion, but relatively junior in their upper-echelon chain of command. I cannot hazard a guess as to why the President chose him for this mission, but I assume it has something to do with that damned missile defense system. It's under the jurisdiction of the American Air Force."

"Then it must be some kind of ultimatum," Magoyan had said worriedly. "General, we should be careful not to show the slightest semblance of concern. In that respect, you must follow my lead . . ."

". . . I trust you had a pleasant flight, Mr. President," Magoyan was saying to Haines. "I'm sorry I was unable to greet you at the field but I left the welcoming amenities to General Balenov, here."

Haines responded, "Very pleasant, Mr. Premier, and General Balenov has been both kind and courteous." He refrained from admitting the flight had been an abysmal bore; the first two hours were spent briefing Silvius on what he intended to tell the Russians, and a subsequent discussion during which the sober-faced general tried to postulate the Soviets' probable reactions. Silvius had then left the upper lounge at the President's request—"I'd like to catch a little cat-nap," he explained—and Haines had waited in vain for the ghost to appear.

I'm definitely on my own here, he thought as he accepted Magoyan's invitation to sit down at a small oval table. *Just as well—even a gambler like Roosevelt, a skilled practitioner of the art of calculated risk, would raise his eyebrows at what I'm trying to pull off.*

"I regret your insistence on total secrecy," the Premier said pleasantly. "It would be a pleasure and a privilege to tender you a state dinner. After all, you're the first American President to visit Moscow since your Mr. Nixon."

Haines said easily, "Perhaps sometime in the future, when relations between our two countries have improved, you could see fit to invite me for more of a social visit."

"Nothing would give me greater satisfaction than to see those relations improve," Magoyan said quickly. "However, the conditions you laid down for this meeting gives me some cause for concern, starting with your request to land at a military field rather than at the Moscow airport. Not even your own people know of this trip—an exceptional feat in itself, given the inquisitive nature of the American press. How are you explaining your absence from official duties?"

"The official explanation is that I'm suffering from a particularly nasty cold and that I won't resume normal activities for several days. By the time the news media starts speculating that I might be seriously ill, I'll be back in Washington. And as for not wanting to land at a civil airport, again I intend this trip to be kept secret."

Magoyan smiled thinly. "That would indicate an unusually brief visit. So I have to ask if you've come in friendship or to threaten us."

Haines said cautiously, "I do not intend to threaten, but merely to state some facts of which you may be unaware. After I state them, the interpretation is up to you."

"If these so-called facts involve your Operation Umbrella, I am fully aware. But let me add that its allegedly successful test doesn't frighten me in the slightest. We have perfected the same impervious system." He glanced at Balenov. "Isn't that true, Comrade General?"

The Soviet officer coughed, caught the Premier's eyes, and said quickly, "We have the same anti-missile capabilities that you do, Mr. President."

Haines said matter-of-factly, "If you want to believe that, go right ahead. But our intelligence reports contradict that claim. It is my understanding that you're two years away from achieving the capability of Umbrella."

Magoyan's voice rose in anger. "So you *are* threatening us!"

"No, although I dare say if the shoe were on the other foot, *you'd* be threatening *us*." Haines missed the sliver of a smile on Balenov's lips, but Silvius saw it and chuckled to himself.

The President continued. "Please believe me, Mr. Premier, when I tell you the thought of waging a nuclear war against the Soviet Union is absolutely abhorrent to me. But you might as well know the truth. The success of Operation Umbrella has prompted many American leaders, including a number of my own closest advisers, to consider an attack upon your country."

"It would be defeated and we would crush you in retaliation!" Magoyan sputtered. "How dare you . . ."

"Calm down," Haines said firmly. "I have rejected this advice even though I've been tempted to accept it."

"A wise decision," Magoyan sneered. "If our anti-missile systems cancel out each other, then we hold the balance of power with our superior conventional forces."

"You can cling to that self-delusion all you want," the President replied, "but I happen to know it's just that—delusion."

"Are you calling me a liar?"

Haines grinned. "I prefer to regard your confidence in Russian anti-missile progress as understandable, perhaps even justified, exaggeration. I might resort to the same self-deception if I were in your position. The point is, Mr. Magoyan, I'm convinced *we* hold the balance of power, or I wouldn't have traveled nine thousand miles to emphasize my conviction."

The Russian permitted himself a sly smile in return. "I suggest that your coming here instead of insisting on my going to Washington could be interpreted as a sign of weakness, not strength. What's the expression—hat in hand?"

"Your command of the English language is admirable, but your colloquialism is somewhat misplaced. Let's say I came with hat in one hand and a sword in the other. Quite frankly, I made the long trip as a gesture of friendship. A willingness to discuss the futures of our two countries. A hope of establishing some kind of live-and-let-live policy."

"The Soviet Union," Magoyan said ponderously, "has never interfered with the internal affairs of the United States. The United States, on the other hand, has consistently tried to interfere with our efforts to assure the existence of governments friendly to us and the goals of socialism."

"Futilely, I'm sorry to say. At least, up to now."

Magoyan's heavy features twisted into an angry scowl. "Again, Mr. President, that sounds like a threat."

"That's *your* interpretation. Let me emphasize, sir, if the Russian people want to live under a communist form of government, that's their choice. The quarrel we have with you is Soviet dominance over millions of people who may or may not want to live under that form of government. If they do, fine—that's their choice and we'd accept it. But they have no opportunity to voice anything to the contrary."

"If you're suggesting, or perhaps demanding, that we allow free elections in every satellite nation, you are wasting your time. Too many people in those countries already have been poisoned by American lies and propaganda. And may I add, Mr. President, that the diatribes and insults heaped on the Soviet Union by your predecessors for years has only contributed to our resolve that the Soviet bloc of nations must stand united against American aggression."

"An excellent point, Mr. Premier," Haines acknowledged, and the Russian's eyebrows lifted to full staff.

"You agree?" he asked in a surprised voice.

"Partially. I agree we fear the Soviet Union and you fear us, whether rightly or wrong on either part is not the issue. I happen to believe, with all my heart, that your fears are unjustified and that ours has far more logic behind it. I readily admit that our words give you cause for fear, but I also ask you to understand that Soviet actions, as well as Soviet words, have given *us* cause for fear. And I don't have to enunciate those actions—you know what I'm talking about."

Magoyan said, "Our actions always have been protectionist, not aggressive. They are defensive measures, taken to guarantee Soviet security."

Haines leaned forward, his voice assuming an intensity that seemed to shimmer the air between the two men like waves of heat. "Taken out of fear. Misguided, tragically erroneous fear but, nevertheless, fear. I will concede this, and I will also concede that for the next two years you have every reason to fear us. Boast of anti-missile equality all you want, but it's an empty boast and *you know I'm speaking the truth!*"

For the first time, the look of arrogant confidence on Magoyan's face wavered. He blustered, "A dangerous assumption on your part," but Haines knew the Premier was shaken.

The President said, "I'm afraid it's no assumption. Let me be candid with you, sir. Hypocrisy is not among my many faults. I detest communism and all it stands for, the total supremacy of the State over the rights and dignity of the individual. But I don't propose to turn this meeting into a senseless debate over our respective philosophies—you'll never understand ours, and God knows, I can't even begin to understand yours. Honesty compels me to state that I hope the day will come when the Russian people themselves will force changes in your system of government."

Magoyan smiled sourly, "I hope the same for the American people, when they realize the basic superiority of socialism over the selfishness and greed of capitalism. But that doesn't mean we have to go to war to prove which system is best."

Haines nodded. "I agree, so let's stop fencing." He looked squarely into Magoyan's eyes and continued calmly, "Mr. Premier, we have the means of badly hurting the Soviet Union and its satellites without resorting to armed conflict."

The Russian stared back, defiance wrestling with sudden alarm.

"May I ask the President in what form this inexcusable aggression would materialize?"

Jeremy Haines said, "We can control the weather over any spot on the globe we choose."

From General Balenov came an audible gulp, the only sound in the ornate room for a long, tense minute. The Premier's harsh, guttural voice broke the uneasy silence.

"I regard this as a scientific impossibility," he declared.

Haines shook his head. "I'm afraid you're wrong. We discovered, almost accidently, the weather-control phenomenon during our work on Operation Umbrella. I won't go into the scientific details but in essence we found that highly concentrated laser beams, generated by the same satellites that constitute Umbrella's anti-missile screen, could be aimed at weather fronts—breaking them up or even changing their course."

He paused, then added ominously, "We can cause droughts of catastrophic proportions."

Magoyan snapped, "We are not without our own laser technology. If you dare to wage a war of weather, we would respond in kind."

Again Haines shook his head, almost sadly. "You persist in a boast we both know is untrue. If you're two years behind in an anti-missile system, you're just as far behind in applying the ancillary effects on weather. Furthermore, Mr. Premier, my own scientists have informed me that such application on a large scale was as difficult to achieve as development of laser defense capability itself. It is their carefully considered opinion that the Soviet Union would need at least three years to perfect a similar system of weather control."

General Balenov found his voice. "Mr. President, assuming you're telling the truth, I submit that drought-generated starvation is as cruel a method of waging war as nuclear destruction. The latter has the advantage of being mercifully quick."

"Precisely," his superior almost snarled. "You *have* come to threaten us! To blackmail us!"

"No," Haines replied, "I've come to plead for

some kind of positive action by the Soviet Union—let's say a gesture of good will, one of sufficient import to enable me to resist those in my own administration who frankly would have me destroy your country by any means possible."

Magoyan said tersely, "A gesture more of surrender than good will."

Balenov broke in. "I would like to ask General Silvius, as one soldier to another, to confirm what his President has told us. Is weather control feasible?"

"It is," Silvius answered.

"Your sacred word of honor, as an officer?"

"I'm a graduate of West Point, General. Its motto is *Duty, Honor, Country*. I do not regard any of those three words lightly, and I hold all three in equal importance. I hope that is sufficient assurance."

Balenov nodded and turned to the President. "Can you end droughts as well as cause them?"

Haines said in a tone of regret, "No, not at present, although our scientists are working on that possibility. I don't pretend to understand the technical reasons, but thus far we've only been able to prevent precipitation, not create it. I hope that achievement will be attained shortly because the benefits to mankind would be obvious."

The Soviet premier rose and walked over to a window, staring out aimlessly before turning abruptly and facing Haines again.

"Do you have a specific, so-called good-will gesture in mind? For the sake of argument, shall we say?"

"I have. A relatively simple one."

"Which is?"

"Permit the unification of East and West Germany. It's something they both have sought for years. A divided Germany makes no sense anymore. Nor would a unified Germany offer any threat to either of us."

Magoyan could not hide his surprise. "You'd regard this as a gesture of peace? A means of relaxing tension?"

"Definitely. It would indicate at least a start toward relaxing the Soviet hold on its satellite countries. Enough to impress those Americans who regard Russia as a permanent, intractable enemy. I need such ammunition, Mr. Premier. And that's why I beg of you not to regard my proposal as threat or blackmail. I suspect we both are plagued by hotheads in our own official families."

The latter was pure blarney, for Haines knew Magoyan was the worst hothead of them all, but he had grasped that the Premier's ego was roughly the size of the Kremlin itself and he was pleased to see Magoyan nod energetically. What he didn't notice, but which Silvius did, was the almost imperceptible smile on the lips of the Soviet air chief.

Magoyan said in a friendly tone, "What you request is not an impossibility. Certainly I'd be willing at least to consider it seriously."

"That's all I ask," Haines assured him, then added, "for the time being, of course."

Magoyan frowned unhappily. "That sounds suspiciously like 'do it or else.' It seems to me you're warning that a unified Germany will not be your last demand. If you intend to hold the sword of Damocles over our heads permanently, there can be no peaceful coexistence between our two countries."

"That sword would be held over Russia's head only for the two or three years it will take you to match Umbrella. I propose to use this period to ease our mutual tensions and to establish not merely an atmosphere of coexistence but one of mutual cooperation."

"What kind of cooperation?"

"Russia's Achilles' heel is agriculture. I don't think it's necessary for me to detail the supporting evidence. But I can promise you that a few peaceful overtures on your part, with German unification as a starter, will result in our willingness to offer the Soviet Union considerable agricultural technological help."

Magoyan snorted, "Agricultural aid is a far cry from an implied threat to wreck our agriculture with this alleged weather weapon."

"The choice is yours, not mine. I don't relish using food as a weapon, but I must remind you that lack of food has been a causal factor in more than one revolution."

For the first time, a look of grudging admiration crossed the broad Slavic features, and the rumble of an irrepressible chuckle emerged from the Premier's chest. "Now *that's* a threat I can understand," he admitted. "A useless threat, I must warn you—the Russian people have proved their endurance and courage time and again—but I admire the subtlety of your, shall we say, approach. Again, for the sake of argument, Mr. President, please elaborate on what you choose to label *a few peaceful overtures.*"

Haines felt like taking a deep breath before replying. There was no way to predict the reactions of this volatile man, so imbued with the paranoic suspicions and blind nationalism of the Russian mind.

"I would suspect," he ventured, "it would favorably impress quite a few anti-Soviet individuals if the USSR finally made some financial restitutions to the families of those who died when you shot down that Korean airliner several years ago."

To the President's amazement, Magoyan registered more surprise than anger. In an almost puzzled tone, he said, "That event occurred so long ago I can't believe you're resurrecting it as an example of Soviet-American tension. Why, I was a minor official in the Politburo at the time. And Balenov, here, was just a colonel. Isn't that right, Comrade General?"

Balenov delivered a cursory nod, as if the whole subject was displeasing—and Silvius knew why. In Paris, after more than one vodka, Balenov had admitted to the American that the Soviets had overeacted to an accidental intrusion of Russian air space. For obvious reasons Silvius refrained from reminding him, but the Premier's next remark stunned all three men.

Half to himself he mused, "I always thought we handled the whole affair badly. The business of not admitting right from the start that we shot it down was a mistake. Then we made matters worse by insisting it was a spy plane—a preposterous claim that was easier to shoot down than the 747 itself." He looked at Balenov. "I seem to remember we decorated the pilot as a hero, didn't we?"

The general nodded.

"Another bit of stupidity. We played right into that

bastard Reagan's hands. Gave him every excuse to call us names. No, it was not a performance that won us respect, not even among our allies. However"—he smiled rather morosely at the President—"I'm afraid there's nothing we can do about it at this late date. The urge to save face, while not an exclusively Russian trait, is too irresistible."

Haines pressed, "It's not too late. A carefully phrased statement to the effect that certain evidence has negated the spy plane theory . . ."

Balenov dryly interjected, "I'd suggest the same ingenuity employed in concocting the reason we shot the damned thing down, perhaps." Magoyan's bushy eyebrows shot up in surprise and Silvius, expecting the Premier to explode, held his breath. Magoyan, however, merely pursed his lips and rose once more to stare out the window. After a few seconds of silence, he wheeled and addressed the President. "You have given me much to think about. Like yourself, hypocrisy is not one of my faults. I deeply resent the threats you've made, but I understand them—the very fact that you saw fit to make this long journey has impressed me. You are brandishing a sword, but I also must examine your motives—and I believe you when you say you are basically a man of peace."

The President murmured, "Accepting my word on that score is a long step toward peace in itself."

Magoyan walked over to him and offered his hand, which Haines shook. "I think this first step calls for a toast. Will you and General Silvius join us in sampling our best vodka?"

The President laughed. "I can't speak for George, but I know damned well I will."

"Good. We can talk further while we drink. You know, Mr. President, I confess a desire to visit your country some day . . ."

Air Force One streaked toward home, aided by a hundred-knot tailwind that eliminated the necessity of a refueling stop at Anchorage. In the upper lounge, Haines and Silvius discussed for a long time the ramifications of the summit meeting.

"I want to thank you for lying in your teeth," the President said. "When Balenov asked you, on your honor as a fellow soldier, if weather control was feasible, you were in one hell of a spot."

Silvius grinned. "Not really, sir. In a sense, adherence to duty and country is a form of adhering to honor. Or am I rationalizing?"

"Probably. Do you think he believed us?"

The general said slowly, "I know he wanted to believe. And that was half the battle . . ."

"Did you believe them?" a vodka-mellowed Magoyan was asking the chief of the Soviet Air Force.

"They both struck me as men of honor," Balenov replied obliquely. "I do know that if they were telling the truth about their ability to create drought, it is something to fear."

"I agree," the premier said sadly, "although I wonder if they'd ever use it. I rather liked that man Haines. I think he's sincere . . ."

The 747 was over Detroit when General Silvius finally left the lounge with the announced intention of spending the rest of the flight in the cockpit.

"Just want to keep Cardella on his toes," he explained. "And knowing Cardella, he'll probably tell me to keep my damned mouth shut and no back-seat flying."

"Go right ahead," the President assured him. "I'll probably doze off. I'm damned tired."

But he knew he wouldn't sleep. Intuition told him the ghost was going to pay him a visit. A final visit, he sensed. One final attempt to convince him that war was the last real chance for peace? A critique on what had transired in that small Kremlin room? A tirade on the futility of trying to do business with a man like Magoyan?

He was sure of only one thing. He was proud of what he had done. The faintest glimmer of relaxed tensions, the tiniest sliver of hope for mutual understanding, were preferable to slaughter. Even one-sided slaughter in a conflict the Russians could never win and that would leave the United States virtually unscathed.

". . . Well, well, Jeremy. Why so pensive? Are you afraid you may have given away the store—as I was supposed to have done at Yalta?"

Franklin Roosevelt was in the familiar chair, an enigmatic smile on his face.

Haines said, "I didn't give away anything. I assume you know what went on."

"I do. I don't know whether to congratulate or to scold you. That business about lasers affecting weather—absolutely audacious! Whether it will convince our Russia friends to be good is another matter. Their own scientists will insist it's impossible and that you were bluffing. If they can convince Mr. Magoyan of that truth, you've accomplished nothing."

The President sighed. "Maybe. Yet he only has to half-believe. One iota of credence on his part is all I need. After all, he does know they're two years behind Umbrella. It's logical for him to assume that if we could be that far ahead of their technology, I might not have been bluffing about weather control. We'll just have to wait and see. I won't be surprised if Magoyan makes some move toward German unification very shortly. He'll do his damnedest to claim all the credit, and he can have it."

"You really think he will?"

"I do. And when he sees the reaction, I figure it won't be the only concessionary move he'll make. In my opinion, he's both scared and, conversely, impressed with me. An ideal situation. Magoyan's a son of a bitch, but he's a pragmatic son of a bitch."

"Thanks to your magnificent bluffing. I do believe, Jeremy, you were playing Russian roulette."

"American poker," Haines corrected. He looked at FDR curiously. "Satisfied?"

"Let's say I share your mild optimism. I don't think anyone can expect more under the circumstances. Vastly preferable to nuclear war."

The President was startled. "That coming from you? I thought you wanted me to push those infernal buttons. You tried your damnedest to talk me into it."

The ghost shook his head. "You still don't get it, do you, Jeremy Haines?"

"Get what?"

"That I was testing you. Judging whether you could act on your own, instead of relying on an apparition for counsel and advice. Leaning on the ghost of a past President just as that president had to lean on his steel crutch. I had to make sure before I left you. For good, I regret to say."

"Wait . . . wait," Haines stammered. "I have to know something."

"You will, my troubled friend. You will . . ."

The face of Franklin Delano Roosevelt wavered, blurred, and contorted into another likeness.

The President of the United States was staring at himself.

He closed his eyes in horror, then forced them open.

The chair facing him was empty.

The truth facing him was insanity.

All in his own mind, he told himself. A frighteningly real hallucination conjured up by a tired, sick brain. A self-created illusion that for months had guided his every move, every action, every decision. And now he had to ask himself if the admission of insanity must brand everything he had done with the stigma of insanity.

He tried to weigh the evidence dispassionately.

Insane or not, I've accomplished miracles. Maybe I've acted with the cunning of a maniac, but basically I've done what had to be done—including this trip to Russia. It's as if mental illness was a kind of catharsis that cleansed my apathy and discouragement, freed me from fear and indecision. Insanity doesn't have to kill instinct, and my instincts have been right.

So what do I do now? Confess what's happened to me and resign? What would that confession do to the programs I've launched? To this new chance for peace? Cover them with doubts and suspicion that everything I've achieved amounts to products of a sick mind? Or am I just deluding myself that I've acted wisely? Am I really capable of judging my accomplishments? Is confidence in my actions a symptom of insanity itself?

I have to ask Jessica all this. Talk it all out with her. Poor Jessica. There can be no marriage now . . .

When Silvius and McNulty came into the lounge before landing, they found him asleep. McNulty leaned over to fasten the President's seat belt and saw glistening moisture on his cheeks. Gently, tenderly, the agent touched the wetness.

"Jesus Christ," he whispered. "I think he's been crying."

EPILOGUE

Jessica peered through the late summer afternoon haze at the mountains nudging the confines of Camp David, then at the man sitting next to her on the porch of Aspen Lodge.

She remarked, "You look ten years younger and you claim you feel twenty years younger, so why the frown?"

Jeremy Haines grumbled, "I keep thinking of that damned ghost—or should I say hallucination?"

She reached over and took his hand. "It's all over, Jeremy. You've been on Air Force One several times since the Moscow trip and there's been no recurrence. For the one hundredth time, hallucination is not synonymous with insanity, not in your case, anyway."

"What you keep telling me seems to be at odds with what I keep telling myself. Nobody could have hallucinated anything that real unless there was something wrong with his mind."

She said with a sharpness that still managed to be soothing, "And I've already pointed out to you that there *was* something wrong with your mind—temporarily. I repeat, oh stubborn patient. You were under an incredible strain that caused your brain to play tricks on you. If you persist in believing you were suffering from actual mental disease, you also must believe that mental disease is not irreversible. In other words, you're cured."

Haines sighed, "I still dream about him—or it."

"Perfectly natural. It was a terrible experience. But remember, the only mental aberration you evidenced was the ghost itself. Your actions during this entire period were totally sane—even brilliant and courageous. Your domestic reforms. The way you resisted Collison and all the others who wanted an attack on the Soviets. The flight to Russia. Look at what's been happening, Jeremy. Germany's going to be a united country again, and there was Peter Frain's column yesterday—those rumors about the Soviets considering some token restitution for that old Korean airliner incident. You told me that might happen."

Her voice had risen in excitement, and Haines smiled. "Jessica, I recall telling myself that attacking Russia would be the height of insanity, and then wondering if deciding *not* to attack could also have been the height of insanity."

She said pedantically, in her best clinical tone, "Seeing a ghost was symptomatic of temporary mental strain. The decision you reached actually demonstrated that the condition was disappearing."

"In effect, then, I was exorcising my ghost."

"Right. And permanently. Jeremy, why are you frowning again?"

"Dammit, Jessica, it was so bloody real! All those long discussions. The voice. The way he reminisced. How in the hell could I have just been talking to myself? I either had to be completely off my rocker or . . ."

His voice trailed off.

"Or what?" she asked softly.

"Or it *was* Roosevelt. You're the parapsychologist, Jessica. You believe in ghosts, or at least concede their existence is possible and even probable. As a matter of fact, at one point you damned near saw my friend."

She smiled ruefully. "I *thought* I almost saw him. But after talking to Colonel Cardella, I realized there were rational explanations for what I experienced. Remember, I was psychologically and emotionally prepared to encounter a true psychic phenomenon. All alone in that cabin, worried about you, actually wanting the ghost to be real, I was a pushover for suggestion, for misinterpreting any kind of visual stimuli. No, the ghost was in your own mind, made real by your knowledge of FDR. And that's the verdict of *both* the parapsychologist and the psychiatrist."

"You seem damned positive," Haines observed.

"I am. Mostly because of what you told me about the last time you saw him. How the face changed from Roosevelt's to yours. That's very significant from a psychiatric standpoint. It shows you fought the whole battle within yourself, from the day the ghost first appeared. You never argued with Franklin Roosevelt. You argued with Jeremy Haines. And that, in effect, is what I said in my letter to Catlin Baxter."

He was surprised. "You wrote Cat? Why didn't you tell me?"

"Well, I didn't really mean to keep it a secret. I knew you were trying to forget the whole episode; showing you the letter would have brought everything back. I've always advised you to look back on it as a kind of persistent, unexplainable fever. FUO, as we doctors like to say, fever of undetermined origin. Incidentally, I've never told Baxter the whole story. How prolonged and frequent your experiences were."

"Or how involved I got," the President murmured.

"Want to see my letter to Baxter?"

"Yes."

"There's a copy in my briefcase, on the living room coffee table. And while you're at it, you can bring me a cold beer."

When he returned, she fished the letter out of the briefcase and sipped the beer while he read, intently studying his face.

Captain Catlin Baxter
Chief of Psychiatry
U.S. Navy Medical Center
Bethesda, MD. 20854

Dear Captain Baxter:

Thank you for your letter in which you requested that I bill the Navy Department, through your office, for services rendered in behalf of the patient you referred to me.

Under the circumstances, I would prefer not to accept any compensation. It was an honor and a privilege to aid you and the patient in whatever way I could . . .

Haines looked up, smiling. "Judging from the amount of time we've spent together, I'd say you've saved the taxpayers a pretty good chunk."

"Shut up and keep reading."

My final diagnosis in this case is identical to the one provided you verbally after my first session. Namely, the patient experienced hallucination under severe stress, resulting in temporary disorientation. Said disability, however, was limited solely to the psychic phenomenon he believed he kept witnessing. I believe it is clinically significant that in all other aspects, the patient retained normal control of his mental faculties and indeed, considering the unusual persistence of the hallucinatory attacks, continued to demonstrate admirable judgment in the performance of his difficult duties.

It is my firm medical opinion, based on a long and close association with this patient, that he is now fully recovered and will continue to function on a completely normal basis.

With every good wish,

Sincerely,

The President's eyes were somber. "Well, I suppose I have to agree with that diagnosis. Naturally, I'd prefer to think I saw a real ghost."

"Which makes no sense. It couldn't have been Roosevelt. FDR never would have tried to force you into destroying Russia. Is that the kind of man he was? That kind of President? Think hard, Jeremy. What you created in your own mind, out of all you've ever read about him, was a perfect replica. Right down to his voice with all its inflections. Right down to his beliefs, his methods, even his own memories of people and events. But only up to a point—when you suddenly rejected his influence and acted on your own."

"You're forgetting something I told you. One of the last things he said to me the last time I saw him. That he was testing me. Testing my judgment."

"I haven't forgotten. You were testing yourself, Jeremy. That's why the last thing you saw was your own face."

He glanced at the letter again and grinned. "While I still have doubts about this diagnosis, I must say the best part is your signature."

"Signature?"

"It reads as well as it sounds. *Doctor Jessica Sarazin Haines.*"

She laughed. "You're the first President of the United States who eloped. Thank God—I couldn't have gone through a White House wedding in front of fifty television cameras. That reminds me, I still have to write quite a few thank-you notes for wedding gifts. Including one to Speaker Rafferty. What on earth possessed him to send us that beautiful thirty-five-millimeter movie camera? I love it, but it isn't a conventional wedding present."

"Conscience, perhaps," Haines said dryly. "Take

that puzzled expression off your face—one of these days I'll explain it to you. Tell you what, wife, finish that beer and let's go for a little walk. And I'll be damned—here comes McNulty. He must have heard me."

The big agent was coming up to the porch, a wide grin on his face. He hadn't stopped smiling, Haines thought amusedly, since he stood by the President's side and listened to a Maryland justice of the peace pronounce the wedding vows.

"We're going for a walk, Mike," Haines announced. "Any chance of skipping the escort?"

McNulty shook his head. "No, sir. But I'll be glad to stay out of earshot—just so long as I have you two in sight."

"Fair enough. Come on, Jessica."

McNulty trailed them down the wooded path, staying discreetly behind them and watching approvingly when he saw their hands entwine. The President had been right—McNulty *was* happy.

So happy that only occasionally did he think about the flight back from Moscow, when he had gone to the upper lounge after landing to make sure the already-deplaned President hadn't forgotten any personal items.

Michael McNulty never told a soul about the steel crutch he thought he saw resting against the arm of the chair facing the President's favorite seat.

The crutch that disappeared as he approached it.

Nor did he ever mention the low, rumbling laugh he could have sworn he heard.